THEODORE TERHUNE STORIES

Seven Clues in Search of a Crime
House with Crooked Walls
A Case for Solomon
Work for the Hangman
Ten Trails to Tyburn
A Case of Books
And a Bottle of Rum
Dead Pigs at Hungry Farm

House with Crooked Walls

BRUCE GRAEME

With an introduction by J. F. Norris

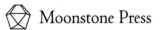 Moonstone Press

This edition published in 2021 by Moonstone Press
www.moonstonepress.co.uk

Introduction © 2021 J. F. Norris

Originally published in 1942 by Hutchinson & Co Ltd

House with Crooked Walls © the Estate of
Graham Montague Jeffries, writing as Bruce Graeme

ISBN 978-1-899000-28-9
eISBN 978-1-899000-29-6

A CIP catalogue record for this book is available from the British Library

Text designed and typeset by Tetragon, London
Cover illustration by Jason Anscomb

Printed and bound by CPI Group (UK) Ltd, Croydon, CRO 4YY

Contents

INTRODUCTION

Theodore I. Terhune,
Occult Detective

House with Crooked Walls (1942) is a marked departure from a straightforward detective story and perhaps the misfit book in the engaging detective-novel series featuring Theodore "Tommy" Terhune, bookseller, crime-fiction writer and serendipitous detective. It most resembles a shuddery ghost story that could easily have come from the mind of Edgar Allan Poe or M. R. James. The title character, as it were, House-on-the-Hill, dominates the action and the psyche of each of the characters. It is a tale of curses, hauntings, ghosts, deeply buried secrets and literal skeletons in the closet... or caverns, in this case. Graeme outperforms even John Dickson Carr, master of the macabre detective story, in this genuinely creepy novel that is not without a murder mystery or two. There are disappearances and corpses, have no fear, but the story, steeped in Gothic excess, is most assuredly influenced by the work of Poe, as well as the British Gothic triumvirate of Ann Radcliffe, Matthew Lewis and Charles Maturin. Graeme also incorporates an oft-used motif found most frequently in the work of H. P. Lovecraft in his exploration of the shunned house and the reasons that certain buildings are avoided, both in person and in conversation.

Without going into too much detail—for the story is best enjoyed by entering its eerie world with little knowledge of the plot—I can divulge that current tenant Dr. Vicente Salvaterra hires Terhune to do research into the house of the title. More commonly known by its nickname, "the House with Crooked Walls", because of its assortment of slanting walls and non-uniform-sized windows, House-on-the-Hill has no real legend attached to account for its being shunned. But Salvaterra is convinced that the mass avoidance by the townspeople and their refusal to talk about the house must be linked to some event that lingers in or around the building. He is sure of a "psychic" explanation, as he says to Terhune: "I think it is possible that some event occurred, probably anterior to living memory, in which House-on-the-Hill played a leading part. That event must have created such intense horror, or hatred, or fear that a modified form of that forgotten emotion still exists, although the cause has long been forgotten." Consulting a variety of reference works and historical manuscripts, Terhune digs deep into the building's past, and is rewarded with a treasure trove of gruesome history.

Lady Kylstone, a recurring character in the Terhune series, herself experienced an "overwhelming feeling of evil" when she visited the house years ago while considering purchasing it for her brother, who wanted to live nearer to his sister. She says: "I did not trouble to see all over the house. I left as quickly as I could escape from the charming but persistent estate agent who had conducted me there." She further elaborates on the possibility of a curse having been laid on the house by its ancestral occupants, and of "wicked depravity" that pervades the building and grounds. House-on-the-Hill is sure to take its place in the hall of infamy alongside such notorious fictional haunted houses as Humphrey Furnival's home in *Cold Harbour* (1924) by Francis Brett Young, Cliff End from *Uneasy Freehold* (1941) by Dorothy Macardle, the eponymous Hill House from Shirley Jackson's famous 1959 novel, and Longwood

House from *The Man Who Could Not Shudder* (1940)—along with nearly every other estate found in the works of John Dickson Carr.

Despite the Gothic setting, the eerie atmosphere and the scandalous and horror-filled history Terhune will reveal, *House with Crooked Walls* is at its core a classic detective novel and a superb bibliomystery. Guided by his curiosity, equipped with several volumes of the *Dictionary of National Biography* and assisted by his frequent sleuthing partner Julia MacMunn, Terhune delves into the house's strange past and stranger occupants.

It doesn't take much for Julia to catch detective fever: "I wish you hadn't told me about House-on-the-Hill," she reluctantly admits to her friend, "…because my curiosity is aroused… [And] that curiosity makes me despise myself for being in a class with you and your amateur detection." Much to Terhune's surprise Julia sets off on her own burrowing into libraries all over England with impressive bibliodetective work that outshines all that Terhune has done on his own. She offers up an "amazing theory", uncovers new books and manuscripts adding more information to what Terhune has already discovered in the handy *Dictionary of National Biography*. Yet together in uncovering a horrible secret which dates back to the 15th century they also set into motion a sinister plot in the 20th century.

Graham Montague Jeffries (1900-1982), better known as Bruce Graeme, was married and had two children: Roderic and Guillaine. Both his son and daughter went on to write books and interestingly also used their father's alter ego surname for their own pen names. Guillaine Jeffries, as "Linda Graeme", wrote a brief series of books published between 1955 and 1964 about a girl named Helen who was a ballet dancer in theatre and on TV. Roderic Jeffries followed in his father's footsteps and turned to writing crime fiction, using his own name and the pseudonyms Roderic Graeme (continuing his father's series about the thief turned crime novelist Blackshirt),

Peter Alding, Jeffrey Ashford and Graham Hastings. In addition to more than sixty crime, detective and espionage novels, Roderic wrote a number of non-fiction works on criminal investigation and Grand Prix racing.

Late in life Graeme gave his Elizabethan farmhouse in Kent to Roderic and his wife. Graeme moved up the road to a bungalow and would have lunch with his son and daughter-in-law once a week. According to Xanthe Jeffries, Bruce Graeme's granddaughter, he remained in Kent while his son's family moved to Majorca in 1972. They remained close even while apart, and Graeme would visit in May every year, on his birthday.

When I asked for any family stories she might share with Moonstone Press readers, Xanthe very politely complied with an anecdote-filled email. I learned that her grandfather kept a couple of marmosets as pets and had inherited a Land Rover from his son when Roderic moved away. She also wrote of his annual visits to Majorca: "If the weather was not to his liking," she reported, "we never heard the end of it. On his last trip to us he became very worried about having to travel back to the U.K. via Barcelona." Apparently he was concerned about Spanish customs law. "When asked why he told my parents that his walking stick was in fact a swordstick!" Clearly, Graeme was something of an adventurer himself.

Whether Theodore Terhune, Julia and Inspector Sampson are ghostbusting or chasing after criminals, the story of *House with Crooked Walls* is a unique entry in Bruce Graeme's fine series featuring his bookseller detective. Devotees of both detective novels and supernatural thrillers will find much to enjoy in this new Moonstone Press edition, a long overdue revival of the varied work of Bruce Graeme.

J. F. NORRIS
Chicago, IL
November 2020

Chapter One

I

One Tuesday morning a car drove into Bray-in-the-Marsh. It travelled evenly along the Ashford road until it arrived opposite Market Square; there, it unexpectedly slowed down as though the occupants were enchanted by the sleepy, old-fashioned, out-of-the-way Kentish village, and were deliberately lingering in the vicinity to savour its charm to the full.

A second or two later appearances were proved deceptive. Behind the chauffeur a hand waved, a tapering, white-fleshed, immaculate hand; and the car moved forward, not to continue along the road, through the village, and so to Wickford or some other quaint, remote corner of Kent (for the road proceeded by nowhere in particular to nowhere at all), but to turn sharp left along the scrap of road which bordered Market Square on the east, and immediately sharp left again, so skirting the Square by its third side. There, having passed by the "Almond Tree," the car came to a halt outside a bookshop.

Why Terhune should have glanced up at that moment was a problem to which, subsequently, he was never able to supply a satisfactory answer. It so happened that he was examining a parcel of books from the library of the Rector of Willingham, which had been submitted for his valuation, and when once Terhune became immersed in a book it usually took some catastrophe, or the tinkle of the shop-door bell, to distract him. Yet, curiously enough, on this Tuesday morning, although he neither heard nor saw anything to attract his attention, he looked up from the first edition of Hardy's *Jude the Obscure*, and through the plate-glass window saw a sequence of events which, in an absent-minded moment, reminded him of a short scene from a film.

He saw, as he looked up, a long, stream-lined car glide forward into his area of vision, and vaguely noted its luxurious, highly polished appointments. He, then saw a chauffeur spring smartly from the driving seat, hurry round the bonnet of the car to the near-side door, which he opened with an unusually obsequious air. A handsome fellow, this chauffeur; he was tall, possessed broad shoulders, and was clad in a tight-fitting dark green uniform.

With the door open, and his view, for the moment, unobstructed, Terhune was permitted a brief glimpse of the car's interior. The upholstery of the car, he saw, exactly matched, in its colour scheme, the chauffeur's uniform; though why this fact impressed itself upon his present, somewhat rambling thoughts and affected him with a slight feeling of irritation he knew no more than why he had looked out of the window in the first instance. But he was annoyed, perhaps because the matching colours suggested ostentation; perhaps because he resented the matching of a human being with the appointments of a piece of unhuman mechanism.

The reflection was fleeting, for he next became conscious of the car's occupants. There were two, a man and a woman. He was unable to see clearly, not only on account of the light reflected by the plate glass of the window, but also because of the comparative dimness of the car's interior; nevertheless, the faces of the two people were so alike as to be startling in their resemblance to one another.

Before he had time for further examination of the two faces, that of the woman was hidden as the man rose and stepped out of the car. By the time he had moved to one side, the chauffeur had closed the car door, and Terhune could no longer see within. Besides, his attention was now riveted upon the one who had stepped out.

A strange little man, indeed. He was not a dwarf, but certainly he was the shortest man Terhune had ever seen. He wore a tall silk hat—a more incongruous sight had not been seen in Market Square for many a year. Beneath this hat his hair was long, and snowy white, it flowed about in the wind like a halo. He wore a long overcoat, and, beneath, an elaborate stock, black with white spots. His trousers were of black and white pin-striped serge. He wore boots.

Terhune grinned as he stared at the little man on the pavement, and imagined what a sensation would have been created in Market Square had he appeared on a Thursday morning. For Thursday was market day, the one day of the week when any real sign of life was to be seen at Bray. Upon all other days—with the exception of Sunday morning, when the younger members of the local society visited the "Almond Tree" for cocktails—it was rare to see more than one car in Market Square, or, maybe, two farm vehicles.

Terhune's amusement was not of long duration, for surprise took its place. The little man was walking across the pavement towards the book-shop with the obvious intention of visiting it. Before there was time to make a move, the door opened, and the high-pitched tinkle of the hanging door-bell echoed round the shop.

"Good morning," the little man greeted in a voice cultured and strangely full for so slight a body. "Mr. Terhune?"

Terhune nodded affirmatively, surprised to learn that his name was known to his visitor.

"Good. I am calling here at the suggestion of Mr. Howard, of Messrs. Howard, Son, and Howard."

Howard was a solicitor whom Terhune had met two or three times in the past twelve months. Surprise at hearing of the recommendation was, however, overshadowed by Terhune's realisation that the little man was not British. True, the few words of English which he had spoken had been excellent, and, despite his diminutive size and old-fashioned attire, the cast of his face was British—Welsh, maybe. Yet, there was an indefinable something in his voice which suggested that he was a foreigner.

Terhune noticed more than this. He became aware of the purity of his visitor's flesh. His complexion, without suggesting ill-health, was milky white, unblemished: a complexion such as most women would have given their souls to possess. His hands, too, were beautiful; narrow, sensitive hands, but they were marred—in Terhune's opinion—by two rings, one on each little finger: the one a massive affair of solid gold; the other a large diamond solitaire.

Terhune nodded again; he could think of nothing that was particularly worth the saying.

"Before I speak of my reason for calling upon you, Mr. Terhune, allow me to introduce myself. Here is my card."

The tapering fingers caressed the inside of the long overcoat, to produce a card which they passed over to Terhune with a fascinating flourish.

Terhune read:

DR. VICENTE SALVATERRA.

Doctor of medicine or of music? Terhune wondered. Whichever it was, the name confirmed that the man was a foreigner, or of foreign extraction.

Salvaterra continued:

"I understand from Mr. Howard that you specialise in buying and selling works relating to local history and personalities; and that you possess a private collection of books about Kent which is unrivalled in the county."

The inflection of the voice was questioning, so Terhune smiled deprecatingly. "Mr. Howard has an exaggerated notion of the value of my collection, Dr. Salvaterra. I am scarcely rich enough to buy some of the rarer volumes which deal with Kentish history."

"But, no doubt, the information to be found in your collection is extensive?" the little man persisted.

"I think I may safely answer, 'Yes.'"

"Then I am going to ask a favour of you, Mr. Terhune. As you must have guessed from my name, I am not a countryman of yours. I am a native of the small Central American State of Panama, although my family came originally, not from Spain, but Portugal. Nevertheless, I am extremely fond of your dear country, and it is my intention to live in England for the next few years—or perhaps for the remainder of my life. Who knows?

"I am particularly attracted by the Garden of England, as I believe Kent is sometimes called. Some weeks ago, in compliance with my instructions, my London solicitors communicated particulars of my special requirements to the principal estate agents of this county, and asked for particulars to be sent of any property likely to suit me.

"Not to bore you with wearisome details, Mr. Terhune, of my visits to one property after another, this week-end I visited a house in this neighbourhood with which, frankly, I was immediately interested, not only on account of its position, but also its extraordinary, not to say fantastic, architecture."

He paused, and glanced questioningly at Terhune, as if to see whether this description evoked an immediate recognition on Terhune's part. He was disappointed.

"Perhaps there are several houses answering to that description," Salvaterra continued, somewhat testily. "I speak of the building with the curious name of House-on-the-Hill. Surely it must be known to you?"

He smiled his gratification upon seeing Terhune's expression.

II

House-on-the-Hill! Of course, the place was known to Terhune. It was known to everyone living within miles of it. It was, indeed, impossible not to be aware of its existence, for it was aptly named. It was situated at the extreme tip of a gently rising slope which covered the surrounding country to a depth of almost three square miles, and because of the peculiar configuration of that area, which resembled, roughly, the virgin breast of a reclining woman, one part or another of the house was visible from every direction.

The prospect, from near or far, was invariably bleak, for the sky was its background, and never mind how the sky changed its aspect, from the bright pink of dawn, or the crimson gold of sunset, to the menacing gloom of approaching thunder, the sharply etched outline of House-on-the-Hill never altered. Whether gilded by the midday sun, silvered by the moon, or caressed by the flecked shadows of cirrus cloud scudding before a sou'-westerly, House-on-the-Hill never softened, never attuned itself to Nature's gentler moods. Sullenly, sombrely, defiantly, it faced all four cardinal points of the compass with an air of being some imperishable brick-and-mortar satyr.

A screen of trees could have transformed this satyr into, at least, a humorous goblin or a puckish gnome, but the nearest trees were far enough from the house to merge unrecognisably into the general green of the rolling fields which comprised the breast of which House-on-the-Hill was, as it were, the nipple. A cloak of ivy might have robbed it of its challenging expression; or a gayer mantle of clematis; or a dainty Dorothy Perkins. But no. For some unaccountable reason, not a leaf, green or brown, not a flower, had, within living memory, ever covered one single weathered brick. Even its crazy tiled roof refused to shelter moss. Local tradition explained this absence of vegetation by crediting the existence of poison in the soil immediately surrounding House-on-the-Hill.

Yet, if House-on-the-Hill was bizarre, Nature alone was not guilty. Man's handiwork was equally to blame, for someone had played queer tricks with its construction. House-on-the-Hill was its official name, but the local inhabitants referred to the place as the House with Crooked Walls. With good reason, for its walls appeared crooked indeed. They rose here, and sank there, where the foundations had shifted. They bulged outwards in one place, inwards in another. No two adjacent rooms were on the same level. Nor, therefore, were the windows, none of which was alike in size, shape, or design. The effect of this complete absence of symmetry was to make the walls appear outrageously crooked—a veritable caricature of a house. So real was this impression of crookedness that several architects, and as many surveyors, had been deceived by it. Again and again House-on-the-Hill had been inspected by experts, but in every case the result had been the same. The walls of the house were not plumb, but their deviation, either from the perpendicular, or the horizontal, was no worse than that of many other buildings in the same district. The exaggerated appearance of crookedness was an optical illusion.

So, reluctantly, announced the surveyors and the architects. But the people of Bray and Wickford and Willingham knew better than the experts. The house had crooked walls, they continued obstinately to assert, and not for a king's ransom would they live in the place. And evidently prospective buyers were in agreement with the local inhabitants, for House-on-the-Hill had been empty ever since Terhune had lived in the district.

III

"So you know House-on-the-Hill, Mr. Terhune?"

"I know of it," Terhune corrected.

"But surely you have visited there? I understand that the lawn facing south is famed locally as a beauty spot, and is used for picnic-parties. Mr. Tuttell, the estate agent, kindly informed me that this was so, and, though it is my habit to discount by at least half everything I am told by an enthusiastic estate agent, on this occasion I was forced to believe him wholly, for the vicinity is littered with empty bottles, and tins, and the remains of innumerable camp fires."

Terhune sympathised with Salvaterra's obvious anger, for careless picnickers had helped to ruin what must once have been a magnificent lawn.

"I have never picnicked there, Dr. Salvaterra, but I have cycled there on several occasions. The view from House-on-the-Hill is reputed to be the most beautiful in south-east England."

"I can believe that," the little man agreed with a gleam in his eyes which now was of enthusiasm, and not anger. "But have you never been inside the house?"

"No."

"No doubt you have peeped in through the broken shutters?" Terhune grinned. "I must plead guilty to that charge," he admitted.

"Why not? I am not without curiosity, which is the reason for my visit to you this morning. But first, would you do me the kindness of telling me what your impression is of the interior of House-on-the-Hill?"

Terhune hesitated before replying to the question, and Salvaterra was quick to perceive this indecision.

"Why do you not answer?" he asked, with a surprising eagerness.

"I have not seen enough of the interior to receive an impression."

"I see." The man from Panama seemed disappointed with Terhune's reply. "I believe you to be an intelligent young man, so I was anxious to know whether you share the popular feeling of aversion in which I gather the place is held. It is held in aversion, is it not?" he added sharply, as if for the purpose of surprising Terhune into making an admission.

"Yes."

"Do you, also, feel aversion towards House-on-the-Hill?"

"Aversion!" Terhune carefully considered the question. "No," he replied at last. "I cannot say that the sight of the house influences me to that point."

"But it does influence you to some extent?" Salvaterra persisted.

"To some extent," Terhune was forced to admit.

"Ha!" the little man snapped out. "Why are you affected? The house is unusual, but it is not ugly?"

"No."

"You would not be too nervous to live there if the property were given to you?"

Terhune chuckled. "Nervous of what?"

"Exactly!" Salvaterra exclaimed sharply. "Of what? You have asked the question which is perplexing me." He paused. "You are not too busy to spare me a few minutes?"

"Thursdays and Saturdays are my only busy days, Dr. Salvaterra."

"Good. Then I will sit down if I may." The doctor pulled a wooden chair towards him, and sat down upon it—Terhune noted absently that only the toes of his visitor's boots touched the floor, although the chair was by no means a high one.

"You have seen by my card, Mr. Terhune, that I subscribe myself doctor, of philosophy. I am deeply interested in all departments of philosophy, and, in particular, I specialise in psychic phenomena.

"I am also practical—and in adding the word *also* I am sure you will not begrudge an old man his jest. I am a rich man. I am prepared to pay adequately for what I want. At the same time, I demand full value for my money. It follows, therefore, that I am not a man to buy what you English describe so picturesquely as 'a pig in a poke.'

"These explanations lead up to my first visit to House-on-the-Hill, Mr. Terhune. I see no reason for concealing the fact that I was immediately attracted by the property. To this extent, indeed, that I was unable to comprehend the reason for its having been vacant for so many years. True, its position makes it particularly exposed to winds blowing from every point on the compass, and, as I am the most intolerant of men to cold winds and draughts, I could understand why the house might fail to appeal to Latins or inhabitants of sunny climes. But Britons have been inured by the custom of centuries to such trifling discomforts, so I found it difficult to believe that anyone able to afford so beautiful a prospect should deliberately refrain from acquiring it.

"True, also, that House-on-the-Hill has an extraordinary appearance from without. I have lived many years, but never have I seen a more bizarre building. Yet it is not un-English. I have seen similar spiral chimneys on a Kentish farm-house; many similar sharp-sloping roofs; similar types of porch; similar half-timbered walls; similar leaded windows. Indeed, I would go so far as to say that I could identify almost every part of the exterior as being similar to the corresponding section of one house or another, all no farther than a mile or so from this village. The chief difference, of course, between House-on-the-Hill and the other houses, lies in its exaggeration. So, upon reflection, again I asked myself: Why had the house been so long unoccupied?

"When I entered the house, the problem became even more inexplicable to me. I found the interior of House-on-the-Hill charmingly picturesque. Had I been a tall man, perhaps my delight would have been qualified, for to crack one's head continually upon the beams of the ceiling no doubt makes one overlook their romance, and remember only their material disadvantage. But I have known tall Englishmen cheerfully develop a permanent stoop through residing in low-ceilinged houses of the fifteenth and sixteenth centuries."

Salvaterra paused, a trifle breathlessly, as if unused to speaking at such length. At the same time he turned slightly towards the window, so that Terhune saw the amused twinkle in his eyes.

"My sister, who accompanies me everywhere, was equally enchanted with the interior of the house," he continued presently. "Like me, she has imagination. She was able to see behind the ruin of neglect, and to disregard the obvious, structural disadvantages of a house that was designed for life in a very different age. She has the intelligence to conceive the house as it could be after renovation and modernisation, so she urged me to buy the property.

"As my reactions coincided with hers, Mr. Terhune, I have decided to open negotiations for its purchase. But, as a practical man, I must first know why the house has remained unoccupied for so many years. To this end, I instituted certain enquiries, and already have learned, not only that the house is known locally as the House with Crooked Walls, but also, that although local inhabitants will cheerfully picnic beneath the shadow of the building, very few, if any of the villagers, would willingly pass beyond its crooked walls.

"Why not? The question has excited the psychic as well as the practical in me. I personally pursued some original enquiries. With this strange result, my dear sir. Although I spoke to many people who admitted quite frankly that they would not enter House-on-the-Hill, none of them was able to give me a concrete reason for this extraordinary disinclination. Again and again I pressed this question: What do you know against House-on-the-Hill which makes you avoid entering it? The answer was invariably: Nothing.

"That is to say, nothing concrete. Children were nervous of the house because their mothers were nervous. Wives had been told never to step inside by their husbands. While husbands remembered, as young boys, being warned by their fathers not to go near House-on-the-Hill on pain of a thrashing.

"The longer I continued my enquiries the more eagerly curious I became, for I was finding myself faced with the strange phenomenon of an entire community of people being nervous of an unknown, and apparently unfounded, dread. I stress the word apparently, for I am convinced that a widespread dread of this nature cannot be without foundation.

"Determined to solve something which was beginning to assume the semblance of a fascinating mystery, this morning I visited Mr. Howard, who is acting on behalf of the present owner of the property, and asked him for an explanation of why House-on-the-Hill has been so long unoccupied. At first surprised by my request, Mr. Howard presently assured me that he had not realised, until that moment, that the property was held more or less in fear by the people of this district. Then he went on to say that he had absolutely no knowledge of any happening or event connected with, the house which might have been the original cause for the growth of local superstition.

"I believed him implicitly, Mr. Terhune. I rose to leave. It was then that Mr. Howard told me of yourself, assuring me confidently that, if anyone can supply the required information, you are that person."

Salvaterra's dark eyes flamed with eagerness. "Will you help me, Mr. Terhune?" he pleaded.

Chapter Two

Much of what Salvaterra had told him, Terhune already knew. It was impossible to live in the neighbourhood of Bray-in-the-Marsh without learning that the House with Crooked Walls was regarded by local inhabitants with a feeling of intense dislike, amounting almost to fear. He had often heard the hope expressed that the property might find a purchaser sufficiently wealthy to pull down the existing house and build another less ugly—although the use of that word was not, in his opinion, justified, for, however bizarre the house might appear, however sombre, however challenging, however any one of a dozen different adjectives, ugly it certainly was not, except perhaps to the purist, because of its incongruity, or to the modernist, because of its antiquity. He had heard people say that they would not care to live in the house even if it became theirs by deed of gift; and still others, that there was something evil about the place. But, until now, he had not realised what Dr. Salvaterra had just made plain—that local aversion towards House-on-the-Hill was founded upon something which went far deeper than an antipathy to crooked walls.

He remembered something he had once heard Winstanley say, speaking of House-on-the-Hill: "Two years before he died, my dear old Paterfamilias told me that his grandfather won the ruddy place during a game of *écarté*, three days after his own home had been destroyed by fire, but, rather than move into it, he exchanged it for a damn fine mare, which later foaled an Oaks winner."

"Considering that he had just lost his own house, why didn't your great-grandfather keep House-on-the-Hill, Stan?" had asked Edward Pryce the artist, also in the "Almond Tree" at the time.

"Don't ask me, old boy. But wouldn't you choose a stud mare in preference to that damned eye-sore?"

"Yes."

Whereupon Major Blye had interpolated: "I didn't know you were a racing man, Edward, dear fellow."

"I am not, but there would be a chance of my selling the animal."

"Ha! So you believe that a black mare is better than a white elephant, what, dear fellow?" And Blye, as always, had laughed heartily at his own witticism.

On another occasion: "Have you heard the rumour about the House with Crooked Walls, Mr. Terhune?" This from Miss Amelia, who looked after the shop whenever it was necessary for Terhune to leave it.

"Is it going to be bought by an American millionaire—the third time this year?"

"Not by an American millionaire, but by a rich Chinaman. I know there must be some truth in that particular rumour," Miss Amelia had continued, with all the excitement of which her placid soul was capable. "Last Wednesday I saw a Chinaman coming out of Mr. Tuttell's office." Tuttell's office was in Ashford; Tuttell was one of the leading estate agents for the district, and he had been trying to sell House-on-the-Hill ever since he had taken over the business from his father.

"But there," she had continued, with a shake of her greying head, "I shall be surprised if we hear that the House with Crooked Walls really has been sold. The Chinaman is no more likely to buy it than are all the other people who have inspected the place during the last two or three years. Mrs. Lawson told me that Mr. Tuttell has vowed to send a cheque for ten guineas to the Hospital on the day he sells the property."

"You don't think the Hospital will get that money in a hurry?"

"I do *not*," she had stated with emphasis. "Not while there are other houses to be bought. I am sure nobody in their sane senses would buy that house."

One memory prompted another; soon many similar remarks about the house jostled one another for a re-hearing—but not one of them supplied a possible answer to the question Salvaterra had asked: what lay beneath this universal dislike of the House with Crooked Walls? Terhune could not remember having heard anyone give a reasoned explanation for their aversion to the house.

Presently he became aware that his visitor was politely, but unmistakably expressing impatience, and realised that he had not yet answered the question implied in his visitor's last words.

"I am sorry to have been so long in speaking, Dr. Salvaterra," he apologised hastily. "I was trying to remember any information about House-on-the-Hill which I could pass on to you."

"So I judged. And have you remembered anything?"

"No."

"I am not surprised. My enquiries have been exhaustive. Indeed, Mr. Terhune, my decision to visit you was not taken solely in order to appeal to your memory. In the light of my information, or, rather, lack of information, it appears to me that the true explanation of the mystery—if I may be excused from using that much misused word?—is psychic. That is to say, I think it possible that some event occurred, probably anterior to living memory, in which House-on-the-Hill played a leading part. That event must have had startling repercussions upon the minds of the people living in the neighbourhood. The sight, or even the mere thought, of the house must have created such intense horror, or hatred, or fear that a modified form of that emotion still exists, although the cause has long been forgotten.

"Such an explanation is not so far-fetched as, at first, it may appear. Many people of to-day still observe picturesque local customs, the origins of which are lost in the fog of antiquity and oblivion. Even in your country, Mr. Terhune, this may be seen. Your Eton College annually plays a strange ball game, of which the origin is, I believe, unknown. You have one village where, on a certain day of the year, it is the, privilege of a small party of chosen men to kiss every maiden living there. You have another where a game of football is played in which many dozens of men take part. And another where the villagers dance through the streets—an unusually un-English display, if you will permit my saying so. Do you know the origin of kissing the Blarney stone?

"I could multiply such instances threefold, tenfold. But, to revert to House-on-the-Hill, were my explanation true, then, as a dabbler in psychology, I am more than ever interested, not only in the house, but also in discovering the origin of the local antipathy." Salvaterra paused suddenly, and craned his head somewhat nearer to Terhune, as if to give his dark, short-sighted eyes the chance of inspecting the younger man more thoroughly.

"I think that I am interesting you, young sir, but if I am mistaken, please speak frankly."

"But you do," Terhune asserted in all sincerity.

"There is a doubt in your mind at the moment."

The accusation startled Terhune, for it was justified. Were his thoughts expressed so obviously? he reflected. Or were the dark, strange eyes of the foreigner more than usually penetrating? He determined to try to keep a better control of his facial expressions.

"Your theory does not explain why House-on-the-Hill remains empty, Dr. Salvaterra. Granted the existence of a very real aversion towards the house, caused, as you suggest by some long-forgotten event, prospective purchasers, from distant districts, cannot have been so affected. Why have strangers refused the property, in spite of its many advantages?"

"By which you mean, I suspect, financial advantages—an unusually reasonable purchase price, for instance, and a low rating assessment?"

"Yes. Besides, although I have visited the house often, I cannot say I have experienced any feeling of repulsion so strong as to make me willing to exchange it, were it mine, for a racehorse. I was not born in this district."

"But you have not been *inside* the house, have you, Mr. Terhune?"

"No."

"Exactly!" Salvaterra exclaimed sharply. "It is not until one enters the house that one experiences that intense aversion which has dissuaded a long succession of prospective purchasers."

"But you have entered House-on-the-Hill, Dr. Salvaterra, and you are willing to begin negotiations for its purchase."

"I!" The foreigner laughed; slyly, yet in a note unexpectedly deep; for the second time, the younger man was surprised that so deep a voice should emanate from so slight a body. "I am an exception," he explained egotistically. "I experienced an unmistakable reaction, probably more acute than that felt by the majority of people who have entered the house, for I am peculiarly sensitive to psychic phenomena. But on me, young sir, the effect was different. Instead of alarming my subconscious, the phenomenon provoked my curiosity and aroused within me that determination to discover its origin which has brought me here this morning."

Terhune was bewildered. He was not interested in psychical research, and had, if not disdain for that and allied studies, at least a disinclination to meddle with them. Why, therefore, had Howard suggested this visit of Salvaterra's? Immediately this question occurred to him, he hastened to voice it, before the other man had the chance of reading it from his expression.

"I do not understand why Mr. Howard suggested your calling upon me, Dr. Salvaterra. My knowledge of matters psychic is scant—"

Salvaterra's dark eyes gleamed with sardonic amusement. "I did not come here to seek your opinion on metaphysical aspects, Mr. Terhune. Perhaps it may appear to you that I am travelling to my destination by too circuitous a route. To be more brief, if I am to study the curious phenomena which appear to surround House-on-the-Hill, I must learn as much of its history as I can. I should, therefore, appreciate your advice as to what books are the most likely to supply such information."

Terhune felt inclined to smile, for if Salvaterra wanted no more than that, then certainly he had used a lot of unnecessary words. Why could he not have asked merely for any books dealing with the history of House-on-the-Hill? In the belief that his visitor lacked a sense of humour, Terhune checked the threatened smile, but not the genuine enthusiasm which the mention of books had aroused in him. Any task connected with his beloved books was real enjoyment, but in this instance the element of mystery afforded an added zest, which made his studious eyes sparkle behind their horn-rimmed spectacles, accentuating the youthful keenness of his expression.

"I have a shelf over here devoted to books of local interest," he told his visitor as he crossed the shop. "One or another of them should contain some information about House-on-the-Hill."

"Will you permit that I join you?" Salvaterra asked courteously from his chair.

"Of course." As he had his back to the foreigner this time, Terhune allowed himself the pleasure of an amused grin. A funny chap, Salvaterra. Not a man to be judged either by appearances or first impressions.

He stretched out his hand for Kerr's *Kentish Houses*. "This is the latest work on Kent," he explained as Salvaterra joined him. "The first edition was published in nineteen thirty-five, but the author brought it up to date, and published a second, post-war edition about a year ago."

"Up to date!" Salvaterra repeated, surprised. "Has much new information come to light between nineteen thirty-five and last year?"

"Not much, but some of the houses mentioned in the first edition no longer exist. Others have been renovated, and are now quite different in appearance from the original illustrations."

"Ah! The war?"

Terhune nodded as he opened the volume at its index. "Hartswell Farm; Hankshill Manor; Heaton, Sir Henry Arthur, Bart.," he murmured, glancing quickly down the list of names indexed under the letter "H." "Heep, Village of; Heep Castle—ah! here it is: House-on-the-Hill, page ninety-four."

He flicked over the pages. "Here we are, Dr. Salvaterra. House-on-the-Hill." He chuckled. "The fellow who sketched the place must have had a shrewd sense of the theatrical. Look! He has given the house almost a human expression of malevolence. He must be a first-rate artist. He has drawn the house just as I have seen it half a dozen times or more—usually just before dusk—but until now I have not realised the effect the place had upon me."

Salvaterra waved away the proffered volume with his long, expressive hand. "My eyes are none too good except in the strongest light. I should need my spectacles to read, which I have not brought with me." A note of interest tinged his voice as he continued: "What does it say?"

"'It seemed as though House-on-the-Hill was cursing me for daring to disturb its selfish, melancholy solitude.'"

"Is that all?"

Terhune realised that he had mistaken the visitor's question. "I thought you were referring to the letterpress beneath the illustration, doctor."

"No, no, young sir. I think that the author must have a perceptive and receptive imagination, for he has chosen his adjectives with cunning skill. Selfish, melancholy solitude! In that short sentence he has drawn a superbly realistic word picture. But I am not interested in either the artist's or the author's impressions. I am capable of forming my own. At this moment I want practical history, not poetic whimsies. What does it say of past history?"

Terhune consulted the volume again, reading silently the author's description of his first visit to House-on-the-Hill—of the setting out from Bray-on-the-Marsh—of the pleasant vista of countryside which bordered the narrow road—the "Hare and Hounds"—the cherry orchard. He began to skip paragraphs, for Salvaterra was expressing irritation at the long pause.

He read on. At last: "'No sooner had I rounded the first corner past Keppel's Farm than I found myself so close to my destination that every detail of it was at last plainly discernible. This was strange, for, although House-on-the-Hill is a landmark visible for several miles, although I had been staring at its long, squat lines almost from the moment of leaving Bray, until I rounded that corner (which I learned subsequently was known as Keppel's Corner), House-on-the-Hill had seemed still very distant. Yet, immediately afterwards, I found myself so close to the house that I was taken aback. A whimsy took me; in those two minutes when the house was hidden from view by that copse which had been the subject of lengthy litigation between Mr. Kepple and Mr. Willoughby, had a kindly fairy moved House-on-the-Hill a mile nearer to me to ease the strain on my pounding lungs?

"'I dismounted from my bicycle, and gazed at the extraordinary building which confronted my astounded gaze. Once more a whimsy took me; one that was eerie and disconcerting, for it seemed as though House-on-the Hill was cursing me for daring to disturb its selfish, melancholy solitude. A sensation of awkward embarrassment possessed me, comparable to that which a homeward-bound reveller might feel upon stepping unexpectedly into a convent chapel.'"

"Well, Mr. Terhune?" Salvaterra's deep, smooth voice interrupted. "So far Kerr hasn't mentioned anything of its past history."

Terhune read on hastily. Writing in much the same strain, the author continued his impressions of House-on-the-Hill, followed by a description of the property. He finished with these words:

"As dusk shadowed the eastern horizon, I rode away from House-on-the-Hill. Only once did I glance backward over my shoulder; that was after I had passed Keppel's Corner. I looked back then, and lo and behold! I might have cycled a mile, two miles, so far away was I from the house which I had only just left. Does distance lend enchantment? Truly it does to House-on-the-Hill. No longer did the House with Crooked Walls terrify me with its unspoken curses. Gathering dusk had softened its malevolence into a forlorn aloofness which would have been pathetic had not the evil memory been still fresh in my mind. I rode away, thankful that I was under no necessity of staying there that night; and no longer curious as to why the house had remained empty for so many years.

"Has House-on-the-Hill, like so many houses, in that part of Kent, a history of its own? No doubt it has, but I know nothing of it. I have not read of its past in any book. Nor have I made any enquiries locally, for I left that neighbourhood with the extraordinary feeling that I had no wish ever to speak of the place again. If anyone wants to know who built the house with crooked walls, and why, they must look for the explanation elsewhere than in these pages."

"I'll be damned!"

"And why, young sir?"

"Listen to this." And Terhune read aloud Kerr's last paragraph about House-on-the-Hill.

Salvaterra nodded his head several times, but Terhune noticed that the expression of his dark, Latin eyes was more that of fervent enthusiasm than of annoyance at this meagre information. "Curious!" he remarked slowly. "Very curious! And how unimaginative of the author, not to have investigated further. But, of course, his impression was similar to that experienced by so many other people. No doubt, other writers have been more enterprising. What made that book your first choice?"

"In the first place, because it is the most recently published book dealing with Kent. Secondly, because Kerr usually delves into the past history of all the places he visits."

"Have you other books on hand which you can consult?"

"Several." Terhune indicated another volume. "*My Heart is Buried in a Cherry Orchard*, by S. Jefferson Dietz."

"The American author?"

"Yes. You know his books?"

"I have read his *South to Panama*, and *Why Pacific?* His style pleases me. In both books he reveals, not only a commendable meticulousness, but also an intense interest in the less obvious. If he visited House-on-the-Hill, it is certain that you will find a trenchant explanation of its continued unoccupancy."

On this point Terhune was less optimistic than his visitor: some years previously he had read *My Heart is Buried in a Cherry Orchard*, but could not remember any particular mention in it of House-on-the-Hill. A quick perusal of Dietz's book confirmed that his memory was not at fault. Ashford was the nearest point to Bray reached by the author during his travels in Kent. From Ashford Dietz had proceeded to Folkestone by the main road, and so had missed that out-of-the-way part of the county of which Bray was roughly the centre.

Terhune then turned to *The Tramp in Kent*, by the Rev. John Dexter, Volume V of the series, *A Tramp in England*. But the Rev. John had concentrated, somewhat understandably, on buildings and monuments of religious interest. House-on-the-Hill was dismissed in a few words: "North of Bray-in-the-Marsh is a house of some antiquity whose only purpose seems to be that of serving as a land-mark for those without sense of direction or compass; and an ideal picnicking place on a warm, sunny day. It has an extraordinary appearance, which has earned it the local nickname of the House with Crooked Walls, but it is scarcely worth a special visit except, perhaps, to those who might be interested in a *mélange* of architec-tural styles which has produced an effect of unpleasing incongruity."

Salvaterra's sardonic gaze followed every movement as Terhune replaced the Rev. Dexter's work and took down another.

"So you are not finding it easy to discover the wanted informa-tion, young sir," he murmured in his deep, soft, voice.

"No," Terhune answered, frowning in perplexity.

"I am not surprised. I have read several modern books on Kent, but in none of them was there special mention of a House with Crooked Walls. Had there been, I might have investigated the mystery long before now. Are all the books on that shelf twentieth-century publications?"

"Not all, doctor. This one, *Wiseman's Antiquarians' Guide to the County of Kent* was published in eighteen forty-eight, five years after this other, *Strange Stories of Kent*, by Ebenezer Mainwaring."

"*Strange Stories of Kent*"! Salvaterra repeated swiftly. "Might that not contain something of interest?"

Terhune turned to the index. There was an entry under House-on-the-Hill which read: "See Fitzwilliam, Sir Constant." And under Fitzwilliam: "Sir Constant buys House-on-the-Hill. Page 231."

Unfortunately page 231 shed very little light on the history of the house. Sir Constant, it appeared, was an old reprobate who had persistently belied his Christian name. During the previous eighty-two years he had achieved a notoriety second to none of his contemporaries in the county. Mainwaring had succeeded in tracing many strange and diverting stories of Sir Constant's escapades, but all of these had taken place while he had been living in a house two miles west of Dover. This house, in 1777, was razed to the ground by fire, the catastrophe being an indirect consequence of Sir Constant's celebrating his eighty-second birthday too well and not wisely. Barely escaping with his life, he purchased House-on-the-Hill, where he lived—still not chastened by Heaven's salutary warning of what his impending future was to be if he persisted in his riotous ways—for the next five years, until his death.

That was all. When Terhune reported this scrap of history to Salvaterra, for the first time that afternoon the Panamanian expressed disappointment. With an annoyed gesture, he glanced at the thin gold watch which he took from his waistcoat pocket, and arose from the pile of books upon which he had been sitting.

"I am afraid I can remain no longer, Mr. Terhune. I have an appointment in Ashford in fifteen minutes' time."

"I am sorry—"

Salvaterra raised his slender hand. "It is not for you to apologise, but me, my dear young sir. I have taken up your time needlessly." He paused, a little uncertainly. "Mr. Howard, in mentioning your name to me, related the interesting story of your successful effort to solve the mystery of Lady Kylstone's vault. You are, I understand, interested in—may I say?—amateur detection?"

Terhune frowned. Damn Howard as a gossipy old woman!

"Mr. Howard has exaggerated—"

"Quite! Quite!" Salvaterra's smooth voice interrupted. "I do not need to be a physiognomist to appreciate your undoubted modesty. But you *did* solve the mystery of Joe Richard's death?"

"I—I—in a way I—helped—"

"Exactly!" Salvaterra exclaimed in a satisfied voice.

And unexpectedly Terhune had a premonition that Detective-Inspector Sampson's prophecy of his being involved in another mystery was about to be fulfilled.

"Please listen to this proposition—" began the Panamanian.

Chapter Three

I

For some minutes after Salvaterra had left, Terhune continued to stand by the window and stare through the plate glass at the far corner of Market Square, around which the foreigner's car had disappeared on its return journey to Ashford. During those minutes, and, indeed, for as many hours afterwards, he was unable to shake off the strange effect which the visit had had upon him.

For instance, his recollection of Salvaterra. The personality of the white-haired, pale-cheeked little man remained vividly in his mind. It was more vivid than many another memory picture, even of people whom he had known for years. Mrs. Mann, for instance. Year in, year out, Mrs. Mann "did" for Terhune. Not only did she keep the shop swept and tidied and his bachelor flat above scrupulously clean, but, as well, she cooked and served both his breakfast and his luncheon. Everything about her was familiar; her broad, shapeless body, her round, red face, the long hairs above her upper lip, almost enough of them to form a moustache (and how often had he felt an overwhelming desire to pull them out?), the birthmark on the lobe of her left ear, the scar on the back of her right hand—all these characteristics he could clearly see in any visual picture of her. For all that, although he could so see her in a hundred postures, doing any one of a hundred different tasks, there was still a vague

formlessness about all such memories. This was not so in the case
of the man from Panama.

Dr. Vicente Salvaterra! Terhune repeated the name aloud,
grinning boyishly as he did so. Dr. Vicente Salvaterra! The name
sounded more like one taken from some book or film rather than
that of a living personage. At least, when heard in a quiet, sleepy,
Kentish market town. In Panama, in Buenos Aires, in Mexico City,
in Los Angeles, in Madrid, in Lisbon—in none of those places
would the name have sounded in any way uncommon or unreal.
But in Bray-in-the-Marsh...

The strangeness of his name was matched by a combination
of appearance and personality. His size, of course, helped first
to arrest and then to hold one's attention. Not merely because
of his stature, however, was one's recollection of him so clear
and indelible. There were at least two men as small as he living
in Bray. One was Joe Maggs, a farm labourer who worked for
George Moore at Three Ways Farm. Terhune had never heard
the name of the second man, but he appeared at the market
every Thursday morning, invariably dressed in a long, brown
overcoat, cloth-topped boots, and an old-fashioned, time-greened
beaver. This man Terhune had seen a hundred times in the past
few years, but, despite the distinctive if incongruous garments,
he could not recollect whether the man had brown eyes or blue;
dark or fair, or even grey, hair; big ears or small, good teeth or
bad...

But everything about Salvaterra was unforgettable. The mane
of spotless white hair, the strikingly black eyebrows, the strong,
prominent, but proportioned nose, the soft, red lips, the perfection
and whiteness of his teeth (except for one gold eye tooth), the almost
transparent, feminine skin, and specially the smooth-shaven chin,
which could be obstinately firm, then, a moment later, weak, then
neither, then both.

The hands, also. One could not forget their beauty. Long, narrow hands, unblemished, graceful, cared-for; with nails shapely and manicured. Nor the heavy, gold rings. Terhune had a feeling that even had Salvaterra no tongue his expressive hands would have no difficulty in speaking for him.

His eyes, too. They had the unfathomable depths of Latin eyes, but also a battery of concealed high lights which exposed, translated and illumined his every thought and feeling. All the concentrated wisdom of the ages seemed to be imprisoned behind those eyes. Other emotions, too, which were not easily interpreted.

Lastly, his voice, with its deep resonance, its carefree lilt, and its slight, attractive accent. The sound of Salvaterra's voice remained as clear in Terhune's ears, as did, in his eyes, the man.

What sort of a man was this Dr. Vicente Salvaterra? Terhune pondered. He was rich, he was a citizen of Panama, his ancestors had come from Portugal, he was deeply interested in philosophy and psychic phenomena, he loved England, and, in particular, Kent. So much Terhune knew of the foreigner, but what else? Was he really as old as his snowy-white hair suggested? His face was remarkably free of wrinkles. The complexion was that of a young man. Or an ageless man. It was also amazingly pink and white for one born and reared in a sub-tropical land. Why was it not olive, sun-burned?

Was he generous? Was he kind-hearted? Was he a humanist? Was he sincere, genuine? Or was he an atheist? Was he tyrannical? Was he a crank?

Exasperation succeeded reflection, as Terhune realised that Salvaterra's inner self was as unfathomable as the future; as inscrutable as the Sphinx. True, his first meeting with the Panamanian had lasted only thirty minutes or so, which was no time at all for knowing a man. On the other hand, Terhune prided himself on a quick and keen insight into character; he usually formed his opinion automatically upon a first meeting—and the occasions were rare indeed when longer knowledge did not confirm first impressions. In Salvaterra's case, there was not one characteristic, good, bad or indifferent, which he could distinguish or identify. Salvaterra was, in fact, as much a mystery as the house which he was proposing to buy.

This reflection brought about a change of thought—or, perhaps, a chain of thought. Terhune began thinking of the House with Crooked Walls. He left the window, returned to the bookshelf containing the books on Kent, and, for the second time, took down Kerr's *Kentish Houses*. He opened it at page 94, and stared at the sketch which Kerr (who had illustrated his own text) had made of House-on-the-Hill.

The drawing was uncanny. In that the artist had used every trick of his trade to exaggerate the evil appearance of the house, it might be said that the impression was more a caricature than a true sketch. Yet the result was unmistakably real. The more he studied the sketch, the more Terhune appreciated this. Again and again had he seen House-on-the-Hill looking exactly as it appeared on page 94 of Kerr's book. The wide, squat front door, framed in red brick walls; with a foot-high crenellated wall in front, enclosing a flower garden. With skilful cunning, the artist had made the dark oak door resemble a half-opened mouth; the red brick surround, lips; the crenellated wall, gnashing teeth. Two upper windows, emphasised by the reflected light of the setting sun, and at the expense of the other windows, which were in shadow, became angry, gleaming eyes. The eaves above, eyebrows. The sloping roof, a hairless skull. Two, conveniently-placed, half-hidden chimney stacks, the ears. Weather-beaten oak beams, high cheek bones. Even the spiral chimney-pots had transformed themselves into horns. For the rest, light and shade played their part in the caricature. "It seemed as though House-on-the-Hill was cursing me for daring to disturb its selfish, melancholy solitude." Absurd? Perhaps. Yet the artist's pen had given the house precisely that appearance, and Terhune, recollecting the house as he had seen it not three weeks previously, could find no fault with the sketch. He could not assert that this window was not really where Kerr had placed it, or that beam, or that stack, or that tree, with its strange, eerie shadows, or the background of ominous clouds.

Terhune was puzzled by this thought. He had seen House-on-the-Hill look exactly as it looked in the drawing; but he had never given its strange appearance an interpretation similar to Kerr's, although it was easy to see, and to confirm, what Kerr had seen. Why was it now so easy to see something he had never seen before, in spite of its having been so obvious? Was it the power of suggestion? Was he rather like a man who, after the fortune-teller has pointed out the object to him, can plainly recognise a ship (or a dog, or a woman's head, or the map of the U.S.A.) in the bottom of a tea-cup, although previously he had seen nothing but tea leaves?

Again, although Terhune had known that House-on-the-Hill was regarded with antipathy by the local inhabitants, why had he not, long ago, been tantalised by curiosity into seeking the reason for their dislike? Further reflection soon supplied the answer to this question. He had not been interested enough in the house to make such enquiries. But it was strange that all the other local residents should be equally disinterested. Why had it been necessary for a stranger—a foreigner, what was more—to visit the neighbourhood before attention was drawn to the existence of what, for want of a better description, Salvaterra had termed a psychological mystery?

Psychological! Mystery! An exaggeration, of course. There was no mystery about House-on-the-Hill. Local people heartily disliked, and even feared, the place, apparently without reason, but was that a—mystery? There had been a time when Terhune had heartily disliked sleeping on a ground floor, and he had reached the age of twenty-six before learning the reason for this finicalness. At the age of five, so said his uncle, an old nurse had read a story to lull him to sleep. With the *un*psychological unconcern (he grinned to himself, remembering his uncle's use of the word) of the old type of nurse, she had chosen a tale about a child who had been killed and carried off by a lion as a consequence of sleeping on the ground floor of an African bungalow. The memory of the story soon faded away. Not so the effect.

If there were no mystery about the lasting impression of a foolish story upon a childish mind, then equally there was no mystery about a parent, consciously or otherwise, passing on a dislike, a repugnance, a fear, to the children. There were, of course, still two other questions to be considered. What had happened, and when, to create this impression? It might be that time alone was responsible for lack of information on this point. But a peculiar imagination was needed to call a natural process of time by the word "mystery."

The only aspect which almost justified Salvaterra's exaggerated description of House-on-the-Hill was part of the last question: Why had prospective buyers, strange to the neighbourhood, and therefore presumably uninfluenced by inherited inhibitions, consistently refused to continue negotiations after having once entered the place? Certainly, that was strange, and might possibly be ascribed to psychic influence. On the other hand, it might be due to natural causes; an understandable disinclination to live in a place which had no right-angled corner, no two adjoining rooms on the same level, low ceilings upon which any man above average height would crack his skull, floors which, quite certainly, sloped from one side of a room to the other, walls which would not stand the test of a plumb line. It would not take a woman five minutes to realise the difficulties of furnishing such a house. Every piece of furniture, every yard of furnishing fabric and material would have to be tailored, as it were, to the house. No two pairs of curtains of the same size, for instance! Furniture having to be placed, not where the mistress of the house chose, but where the peculiarities of the house permitted.

To say nothing of the heartbreaking task of keeping clean a house that was a succession of passages and of steps up or steps down.

There were other reasons, too, liable to make one pause before buying the place. One man might genuinely dislike the appearance of a house which looked crooked. Another might prefer not to live in a house open to all four winds. Another might think it too old-fashioned. Another might think of the expense incurred in keeping a house, several centuries old, in repair. Were such reasons psychic? Did they suggest mystery? Most certainly they did not.

Yet, even if there were no genuine mystery as to why House-on-the-Hill remained empty, Terhune was none the less interested in the problem—what was responsible, in the first place, for the local deeply-rooted repugnance to entering the house? This reflection led his thoughts to the proposal which Salvaterra had put forward.

The proposition was a simple one. In effect Salvaterra had said: "Bring me a complete history of House-on-the-Hill, including, as far as possible, the biographies of all previous owners, also the answer to why local people fear the House with Crooked Walls, and I shall be happy to send you a cheque for fifty pounds."

Fifty pounds! A welcome amount to add to his small bank balance Terhune accepted the proposition, not so much on account of the proffered reward, but because of his own eagerness to know more of the past history of House-on-the-Hill. After all, as far as he was concerned, literary research was a pleasure, not a task. And he certainly had enjoyed his previous venture into amateur detection...

I I

Filled with enthusiasm, he returned to the row of books dealing with Kent, leaving until later his examination of the parcel of books from the Rectory. Now that there was no need to satisfy the immediate requirements of an impatient client, he decided to reverse the order which he had previously adopted, and, instead of referring first to the most modern publications, he opened his oldest volume.

This was, *A Compleat Topographical and Geographical Survey of Ashford and Its Environs*, by J. W. Mason, printed in London by *I. Dawks*, for, and Sold by *John Pemberton*, at the *Buck and Sun* over against *St. Dunstan's* Church in *Fleet-Street*, 1712. The book had neither index, nor chapter headings; the only method of tracing any particular place or district was the laborious one of skimming each page.

He carefully turned over the pages, which the years had made brittle and brown. Ashford itself was dealt with at great length, but Terhune ignored these pages, and arrived at the chapter where the author began his series of excursions into the countryside surrounding the small town. Kennington, Hinxhill, Willesborough, Sevington, Mersham, Smeeth, Sellindge. He turned over more pages, marvelling at the writer's perseverance and industry. He had entitled his book "Compleat," and complete it was. As far as it was possible to judge, every building with any claim to antiquity, or anecdote, was mentioned, and often described.

Willingham at last! Or rather, Willinshame. The author arrived there one 3rd of May, "a balmy, beautiful summery day that, methinks, no other country in the world could equal." First, to Willinshame Church: "'Real old, that church be,' says John, pointing with his whip at a creeper-covered stone edifice whose rustic simplicity brought tears to my eyes, in between whoa-ing Mary and bringing her to a gentle halt." Two complete pages were allocated to a description of the Church, and its history; and as many paragraphs to the Kylstone family vault—the vault which had been indirectly responsible for Terhune's achieving local fame as an amateur detective, and also more particularly for his having made a host of friends.

From the Church the author went on to speak of Willinshame Manor, now the home of the Hon. Mrs. MacMunn, The Mill (now Old Mill House, occupied by Sir George Brereton), Rockaway Cottages, then being rebuilt by Sir Piers Kylstone, for the use of his tenants, the Posting Inn (now the "Hop-Picker"), and by way of two or three houses which no longer existed, to Turnpike House, and House-on-the-Hill.

Terhune was interested to note that, as long ago as 1712, House-on-the-Hill was known by that same name. He read on, eagerly, but the author had less to say about House-on-the-Hill than he had hoped. According to Mason, House-on-the-Hill stood on the site of a Norman Keep, erected by William the Conqueror to garrison a small company of soldiers under one Fitz-Osbern the Bald, nephew of William Osbern, afterwards one of William's regents when he returned to Normandy.

Since that time, continued the author, only three other buildings, it is said, have occupied the site. The first, a cell and grotto, built in the later years of the twelfth century from the ruins of the keep, and occupied by one Robert the Hermit; three cottages by Sir Godfrey d'Angillon (1393–1432), and a large manor, incorporating the cottages, with additions thereto, by Cecil Mulholland, a burgess of the City of London, and completed in the year 1596. Another wing was added in 1621 by Charles Mulholland, son of Cecil. In 1673, died the last of the Mulhollands, whereupon the property passed into the possession of Silas Ingleton, nephew by marriage of the last Mulholland.

"At the present day, House-on-the-Hill is owned by Nathaniel, son of Silas, a pleasant, homely gentleman who lives there with his wife, and five healthy children. Upon my stating the purpose of my visit, and soliciting the honour of being shewn over the house, I was received most charmingly by Mr. and Mrs. Ingleton, whom I found to be truly affable. Not only were they agreeable to my request for information, but Mr. Ingleton further revealed his sympathetic interest in my book by promising to subscribe for two copies of same upon publication.

"The previous history of House-on-the-Hill I have already passed on to my readers. The house itself I found to be commodious, while still retaining an enviable homeliness. One strange habit of this household, which I cannot forbear mentioning, is that each child occupies a bedroom of his or her own; a custom to which I cannot wholeheartedly subscribe, for surely the sharing by brothers of a common bedroom is the core of fraternal love and affection, whereas, methinks, the occupying of a bedroom by one person only, except one who has reached an age of maturity, must lead perforce to a dangerous spirit of independence, and even selfishness."

The author had more to say on this subject, but Terhune skipped the passage, and resumed his reading at the point where Mason continued his description of the house, which was both brief and disappointing. In so far as it was possible to judge from an account written in the knowledge that the charming Mr. Ingleton had subscribed for two copies of the book, House-on-the-Hill, in the year 1712, was very little different from the scores of surrounding houses visited by the indefatigable Mr. Mason. There was no hint of crooked walls or of a local distaste or fear of the house. Furthermore, it seemed that between the years 1596 and 1712 the house had been in constant occupation.

An interesting discovery. Whatever was at the root of the present instinctive aversion apparently dated from some time after 1712. So much the better, Terhune thought, for, doubtless, it would be easy to unearth that root. He stretched out his hand for another volume...

"Well, Theo, my sweet, have I to stay here *all* the morning before you will condescend to notice me?"

Terhune recognised the bitter-sweet voice of Julia MacMunn.

Chapter Four

He had not seen Julia since the day before she had left Willingham for a trip to the Canary Islands. He jumped hastily up from the pile of books on which he had been sitting—the same pile as that previously occupied by Salvaterra. He held her two hands within his own, and gazed at her through his horn-rimmed spectacles.

"Julie! This is a surprise. I thought you were not due back for at least another four weeks."

"Mother insisted upon returning. She said she would be ill herself if she looked at another banana, smelled any more garlic, or tasted olive oil again."

"Was it as bad as that?"

"Of course it was not, but you know what an old stick-in-the-mud Mother is. Every day spent away from home is a day of agony for her."

"You—you didn't mind coming home, Julie?" he asked awkwardly.

"Naturally I minded," she replied testily.

"I think your mother might have considered your feelings just for once. After all, it—it was for—your—sake—" He broke off, embarrassed.

She snatched her hands away from him. "Why are you staring at me so solemnly?" she demanded acidly. "Am I looking better than your lordship believed possible?"

The question did not help to ease his embarrassment, for she had correctly divined his thoughts. She was looking far healthier than on the occasion of their last meeting. Then, beneath the tan of sun and wind and rain, her cheeks had been pale and drawn; her left eyelid had developed a nervous twitch, and her expression, bitterness.

During her absence in the Canaries, not only had her cheeks filled out, but they had also lost that underlying paleness. The twitch, too, had entirely disappeared. But the bitterness? He was not sure. There was a flame in her eyes which could have been bitterness, or resentment, or even anger—but then Julia had a nature which had always been notoriously intolerant, hypercritical and sardonic; a nature, indeed, which events previous to her trip abroad were scarcely calculated to improve.

For what had happened? One foggy night, some months previously, while cycling home from Wickford, Terhune had run headlong into adventure. Nothing particularly dramatic, or even heroic—just five men assaulting a solitary girl in a car. Jumping from his bicycle, he had cheerfully attacked the five men, only to be knocked out after a brief, but spirited struggle. Fortunately, a local constable, also on a bicycle, arrived at that moment, so the five men promptly vanished in the fog, and that—so it seemed at the time—was the end of that little episode.

It was far from the end, as subsequent events proved. Terhune's interference with the plans of the five men had many consequences—his friendship with the girl he had saved, Helena Armstrong; her employer, Lady Kylstone; the Honourable Mrs. MacMunn; Julia; and many others. Another consequence was his discovering, first, a murder, and later, the murderer. But, in doing this Terhune had brought distress to the proud, arrogant Julia, for he had sent her friend to the gallows; the man whom local gossips had been certain that she would marry.

What effect the execution had upon Julia's heart was known only to herself, but most people were tempted to add two and two together, for Julia subsequently became ill, and the doctor was forced into bullying her mother to take her abroad to recuperate. Others, who liked Julia in spite of her caustic tongue and brusque manner, believed that her pride had suffered more than her heart, and were even more sympathetic in consequence, arguing that it could not be pleasant to learn that one had been freely consorting with a cold-blooded murderer, going everywhere with him, making him one's confidant.

"You are looking fine, Julie," Terhune told her, ignoring her question. "I am glad."

His undoubted sincerity restored softer lights to her eyes. "Returning home has some compensations," she said, glancing round the shelves of books which all but surrounded her. "I have missed your cheerful grin, Theo, and all your funny little ways. You are an ingenuous soul, my pet, with your deep love of books, and your selfish, narrow-minded contentment…"

"Thank you." He grinned happily. There spoke the Julia of old; proof enough, to his own satisfaction, that she had largely recovered from her recent shock.

"Well, you are narrow-minded. Only a narrow-minded man could remain content living in a stuffy little town like Bray-in-the-Marsh."

"So you have told me before…"

"Without effect, apparently."

"Exactly. And why am I selfish? Because I do not grant the rest of the world the honour and privilege of knowing me?"

"Idiot!" She quickly changed the course of conversation, apparently in the belief that it was approaching a danger point. "You must have been tremendously interested in the book you were reading when I first entered. I stood here more than five minutes before I dared to interrupt you."

"Five minutes!"

"Not a second less," she assured him firmly. And, rightly interpreting his incredulous expression, she added appealingly: "Honestly, Theo."

"Not a second less than *five* minutes?"

"*Five* minutes."

He believed her, so he ruffled his hair, which was, as usual, already untidy. "I can't understand how you could have been there all that time without my knowing. And how did you get in without the bell jangling?"

"But it did! It made its customary noise." Seeing his expression of confusion, she laughed. "I believe you were reading a naughty book, my pet, and are feeling embarrassed at being found out."

"I was not," he denied indignantly, and she laughed again, because he had risen to the bait so innocently. "As a matter of fact I was reading a book entitled *A Compleat Topographical and Geographical Survey of Ashford and its Environs*."

"Heavens! And you found *that* absorbing? It would bore me even to read the title."

He grinned, for Julia MacMunn, like her mother, had a notorious distaste for any kind of reading. "I was looking up the history of House-on-the-Hill."

"That terrible place!" She stared at him. "What on earth do you want to know its history for? Surely you are not proposing to buy the property?"

He realised that the question was not put to him seriously, so he did not answer. Instead, he asked: "What made you describe House-on-the-Hill as a terrible place?"

"Don't you think it is? Surely you do not *admire* that atrocity?"

"I do not. But tell me, seriously, Julie, why did you scoff at House-on-the-Hill immediately I mentioned it?"

"Because it is an atrocity," she answered promptly.

"But is it? Try to answer without prejudice. Don't you think that, if it were a little smaller and if it were in a valley, surrounded by trees, you might call it romantic, instead of atrocious. After all, most of the old houses round about bulge here and there."

"*I* should not describe it as romantic, never mind what its surroundings might be, but then I prefer the twentieth century and comfort to the seventeenth century and romance. Still, I see what you mean, Theo. Why do you ask?"

"The place repels you, but you cannot say why?"

"No."

"And your mother? What does she think of it?"

"She loathes it, naturally."

"Why do you say, naturally? Your mother usually has a penchant for anything unusual or *outré*."

Julia showed signs of irritation. "For Heaven's sake, Theo, are you going to spend the rest of the morning asking stupid questions? If you were a gentleman, you would suggest taking me to the 'Almond Tree' for a cocktail."

"If you were a lady, you would not drink a cocktail."

"Come back from your journey to the seventeenth century," she snapped, adding, after a pause: "Why the sudden interest in House-on-the-Hill?"

"Because there is a possibility of its being sold."

She laughed scornfully. "That rumour has been circulating for years, but the place is still empty. Every time a prospective purchaser sees the inside of the house he decides to live elsewhere."

"Not so this time, Julie."

"Do you mean to say that somebody still wishes to buy the place even after having seen it?"

"Yes."

"He must be crazy."

Terhune chuckled. "More than that, he is not buying the property in spite of its crooked walls, but because of them."

Julia angrily pursed her lips. "If you would stop looking mysterious, and not talk in riddles, I might be able to take an intelligent interest in what you are saying."

"I am not talking in riddles. You won't give me a chance of explaining..."

"I shall take myself to the 'Almond Tree' unless you explain quickly why you are asking so many questions."

He realised that her temper was too touchy to endure further teasing. "I am trying to," he explained quickly. "What happened is that the prospective buyer, upon learning that House-on-the-Hill has been unoccupied for many years, and not understanding why, took the precaution of instituting enquiries into the matter. As a consequence, he learned, not only that clients had refused to consider buying the property after having once entered it, but also that everyone living locally hates and fears the house to such an extent that nobody would accept it as a free gift."

"It cannot have taken him long to find that out."

"Probably not, but what he has not yet learned is the reason for that local fear."

"Reason!" Julia's wind-coppered forehead wrinkled. "Is not the house itself reason enough?"

"Are you afraid of everything you hate?"

"Of course not!"

"Besides, you admitted, a few minutes ago, that you could not explain precisely *why* you hate House-on-the-Hill. What applies to you applies equally to everyone else. Everybody appears to hate the house, but only by instinct."

"Doesn't one usually hate by instinct? I hate tea served from a silver teapot, but I cannot give you a specific reason for that particular hate."

"That particular hate, as you call it, is individual. Not everybody hates tea from a silver teapot, but, as far as can be learned, everybody knowing House-on-the-Hill has some sort of an adverse feeling about it. Dr. Salvaterra—"

"Who?"

"The prospective buyer. The doctor, being interested in metaphysics, is convinced that something happened in connection with the house, probably a good many years ago, which so affected local people that it has been feared and disliked ever since, although the original cause for that feeling has long been forgotten."

For many seconds there was silence in the bookshop. During this time Julia stared at one or another of the books which filled the shop, but the expression in her gipsy-dark eyes revealed her profound interest in all that she had just heard. Presently she nodded her head, and spoke, in a voice more vivacious than it had been since her entry:

"I am beginning to comprehend what Dr. Salvaterra—I suppose he is a foreigner, Theo?"

"A Panamanian."

"Good Heavens! I have never before heard of a Panamanian! As I was saying, I think I realise why he is so curious about House-on-the-Hill. I cannot remember ever having heard anyone give what you call a reason for his or her feelings towards the house. But what have you been looking up in your musty old books?"

"Its history, Julie, in the possible hope that the past will supply an answer. Salvaterra has promised me fifty pounds if I find it."

"Dr. Salvaterra—you—Why you, Theo?"

He began enthusiastically: "Because Howard told him I was a bookworm, had a collection of old books about Kent, and was by way of being interested in amateur detect—" He stopped abruptly upon seeing the bleak expression which sprang into Julia's eyes.

"Oh, Julie! I—I am—sorry. I was not thinking what—what I was saying…"

"Haven't you done enough harm through dabbling in matters which should not concern you?" she asked in a low, bitter voice.

"*Harm?*" he repeated in a reproachful voice. Harm, that a criminal and murderer had met with just retribution!

She was quick to sense his reaction. "I am sorry, Theo," she said flatly. "I did not mean to say that. I spoke without thinking…" She made an effort to dispel the atmosphere of tragedy which had so unexpectedly invaded the bookshop. "Tell me more about House-on-the-Hill. Have you found anything in its history to account for local sentiment?"

"Not as yet. What I have learned is that the house was occupied, apparently continuously, between the years fifteen ninety-six and seventeen twelve."

Her face reflected her newly-aroused interest. "Did it become empty after that?"

"I cannot say. At the latter date Nathaniel Ingleton and his family were installed there, but the next pertinent date is seventeen seventy-seven, when Sir Constant Fitzwilliam moved in. He remained there until his death five years later. I have not yet found out what happened between seventeen twelve and seventeen seventy-seven."

"Then the house had not its present reputation in seventeen eighty-two?"

"Apparently not, Julie, although Sir Constant appears to have been something of an old reprobate; he might easily have been a character ready to thumb his nose at Mephistopheles himself, and not care a damn where he lived, so long as he had a bed to sleep in, a pipe full of baccy, and a tot of rum."

Julia's interest increased. "You haven't discovered when House-on-the-Hill first became an object of hate among the local inhabitants?"

"No, but Winstanley can supply a clue."

"You mean his story about his great grandfather's being given the place in settlement of a gambling debt, and exchanging it for a Derby winner?"

"The animal was not a Derby winner, but the dam of an Oaks winner," he corrected drily.

"I am sure Stan mentioned the Derby when he told the story to me. When was the exchange supposed to have taken place?"

"I have never heard a date mentioned, but as Great-grandfather Winstanley lived three generations ago, and three generations roughly equals a century, probably the date of the transaction can be placed between eighteen forty and eighteen fifty."

Julia's eagerness to know more was good to see; her lips parted slightly, and in doing so, lost all the hard cynicism which normally spoiled their otherwise attractive shape.

"Then the period to be investigated is that between Sir Constant's death, in seventeen eighty-two, and eighteen forty?"

"Probably."

Her eagerness vanished; she began to look dubious. "How can you possibly obtain information about something which may have taken place between one hundred and one hundred and sixty years ago?"

"By going to the source which has already supplied what knowledge we already possess."

"Books?"

He nodded. "Books, old manuscripts, records, and other similar papers in the British Museum and other repositories of historic documents. As you are not fond of reading, it would surprise you to know how much information about the past has come from private diaries."

"I did not entirely fritter away the time I spent at Roedean and Girton," she said drily.

"I was not referring to Pepys, Evelyn, Grenville, and all the more famous recordists, but to others, whose papers one would not expect to find at Roedean." He grinned happily. "William Hickey, for instance, and I do not mean our contemporary columnist," he added, observing her expression of bewilderment. "It is surprising how much is now known of some most insignificant people, whose doings would have been unknown to posterity but for some dear, garrulous old lady or gentleman writing in a diary: 'To-day, tea with dear Mrs. MacMunn, in whose drawing-room I had the pleasure of meeting her charming daughter Julia, and a solemn young man by the name of Theodore Terhune who runs a book-store and library in the neighbouring town of Bray-in-the-Marsh.' In the next century that entry will inform enthusiastic biographers of the famous Secretary for War, Mr. Nicholas Terhune, that his great-grandfather was a resident of Bray-in-the-Marsh."

She laughed. "You are a fool, Theo; and if that is meant as a hint—well, it all depends how well you behave during the next hour."

"The next hour! My dear girl, I know I am not exactly over-worked on a Tuesday morning, but you must realise that I cannot leave this place to run itself while I escort you to the 'Almond Tree.' What do you think Sir George would say if he came in to buy another book on fly fishing, and found nobody here to listen to the story of the trout he almost caught last Friday?"

"Don't jump to conclusions, my pet. I was not suggesting your leaving the shop. I am going to stay here with you, while you rummage among your musty old books for information about House-on-the-Hill."

He tried to dissuade her from this course, for he knew the gossip which would begin to circulate if once it were known that Julia MacMunn had spent all the morning in Mr. Terhune's book-shop. His efforts met with no success. Julia had a nature that was as obstinate as it was independent. Her curiosity about House-on-the-Hill had been aroused by his story, and she was eager to learn more about the place at the earliest possible moment. She laughed at his warnings about what the gossips would have to say on the subject of her long visit to the shop, settled herself comfortably on the only chair, and coolly ordered him to proceed with the work her coming had interrupted.

There being nothing else to do in the circumstances, he walked slowly back to the bookshelves. But not altogether with good heart. He was glad of her company. Very glad. He was also pleased to know that the happy camaraderie between Julia and himself had not been destroyed in consequence of his having solved the mystery of the Kylstone family vault. But, equally, he did not care to reflect upon what effect the gossip would have on Helena—when it reached that far, as inevitably it would. Where Julia MacMunn was concerned, Helena was apt to become somewhat—well, sharp-tongued.

Julia's presence proved no mascot to him. During the next thirty minutes he looked through some half a dozen books, but the only new item about House-on-the-Hill to come to light was a paragraph mentioning that, according to one of Mrs. Elizabeth Maxwell's letters, Lord Kenelm Chisswell was rumoured to have spent the Christmas of 1793 at Caroline's house in Kent, House-on-the-Hill, near to Ashford.

Caroline—whom? Alas! There was no further mention of Caroline in the book. Nor was there any person indexed whose Christian name began with a "C." But the mention of Lord Kenelm Chisswell was a clue to be followed up. Across the other side of the shop was a complete set of the *Dictionary of National Biography*, in which, no doubt, further information concerning Lord Kenelm was likely to be found. He took one step in that direction. Before he could take a second, Julia's sharp voice rang out.

"Theo!"

The excitement in her voice made him glance at her with astonishment. It was rare to see Julia excited, for normally she was entirely imperturbable.

"What is it, Julie?"

"Grandfather's book!" she exclaimed.

Terhune swore silently. Why the devil hadn't he thought of that before?

Chapter Five

O utside the MacMunn family, nobody knew more about "Grandfather's book" than Terhune himself. "Grandfather" was the late Baron Fulchester; his "book" a painstaking and exhaustive genealogical history of every family of importance living in the neighbourhood of Willingham. During the last ten years of his life, and following the death of MacMunn, Lord Fulchester had lived with his daughter at Willingham Manor. Prompted by a love of genealogy and heraldry, he had occupied and amused himself during his last years in compiling local genealogical, heraldic—and, one might add, anecdotal—biographies, which he had himself written on parchment specially bound for this purpose. These biographies he had illustrated by coloured reproductions of armorial bearings.

The work was alphabetical. It was also uncompleted, the author having been overtaken by death while finishing the last entry under "T." The book, having thus been deprived of its ending, subsequently lost its beginning. One day, a year before Terhune became involved in the affair of the Kylstone family vault, an unknown vandal had gained-access to Mrs. MacMunn's library, and had deliberately torn out all biographies appearing under the first four letters of the alphabet. It was Terhune who, later, proved that the theft of these pages was linked up with the theft of the key of the Kylstone vault, and in doing so, had disclosed the details of an unsuspected murder.

Lord Fulchester had done his work meticulously. From one source or another—as often as not from the private records of actual families, with whom he was friendly—he had garnered almost every scrap of interesting material concerning the lives of past and present members, even to the extent of including briefer biographies of other families connected by marriage, but not otherwise resident in the neighbourhood. If any source extant were likely to contain information relating to past occupiers of House-on-the-Hill, Lord Fulchester's manuscript was that source.

Seeing the eager expression which immediately flowed across Terhune's face at the mention of her grandfather's book, Julia followed up her suggestion to consult the work by inviting him to dine with her that night. He accepted gladly, and not solely on account of the opportunity to continue his investigations. For all her faults, he liked Julia immensely, so the prospect of spending an evening with her was agreeable, even if it did mean enduring her mother—Alicia MacMunn was a dear person, but she had a tongue which was rarely at rest, and a brain that was incapable of concentrating upon any one subject for more than two minutes at a time. Usually Alicia's conversation would flit from one unrelated topic to another with all the blithe inconsequence of a butterfly flower-visiting on a sunny day.

Having accepted the invitation, Terhune found he had to pay a price for Julia's good nature. For once in his life he was to leave the shop to take care of itself while he escorted her to the "Almond Tree" for the promised cocktail, not in an hour's time, but at once. She bolstered up her command by the tempting argument that Winstanley was sure to be occupying his usual seat at the hotel, and that the moment was as good as another for interrogating him about his ancestor's brief ownership of House-on-the-Hill.

Terhune argued feebly against this course, but Julia was adamant, and, as Mrs. Mann was upstairs, cleaning one of the rooms, he compromised by promising to escort her to the "Almond Tree" in thirty minutes' time, when Mrs. Mann would be able to keep an eye upon the shop until it was time to close it. Meanwhile, he could spend the intervening thirty minutes in looking through the *Dictionary of National Biography* and other books, in the hope of discovering further information of value.

Julia promptly agreed to this proposal, so Terhune went upstairs to make the necessary arrangements with Mrs. Mann. She was—using the word plainly expressed by her eyes, if not by her lips—"flabbergasted" by his revolutionary resolve to leave the shop in order to visit the "Almond Tree" on a *Tuesday* morning (Sunday mornings alone were permissible by her code of ethics), but her heart was as large as her body, and she agreed readily to take charge of the shop during his absence.

The next thirty minutes he spent in consulting the *Dictionary of National Biography*. First, opening the Index and Epitome, he turned up Lord Kenelm Chisswell. To judge by the amount of space devoted to his biography, Lord Kenelm had been a person of no great importance. Lord Kenelm, it seemed, was born in 1768, the third son of George Perfect Chisswell, second Marquess of Hamble; educated at Eton and Christ Church, Oxford; B.A., 1790; patronised the Arts; died, 1794.

Page 264 of Volume 10 of the series contained a fuller biography, but reference to it shed little further light on the life of Lord Kenelm Chisswell. This was not so regarding his death, for Lord Kenelm had died at his own hand, on January 7th, 1794, in Maidstone, Kent.

January 7th, 1794! Terhune's face must have been vividly expressive as he appreciated the possible significance of this date, for Julia asked sharply:

"What have you just read, Theo?"

"This Lord Kenelm Chisswell I mentioned to you just now committed suicide on the seventh of January, seventeen ninety-four."

"Well?"

"The date may be no more than a coincidence, but it is strange that he should have killed himself within two weeks of having spent Christmas at House-on-the-Hill."

"Theo!" During some seconds' silence she considered his inference. Presently she spoke; there was a suggestion of excitement in her voice which, normally, was aggravatingly self-controlled.

"Do you think that his suicide may be not unrelated to his stay there?"

Spoken aloud, the theory no longer sounded reasonable. Indeed, the question introduced a note of ridicule, although he knew that such was not the intention. He realised that he was falling into an error, common among all enthusiasts and addicts to arm-chair criticism: he was trying to make his facts agree with a theory, instead of basing his theory upon a firm foundation of fact. Any one of a dozen reasons might explain Lord Kenelm's suicide; it was absurd to deduce, in the absence of further information, that his suicide on January 7th was connected with a holiday spent, two weeks previously, at House-on-the-Hill. Give a dog a bad name—That was what he, Terhune, was doing to House-on-the-Hill. Because he had heard, for the first time that day, that House-on-the-Hill was notoriously repugnant to local inhabitants, he was already trying to hang on the place the blame for a death which had taken place twenty-three miles away, an unknown number of days later.

Julia was less critically minded—at that moment. "Did he commit suicide in House-on-the-Hill?" she continued eagerly, evidently taking his silence to mean that his answer, had it been voiced, would have been in the affirmative.

"No. At Maidstone."

A disappointed "Oh!" Then: "Tell me more."

"There is no more."

"Doesn't it say why, or how?"

"Not in this publication. I doubt whether the biographer himself knew the answer to those two questions. Probably he learned from some parish record or other, or perhaps from the family, that Lord Kenelm died on the seventh of January, and was buried at So-and-So, a burial service being held in such-and-such a church, and that was all. He recorded the fact in the *D.N.B.*, and, because our Kenelm was a nonentity, neither he nor anybody else subsequently troubled to find out more of the actual details of his death."

"In view of the reputation of House-on-the-Hill, I still think it strange that his death should have followed so soon after his visit there."

"You forget, Julie, as far as we have yet learned, House-on-the-Hill did not have its present reputation back in seventeen ninety-four. On the contrary, if one takes into consideration the fact that the unknown Caroline was living there, and not alone."

"How can you make that assertion? She might have been a recluse—another, more modern, Robert the Hermit."

"If Caroline had been young, and living alone, would Kenelm have offended so openly against the proprieties by staying with her over the Christmas holidays? Indeed, would the proprieties of that period have permitted a young girl to live alone?"

"She might have been middle-aged, or even elderly."

"Then I doubt that Kenelm, who was still in his early twenties, would have spent with an elderly woman what is generally a time of festivity, in which youth comes into its own."

Julia's eye twinkled. "You are very logical, my pet. So, if Caroline were not a recluse, then she must have been one of several other people living in the house. In which circumstances, you think it unlikely that a family of several people would cheerfully have occupied a house which had achieved a reputation equal to that which it possesses to-day?"

"Don't you agree, Julie?"

"I suppose so. The theory sounds feasible, and is worth considering until it is disproved." She pursed her lips, almost angrily. "I wish you had not told me about House-on-the-Hill."

"Why not?"

"For two reasons. The first, because my curiosity is aroused, making me want to know why that poor boy, Kenelm, committed suicide."

"And the second reason?"

"Because that curiosity makes me despise myself for being in a class with you and your amateur detection."

Terhune chuckled. "So at last you are beginning to understand the fascination of solving mysteries! The next thing to happen will be your coming to me and asking the name of the latest Peter Wimsey, or the latest Mr. Fortune."

She appeared not to hear his raillery, for she continued meditatively: "If one could find out Caroline's surname, one might learn more of Lord Kenelm from her biography. How could it be traced, Theo?"

"Only by luck, I am afraid. Of course, if she were a queen, I could look under the Carolines—"

"Theodore Terhune!" she snapped. "If you make fun of me, you shall not come to dinner to-night."

He thought it better to be diplomatic. "I wasn't making fun of you, Julie. Honestly, I don't know how to begin looking for Caroline. Later on, I might come across a lead to her—for instance, tracing back the past owners of the house. Meanwhile, all I can do is to ignore her, and pretend that Lord Kenelm committed suicide on account of an accumulation of gambling debts."

She smiled, a trifle wistfully. "You are almost making a convert of me, after all. I am beginning to appreciate that books can sometimes be useful…"

"Only sometimes? And only useful? Won't you admit their entertainment as well as their utility?"

"I might admit that where books of history are concerned—which is a generous admission on my part, for I have always hated history even more than I have hated reading. But now that you have lifted the veil of the past, and permitted me the tiniest peep into the history of House-on-the-Hill, I must confess that I am anxious to see more. Are there any other names you can turn up in the *Dictionary*?"

"Several. Shall we look up the names in chronological order?" She nodded. "Then Fitz-Osbern is the first."

He carried the Index across the room, and laid it flat upon his table, where the light was better. She followed him there, and as he turned over the pages, she approached close to him, and peered over his shoulder.

"Here are the Fitzs," he muttered. "Fitzgerald—Fitzgerald—Fitzgilbert—Fitzmaurice—Here we are! Fitz-Osbern, William, Earl of Hereford. That is our Fitz-Osbern's uncle. We want the nephew. Here he is, in the next column. 'Fitz-Osbern the Bald, nephew of the Earl of Hereford, came to England with William the First; rewarded by a grant of land in Kent; killed during the Baron's rising, 1074.' Nothing there, Julie, to make us excited.

"Who was next? Robert the Hermit." He turned over the pages again, until he reached the Roberts. "Good Lord! Look at all those Roberts. I didn't know there were so many Roberts in English history. Robert the Staller, Robert d'Oilge, Robert the Englishman, Robert the Scribe, Robert, Abbot of Glastonbury—"

"You are looking for Robert the Hermit," she reminded him.

"So I am." He turned back to the previous page. "Here's our man. Robert the Hermit; entered the Benedictine abbey at Whitby, in 1173, but renounced the monastic way of life in 1189, to establish a hermitage near Guillinshame (Willingham); accused of strange practices; disappeared in 1203."

"Strange practices! Disappeared!" Julia repeated sharply. "What does that mean?"

"We will soon see." With mounting excitement, Terhune again consulted the volumes of the *National Biography*, collected Volume 68, and returned to the table. Laying the volume on top of the opened Index, he turned to page 358.

'Robert the Hermit, a Norman by birth, accompanied his father to England in the year 1171. When his father died, two years later, Robert entered the Benedictine abbey at Whitby, at the age of thirteen. In 1183 he was ordained, but finding monastic life too irksome, in 1189 he obtained his abbot's permission to renounce monastic life and become a hermit. Proceeding to the village of Willingham in Kent, he established himself on the site of a disused keep, and used material from the ruins to build himself a hermitage, in which he lived for the next fourteen years. In 1191 he constructed a grotto, which became known as a holy shrine to which sterile women could make a pilgrimage to offer prayers for fecundity. Successful results of these pilgrimages having been reported by grateful mothers, the hermit's grotto became famed both far and wide, and many women were recorded as having travelled distances ranging from fifty to one hundred miles to pray in the grotto of Robert the Hermit.

'During the first year of the new century, strange stories began to circulate that the new-found fecundity of the pilgrims was not to be ascribed solely to prayer. Early in 1203 the serfs of the neighbouring villages of Willingham and Bray implored their rector, William de Wiseham (d., 1221) (*q.v.*) to take action against the hermit for practices alleged to be incompatible with his spiritual duties. Before the rector could communicate this complaint to his bishop, it was learned that Robert had disappeared from his hermitage. Nothing more was ever heard of him.

'(Leland's *Comment. de Scriptt.* 203; Wright's Biogr. *Brit. Litt. Anglo-Norman,* p. 270; Coxe's *Cat. MSS. Coll. Aulisque Oxon; Gent. Mag.,* 1817, i, 320).

G.M.J.'

Terhune laughed as he looked up from the desk. "A picturesque character, our Robert. But though his biography is an amusing one, Julie, I do not think it throws fresh light on the problem which we are trying to solve, except, perhaps, to confirm that the feeling against the house—or rather the site—is a modern development. Far from dreading the spot, the local womenfolk of those days were apparently eager to visit it."

"I wonder if you are justified in dismissing the biography of Robert the Hermit quite so easily," Julia commented thoughtfully.

"What do you mean by that?"

Julia placed her forefinger on the last paragraph of the biography. "According to this biography Robert the Hermit disappeared from his hermitage before the Rector of Willingham had an opportunity of passing on the villagers' complaint to his Bishop. One might assume that, in consequence, nothing more was done in the matter. I wonder if that were really so."

"Seeing that our Robert wisely disappeared, what more could have been done?"

"My knowledge of religious matters is not particularly brilliant, but I believe that, in Mediæval days, religion was based largely on superstition. It was also practised far more sincerely than it is in these days. Religion, then, was something very real; and perhaps something rather terrifying. Robert's grotto may not have received the official blessing of Mother Church, but it is possible that, at one time, it was recognised as being, if not a holy shrine, at least a place of quasi-holiness." She paused, to glance questioningly at her companion.

"Well?"

"If so, Theo, it is likely that the disappearance of Robert would not have prevented the Rector, or perhaps the Bishop, from investigating the accusations made against the hermit, not so much on account of Robert's own misbehaviour, but because, if those accusations were substantiated by reliable evidence, a holy or semi-holy place had been profaned. Therefore, one of two courses might have been followed. The grotto may have been officially exorcised to expel the evil spirits which had been attracted there by the hermit's profane practices, or the local priest may have cursed it from his pulpit, to stop further pilgrimages to the grotto for the offering of, possibly, surreptitious prayers. If either of these alternatives were followed, the effect would have been the same. The serfs, henceforward, would have shunned the site as they would a leper. Of course, I may be utterly wide of the mark, but some such sort of thing might account for the existence of the present-day local fear of the place."

"It is an amazing theory, Julie, and I hate to criticise it——" He paused uncertainly.

She frowned. "Don't be such a beastly pig, my pet, as to judge me incapable of accepting criticism. I can take it as well as give it."

"I have only one fault to find with it," he hastened to assure her. "I think it more than likely that the grotto was either exorcised or cursed, and that the peasants, therefore, never went near the place. But I do wonder whether the effect of that curse could have persisted for nearly seven hundred and fifty years. One hundred and fifty, perhaps, but seven hundred and fifty——"

"I suppose not," she agreed presently, in a disappointed voice. "In my enthusiasm, I forgot that Robert had lived so many centuries ago."

"Besides, Julie, many people have lived there since. The peasants who occupied the three cottages built by Sir Godfrey d'Angillon— the Mulhollands—the Ingletons——"

"Look up the other people," she interrupted eagerly.

"All right," He moved Volume 68 to one side, and again consulted the Index. He looked up Sir Godfrey d'Angillon. There was quite a long epitome of Sir Godfrey's biography, but beyond a brief mention of Sir Godfrey's having received a grant of lands in Kent and Sussex from his grateful sovereign, as a reward for services rendered during the fifth Henry's conquest of Normandy, there was nothing of interest. Nor was the biography itself any more helpful. One paragraph mentioned the fact that Sir Godfrey was famed for his philanthropy, and the great kindness with which he treated his servants and retainers. Another spoke of the many cottages he built in Kent, Surrey and Sussex. But that was all.

Terhune then turned up the Mulhollands, only to find that the Index listed only one man of that name—one Andrew Mulholland, who was born in Ireland at the end of the eighteenth century, where he had lived most of his life. From this Mulholland to the Ingletons—with a similar lack of success: not one Ingleton was indexed.

The expression in Julia's gipsy-brown eyes changed from eagerness to disappointment. "I had hoped you might make some new discoveries," she confessed. "Does the omission of the Mulhollands and the Ingletons from the *Dictionary* mean that you are not likely to find out anything about them?"

"Not necessarily. Only people more or less in the public eye have their biographies in the Index. What it does mean is, that it will prove harder to trace their names in contemporary records because I do not know what sources or authorities to look up for a start. It may mean days of laborious searching through masses of indices at the British Museum before discovering the source of information used by the writers of the earlier books we looked through just now."

"Could I help you do that?" she asked abruptly.

The request astonished him. For Julia to offer to help in monotonous research work was a surprising revelation of yet one more facet of her complex, unpredictable character. Julia, with her deep-rooted and inherited distaste for books; Julia, so scornful of his enthusiastic dabbling in amateur detection; Julia, who had not done a day's work since her war service in the W.R.N.S....

What impulse prompted her offer? he reflected. Was she genuinely interested in learning more of the strange problem? Or was she taking advantage of a situation which might offer her distraction from bitter memories of her friendship with a criminal and a murderer? (Though, surely, by now she should have recovered from that shock?) Or had her first introduction to the real realm of books, and the fascination of historical and literary research, given her a taste for hitherto unsuspected pleasures?

Whatever her reason for making the offer, he hesitated to take advantage of it. To-morrow she might regret her impulse, though she would honourably keep to the spirit and letter of her offer. Apart from any other consideration, he was unwilling to let her undertake the most tedious part of the work, for if a sudden taste for books were the real cause of her request, the searching of a score, or even a hundred, indices would scarcely help to foster it.

Before he could answer her, he was interrupted by the telephone. The receiver was near to hand, and he picked it up.

"Mr. Terhune?"

The soft, deep voice was unmistakably Dr. Salvaterra's.

"It is, doctor."

Salvaterra chuckled at his quick recognition of his voice. "Forgive me, my young sir, but can you spare me an hour of your time this afternoon?"

Tuesday afternoon! Tuesday was never a busy afternoon.

"I think so."

"Good! Then I will call for you about three-thirty, if that time is convenient."

"I will make it so, doctor, but did you say you would *call* for me?"

"Yes, We are going to pay a visit."

"A visit?"

The note of surprise in Terhune's voice made the other man chuckle.

"Yes, my dear young sir. A visit. To the House with Crooked Walls."

Chapter Six

I

In his enthusiasm to see the interior of House-on-the-Hill, Terhune had accepted Dr. Salvaterra's invitation, and had disconnected, before ascertaining whether he could make the necessary arrangements to leave the shop. Mrs. Mann was never free during the afternoons, for she had a large family, and the afternoons she devoted to her own home. On the other hand, it was, fortunately, a Tuesday, so there was Miss Amelia to fall back upon. Miss Amelia was sometimes free on a Tuesday afternoon, and it was always she who tended the shop whenever Terhune went to London on business.

With a word of apology to Julia, he hurried across Market Square to Miss Amelia's rooms. He found her in, and, arrangements having been satisfactorily completed, he returned to Julia. She immediately demanded his answer, but when he gave it, her temper flared up.

"If you refuse to let me help you, Theo, I will never speak to you again," she threatened heatedly. "You did not object to being helped by Lady Kylstone and Helena Armstrong when you visited America. If Helena could come to this shop, day after day, to do your work, why shouldn't I be permitted to help you?"

The question was not an easy one to answer, and while he was still trying to think of the reply, she continued:

"You only go up to Town once a month, do you not?"

"Yes."

"Is your principal reason for going there to buy books for your library?"

"Yes."

"How much time have you to spare after doing your usual business?"

"Two hours or so, as a general rule. Sometimes three."

"Three hours per month!" She laughed scornfully. "How many years do you think it may take you to look through a hundred indices in the hope of tracing the Mulhollands and the Ingletons?"

Her questions made him feel foolish. More than that, her scornful manner, and her sharp voice reminded him, unpleasantly, of the Julia of their first meeting; the Julia whom most people avoided in so far as etiquette and good manners allowed; the Julia who alienated one friend after another because she contemptuously refused to keep in check her caustic tongue.

Not only his words, but also his boyish, open face pleaded with her as he tried, stammeringly, to explain his reasons:

"Have a—a heart, Julie! It was on your own account that I refused your—your offer. How many times have you told me that you hated reading? Even for anyone who loves books and enjoys reading, looking through indices is one of the most boring jobs there is. If I let you do as you suggest, you would hate every moment you were at the Museum."

Her expression lost something of its acrimony. "Was that your only reason for not wanting me to help?"

"Yes."

"Then I am sorry, Theo, for saying what I did. But I still want to help. My dislike for reading hasn't altered, but I am ready to endure being bored—"

"And exasperated," he interrupted, with a grin.

"And exasperated, too," she added, "for the sake of satisfying my curiosity, and of having something to occupy me. Having had a taste of something I have wanted all my life to do—travel—it is not going to be easy for me to settle down again to existence in Willingham. When do you go to Town again?"

"Next Tuesday."

"Then let me go with you, Theo, so that you can take me to the British Museum, and show me how to set to work. Once I know how to begin, I can travel up to Town as often as is necessary to find out all we want to know."

The offer was tempting. If she faithfully carried out her self-appointed task—and hers was a character one could rely on, once she had given her promise—if she acted as his eyes, as it were, the partnership might easily prove a short-cut to the wanted information.

"All right, Julie. That is a date," he agreed. "Next Tuesday as ever was."

I I

On entering the smoking room of the "Almond Tree," Julia and Terhune found Winstanley already there. He was with Arnold Blye and Jeffrey Pemberton, both of whom gave a whoop of joy upon seeing Julia, for these two men were both possessed of thick skins, against which the barbs of her sarcasm had a habit of harmlessly blunting themselves. It had been rumoured, though never confirmed, that, before the arrival of Gregory Belcher, Jeffrey Pemberton had proposed marriage to her, apparently without success, for she still held the youngest son of Mr. Justice Pemberton at a metaphorical arm's-length.

"By all that's wonderful! Julie!" Arnold shouted out cheerfully. "When did you get back, old girl?"

Jeffrey greeted her with: "Hullo, Julie! I didn't know you were home again."

She addressed them both with the one remark. "We arrived back at Willingham yesterday afternoon."

"Just in time for Isabel's yearly hop to-morrow night," Jeffrey said hurriedly. "Any chance of your being there?"

"Never mind to-morrow night, Julie. Jeffrey only wants to snaffle you for himself. The more important point is, at the moment, what are you drinking? Name your poison. And yours, Terhune?"

"Hullo, Terhune," Jeffrey added.

"I am drinking with Mr. Terhune," she informed them with asperity. "Besides, we have come to talk to Win, not to you two. Good morning, Win."

Winstanley was seated at his usual corner of the bar, a spot which no other local inhabitant would have dared usurp, for years of occupation had made that particular high, leather-covered stool sacrosanct to him.

Winstanley was a law unto himself in Bray. Generations ago the Winstanleys had been the largest landowners in the district; and Bray had been built in the Manor of Brazing, of which the then Winstanley had been the lord. But the passing years, and themselves, had dealt hardly with successive generations of Winstanleys. From some forgotten ancestor they had inherited a strain of wildness which had appeared and reappeared in different guises, of which the most persistent had been a passion for gambling. One by one they had gambled away their patrimony until no more of it existed than was enough to maintain one person in a minimum of comfort.

The present Winstanley lived on that minimum, refusing positively to augment it by working. But nobody despised him on that account, not even the farm labourers, who toiled from sunrise to sunset for a weekly wage that was little more than the sum

Winstanley passed across the bar of the "Almond Tree" in that same period of time. For there was nothing about him to dislike. Besides, he was a Winstanley, and Winstanley still remained an honoured, almost traditional name in that forgotten corner of the county which had once belonged to his distant ancestors, and where the local inhabitants remained loyal to the traditions of the past.

"Good morning, my dear," he greeted her, nodding genially at Terhune at the same time. "What can I do for you?"

"It is not what you can do for me, Win, but for Mr. Terhune. He wants you to give him some information, if you will."

Winstanley chuckled. "I didn't know I was the happy possessor of any knowledge not already known to scholars of the fifth standard, but if I am—" With a significant gesture he drained his glass, and replaced it on the bar with a slight thump.

Terhune took the hint. As soon as George, the barman, had pushed the three glasses across the bar, Winstanley lifted his to his lips, and with a courtly gesture in Terhune's direction, half drained its contents.

"What do you wish to ask me, my dear chap?" he asked presently.

"Something to do with House-on-the-Hill," Terhune began.

"House-on-the-Hill!" Winstanley raised his sparse, greying eyebrows. "What am I supposed to know about the place?"

"Is it true that your great-grandfather once came into possession of the house in settlement of a gambling debt?"

"It is, but the old rascal exchanged it for a damn fine mare, which later foaled an Oaks winner. And this exchange, mark you, my dear chap, took place three days after his own home had been destroyed by fire."

"In those circumstances, why didn't your great-grandfather keep the house, and move into it?"

Winstanley laughed jovially. "Probably he believed the mare would be of more use to him—as the brute would have been if the old boy hadn't sold the filly before she won the Oaks. Besides, wouldn't any sensible chap choose a stud mare in preference to that damned eye-sore?" He jerked his head in the direction in which the house stood.

"I shouldn't, especially if I had just had my own house razed to the ground. I should consider the winning of another house as something miraculous."

"You mean, something devilish," the other man corrected. "I have heard my father say that great-grandfather often cursed the day he won that damned house."

"Why?"

"From the day he won it, nothing ever went right with him again, although, previously, life had been very kind to him."

"Except as regards the destruction of his house," Julia interpolated.

"Oh, that!" Winstanley shrugged his shoulders. "He didn't worry about the house burning down, especially as, in the previous twelve months, he had won enough money not only to build a new house, but also to re-purchase some of the Winstanley lands which his father had sold some twenty years previously."

"What happened after he had won House-on-the-Hill?" Jeffrey asked.

"Although he had only possessed the damned place for three days or so, from that time his luck turned. He lost all the money he had won during the previous year, and more besides. He became so desperate for cash that he even sold the filly I have mentioned, although it was already promising well. Finally, within two years of winning the house, and despite the fact that he was perfectly healthy, and in the prime of life, he died."

"From what cause, Win?" Julia asked.

Winstanley laughed hoarsely. "From a kick in the jaw from that same damn mare."

"Then he would scarcely have been worse off for keeping House-on-the-Hill," Terhune suggested.

"I hadn't thought of that." Winstanley stared into the bottom of his glass as if seeing pictures there. "But why are you so interested in my great-grandfather's doings, Terhune?"

"I am trying to discover something, of the past history of the house."

"You literary chaps! Always wanting to find out something about everything. Do I remember somebody telling me you do a bit of scribbling on your own account?"

"Sometimes."

"Don't tell me you propose writing a book about House-on-the-Hill?"

"Why shouldn't he, Win, if he wants to?" Julia snapped unexpectedly.

Winstanley's unnaturally sallow but still likeable face wrinkled into a sly grin. "Why not, of course, my dear? But I do not think that, beyond giving pleasure to its author in writing it, a book about House-on-the-Hill would interest more than a handful of morbidly minded people. However, you know your own business best, my dear chap, so if I can help you in any way, I am only too pleased to do so. What do you want to know about my great-grandfather, the old rascal?"

"Can you tell me the name of the man from whom he won the house, also the name of the man with whom he afterwards exchanged it for the mare?"

"I know the answer to the second part of the question," Winstanley answered promptly. "It was Patrick O'Malley himself, begorral and him all the way from Donegal in Auld Oireland. The old boy and O'Malley met in White's. One night when O'Malley was in his cups he announced loudly that he had a mare in foal by the previous Derby winner, which he was willing to sell to the highest bidder. As soon as he heard this the old boy—my great-grandfather, I mean—wheedled the Irishman into exchanging his mare for a house in Kent. O'Malley jumped at the offer, saying that he had no objection to owning a house in Kent, and adding that he would carry on exchanging horses for houses for as long as there were fools with country houses to exchange."

"Did O'Malley move into House-on-the-Hill?"

Winstanley laughed—his fruity, boisterous laugh was famous in the neighbourhood; even if it were born of good nature out of alcohol, it remained highly infectious; wherever Winstanley might be, there, too, were high spirits and conviviality.

"According to Great-grandfather's story, the O'Malley took one look at the house, then fled back to Auld Oireland as quickly as coach and packet could take him. According to Great-grandfather, O'Malley had seen a banshee looking at him out of a window, which was enough to make him want to put the width of the Irish Sea between him and his new possession."

Although it was Terhune to whom Winstanley was chiefly addressing himself, Arnold Blye impulsively interpolated a question.

"What did O'Malley do with the house after returning to Ireland, Stan?"

"Sold it for a song just as soon as he found a buyer fool enough to take it off his hands."

"Do you know who that was?"

"Yes. An American by the name of Reuben Douglas. Having spent three-quarters of a lifetime in the U.S.A. amassing a fortune, he decided to finish his life in spending it in the country of his forefathers—which isn't a bad idea, when you come to think of it." Winstanley paused reflectively, and again stared into the bottom of his empty glass.

"Well, what happened then?" Julia prompted impatiently.

Winstanley sighed; none of his audience knew why. Perhaps it was because his glass remained empty. "Douglas, apparently, had no objection to living in a house which looked as if it had stepped straight out of some crazy architect's nightmare. He spent God knows how many thousands of dollars in renovating House-on-the-Hill, moved into it, and promptly—vanished."

"What!" Terhune's glass slipped through his fingers, and crashed on the flagged floor, where it splintered into a hundred pieces.

"What is the matter, Terhune?" Winstanley asked mildly. "Haven't you heard that story before?"

"No."

"Nor have I," Julia added breathlessly. "You are not joking, Win?"

Winstanley chuckled. "Cross my heart, cut my throat. Ask Jeffrey; I'll bet he has heard about Reuben Douglas's disappearance."

Jeffrey nodded. "I have often heard the old man discussing that story with his cronies."

"What happened to Douglas?" Terhune questioned trenchantly.

"Search me, my dear chap! All I know is that he just vanished, and was never heard of again. And didn't his relations in the States raise Cain! Not that I blame them." Winstanley slowly pushed his glass across the bar. "Set them up, George," he muttered ruefully.

"This is my round, Stan," Arnold said quickly.

Winstanley sighed his relief. "If you insist—"

"Do you know what happened to the house then?"

"Douglas's heir—his son, I believe—ordered the place to be put up for sale again, but he hadn't a hope. Even before Douglas's disappearance, the house had had a reputation, but afterwards—" Winstanley shrugged his shoulders, and half emptied his re-filled glass. "For forty years the house remained untenanted."

"Only forty years! Wasn't it a century ago when your great-grandfather made the exchange with O'Malley?"

"Yes, but the house has had one tenant since then, a grand old character, according to my father. Name of Oliver Finlayson. He was a retired African explorer. At the age of seventy he came back to England, and looked around for a place in which to spend the last few years of his life. He was offered House-on-the-Hill cheap. When he asked the reason for the low rental, someone was honest enough to tell him. He was taken to see it, and was delighted with the view. He said that the look of the house didn't worry him; it was the view from it that mattered. As for the superstitious fear in which the place was held by the local people, he said that, having had to deal with African ju-ju and native witchcraft for fifty years or so, a touch of white superstition didn't mean a thing to him. Besides, he hadn't many more years to live, anyway. So he arranged a yearly lease, and moved in."

"What happened to *him?*" Julia asked.

"He died—twenty-one years later, at the ripe old age of ninety-two," Winstanley replied drily.

"Well, I'll be damned! So much for superstition," interjected Arnold Blye. "Why haven't you told us this story before, Stan?"

"Because nobody asked for it, my boy."

"And after Finlayson's death?" Terhune prompted. "Did his long tenancy help to counteract local superstition?"

"Not a bit of it! The American owners put it on the market again, but it remained unsold and empty for another eleven years. Then it was bought 'blind' from the estate agent's description by an Anglo-Indian who was about to retire from his tea plantation, or something of that sort. When he landed home and saw what place he had purchased, he very nearly assassinated the estate agent. At any rate, the agent brought and won an action for assault and damages against the buyer, and the judge made some very nasty remarks about the foolishness of people buying properties without first inspecting them. He hadn't much sympathy for the defendant, he continued, especially in view of the fact that he had bought it cheaply.

"The poor devil—I think his name was Noel Middlemass—never lived in the house he had purchased so rashly. Instead, he went to live in a private hotel at Bournemouth. When he died the property descended to James Middlemass, his son, who still owns it, to the best of my knowledge."

"Very many thanks," Terhune said gratefully. "There is just one more question—"

"Well?"

"From whom did your great-grandfather win House-on-the-Hill?"

"Ah! There, my dear chap, you have me. I have never known the name."

"You should be able to get the name from the title deed Terhune," Jeffrey suggested.

Winstanley shook his head. "I am afraid not, Jeffrey. The man—whoever he was—from whom my great-grandfather won the place possessed it by squatter's right."

"Then the present deeds must have started from him, so his name would still be on the title deeds," Jeffrey persisted, thus proving himself a true son of his father, the Judge.

Again Winstanley shook his head. "Nothing about House-on-the-Hill is quite as simple as that. In consequence of O'Malley rushing back to Ireland as if the devil himself was behind, the title deeds never passed. When O'Malley sold to Reuben Douglas, the solicitor approached my great-grandfather for the documents. Unfortunately the old boy had been done to death by that damned mare, and his son was neither able to find the deeds nor remember the name of the squatter. He had to sign an affidavit that his father had come into possession of House-on-the-Hill as payment of a gambling debt, and had exchanged it for a mare. Probably there never was a more imperfect title to real estate, but time eventually put that matter right. Anything more I can tell you?"

There was not.

Chapter Seven

I

Presently, the conversation passed on to other subjects, and shortly afterwards Terhune left the "Almond Tree," to return to his rooms for luncheon.

His was a happy and contented nature. Every minute of the day, from the moment of waking up in the morning to that last, dreamy moment before falling to sleep at night, was, on ninety-nine days out of every hundred, a minute of pure enjoyment. This was largely due to the pleasure which he derived from his work. He loved books. He loved handling them; he loved owning them; he loved reading them. He also enjoyed writing them. Unambitious for worldly goods, he asked nothing more of life than that he should live it in the company of books. It was little wonder, therefore, that his hours in his bookshop and library were as nigh to being blissful as work hours possibly could be.

Even when he closed the shop for the luncheon hour, that interval still afforded him sixty minutes of pleasure. He thoroughly enjoyed his meals, not only because he had a healthy appetite, but also because it was his habit to prop a book up on the table before him while he ate, and indulge himself in an hour's uninterrupted reading—an unsocial delectation which only those who live alone are able to appreciate.

After he had closed for the night, he found the remaining hours even more pleasurable, for one of his four rooms above the shop was fitted up as his study. In that small, cosy room, surrounded by yet more books, those forming his private library, he either read or worked at a short story (he had sold several in the U.S.A. to the *Saturday Evening Post*), or at his first novel, which was nearing completion.

Following his conversation with Winstanley at the "Almond Tree" for once he found no pleasure in reading while he ate. He was half-way through a new detective story, but somehow it had become far less absorbing than it had been when he had commenced reading in bed the previous night. Compared with the strange circumstances surrounding the House with the Crooked Walls, the story of the novel was now something rather unreal, rather artificial, something which still smelled, metaphorically speaking, of printer's ink and bookbinder's glue. He tried to persevere with it, but without success. His eyes read the printed words, but his consciousness rejected them in favour of House-on-the-Hill. At last he closed the book, and concentrated on the more vital problem of the house.

Certainly, a strange series of occurrences was connected with House-on-the-Hill, each happening of little significance when judged on its own, but serving, in conjunction with other, apparently unimportant events, to build up a very unusual history. The disappearance of Robert the Hermit. The suicide of Lord Kenelm Chisswell. The extraordinary behaviour of O'Malley. The disappearance of Reuben Douglas.

Two disappearances. One such disappearance was fortunately rare, but two... A fantastic coincidence! If it were a coincidence, suggested a fleeting thought. A very fleeting thought, for common sense refused to admit of its being anything else. Six hundred years separated the two disappearances. What possible connection could there be between them? Obviously none. Besides, was Robert the Hermit's disappearance really something extraordinary? What probably had happened was that the hermit had received news that the peasants had complained about his practices and, aware of the possible consequences to him of that complaint, had wisely taken the precaution of fleeing from the neighbourhood while he still had the opportunity. Whence he had subsequently proceeded was a question that was likely never to be answered, but in those days of illiteracy and lack of communications he could easily have "disappeared" merely by travelling to another district fifty miles or so distant.

Douglas's disappearance, on the other hand, was definitely more mysterious. Douglas, unlike Robert, had—as far as was known at present—no reason for vanishing. One does not spend many thousands of dollars on buying and renovating and moving into a house only to vanish very soon afterwards. Besides, whereas it was a simple matter to "vanish" in the first years of the thirteenth century, by the middle of the nineteenth century the growth and amenities of civilisation had already raised many obstacles in the way of a truly genuine and successful disappearance.

Why had Reuben Douglas vanished (to say nothing of how, or where!)? Why had O'Malley rushed back to Ireland immediately after seeing the house which had come into his possession at so small a cost? Why had Lord Kenelm committed suicide so soon after his holiday there? Was it just coincidence, again, that the affairs of Great-grandfather Winstanley had changed from good to bad following *his* brief possession of the property?

Terhune stirred uneasily as he recollected the explanation which Julia had put forward to account for such a series of inexplicable happenings. Had the site been cursed by the Rector of Guillinshame or some other militant churchman? Had this curse persisted through the centuries, affecting all who came into contact with it? Perhaps O'Malley was more sensitive than most to psychic influence, and, having sensed the curse, had fled to his own country rather than take the risk of being touched by its influence. Had the curse been responsible for Lord Kenelm's suicide?

He frowned, annoyed that he should have given the suggestion a second thought. His normal outlook was far too realistic to admit the supernatural. Besides, the general history of the house, as opposed to detached episodes, ridiculed any such explanation. The Mulhollands had lived there from 1596 to 1673. A period of roughly eighty years. And after the Mulhollands, the Ingletons, who had occupied the house from 1673 to—when?—but certainly to 1712, when the author of *A Compleat Topographical and Geographical Survey of Ashford and Its Environs* had visited there and had tea with Nathaniel. Another substantial period, this time of forty years. Again, Sir Constant Fitzwilliam had lived there from 1777 to 1782—five years—and Oliver Finlayson, from 1861 to 1882—twenty-one years. During none of these separate periods had anything of a, tragical, calamitous, supernatural, or mysterious nature occurred, so it would appear that the curse, if any, was not particularly effective.

Whatever the solution might be, the problem was undoubtedly fascinating; Terhune felt that he owed a debt of gratitude to Salvaterra for having introduced it to him. Reward or no reward, he knew that he would not rest satisfied until he had exhausted every possible source of information.

Meanwhile, he impatiently awaited the hour of three, and realised that he was immensely curious to see the interior of the House with Crooked Walls.

II

Salvaterra's car drew up outside the shop precisely as the distant church clock chimed three. Through the glass panel of the door

Terhune saw the chauffeur descend from the car, cross the pavement towards him, and open the door.

The man touched his cap. "Mr. Terhune?"

"Yes."

"Dr. Salvaterra is awaiting you in the car, sir."

"Right." With a quick nod to Miss Amelia, who was fluttering around, trying to obtain a discreet glimpse of the "mysterious" foreigner—being a foreigner, he was automatically mysterious in the eyes of Miss Amelia, and of most of the villagers, too—he followed the chauffeur out, and advanced towards the car door, which, meanwhile, the chauffeur had opened.

"Good afternoon, young sir," Salvaterra warmly greeted Terhune. "Will you sit opposite me?" He gracefully waved his white, tapering fingers towards the tip-up seat.

As Terhune stepped into the car, he saw that the off-side rear seat was again occupied by the woman he had noticed earlier on.

"My dear!" Salvaterra turned towards her as Terhune settled himself. "This is Mr. Terhune, the nice young man whom I have already described to you. Mr. Terhune, my sister, Señorita Salvaterra."

She acknowledged him with a slight, graceful bend of her head. "Good afternoon, Mr. Terhune. It gives me great pleasure to have this opportunity of meeting you. Vicente told me about you at the luncheon table; I could not persuade him to speak of anyone else."

Scarcely conscious of what he was saying, Terhune muttered some polite pleasantry. His thoughts were muddled with confused amazement. The brief glimpse he had had, earlier, of the two Panamese had prepared him, to some extent, for their being alike. But not for quite such a fantastic similarity.

He could not shift his gaze from the señorita's face. Her hair was as luxuriant, as snowy white, as her brother's, and, despite its added length, it was cunningly dressed so as to create a similar halo-like effect. Her Latin-black eyes had the same mysterious depths, the same sparkling vivacity. Her flawless, unblemished complexion possessed the same startling, almost transparent pallor. Her mobile lips, untouched by cosmetics, were of the precise tint and the precise shape of his. Her hands, too, were narrow, long and graceful.

If there were differences between them, apart from their clothes, such differences were not easy to detect. Neither wore a hat; as they sat, side by side, Terhune judged them to be of similar height and build. The forehead, nose, chin and shoulders of each were in perfect alignment with the other's. And though she had a bust, it was extremely slight. He, on the contrary, had a broad chest somewhat out of proportion to his size.

Terhune found it hard to believe that the two people could really be of different sex. For instance, her mouth was inclined to be a trifle too masculine. But his, on the other hand, approached perilously close to being feminine. His hair, it was true, was trimmed in masculine style—but it was more luxuriant and longer than that worn by the average man. Even their voices were the same; soft, musically deep, with only an attractive lisp, and an oddly worded phrase to betray their foreign extraction. An absurd notion occurred to him that if they should ever appear before him dressed alike— either as men or as women—he would be unable to distinguish one from the other.

How long he would have gaped at them like a witless fool (as, subsequently, he mentally accused himself of doing) there was no knowing, for his confused reverie was interrupted by Salvaterra's laughter.

"Well, young sir?"

Terhune realised the extent of his impoliteness. Stammeringly, he began to apologise, but Salvaterra shook his head, and raised his hand in a commanding gesture.

"You do not have to apologise. My sister and I were long ago inured, by *force majeure*, to the embarrassment of being stared at as if we were wax dummies. In fact, we have come to enjoy watching the confusion expressed by people meeting us for the first time, and should be extremely disappointed if we encountered someone too polite or too *blasé* to expose his real feelings. Of course, we are twins. We have lived together all our lives, so it is not surprising that we have become even more alike with each passing year. Indeed, we have even come to think alike, have we not, my dear?"

By the way he looked at her, by the tone of his voice, by the expression of his eyes, Terhune realised that Salvaterra loved his sister with an unsexual emotion transcending the more brittle rapture of passion.

"Vicente does not exaggerate," she confirmed—it seemed almost unbelievable that the stream of conversation could have been diverted, so constant was the voice, in pitch, tone, and expression. "Sometimes we converse without speaking one word aloud."

"Of course, it is only by comparing notes afterwards that we become aware of this fact," continued the voice—but Terhune was startled to see that now the brother's lips were moving. "Perhaps I should explain. Maybe I grow tired of reading my book of an evening, and suggest to myself that I should ask Inez to play a game of cribbage with me. Before I can open my mouth to speak the words, I know that she is anxious to finish her knitting first, so I continue reading."

Señorita Salvaterra nodded her head. "Although he says nothing to me aloud, I know that my brother wants to play cribbage with me, so I think: 'As soon as this row is finished, I will play.' And when it is finished I say, perhaps aloud this time, 'Now I am ready for the game of cribbage, Vicente.' It is then we realise that we have read each other's thoughts."

Salvaterra took from an inside pocket a cigar case filled with long, thin cigars, almost black in colour, which he offered to Terhune.

"Not for me, thank you, doctor. I smoke only cigarettes, and then not often."

The Panamanian sighed. "These cigars are my weakness. I am only truly happy when I have one between my lips. Have you any objection to their being smoked in your presence?" When Terhune replied that he had not, Salvaterra did not immediately take one from his case. Instead, he offered them to his sister. To Terhune's amazement, she accepted one, and placed it in her mouth.

Salvaterra's sharp eyes did not miss the expression which flashed across Terhune's face.

"Are you shocked, young sir, at the idea of my sister's smoking cigars?"

Terhune knew it was useless to try to deceive the foreigner. "Not shocked," he corrected. "But perhaps—surprised."

The doctor laughed. "Inez shared my first cigar, and enjoyed it as much as I did."

"I do not smoke as many as my brother," she added.

"You would if I permitted, *querida*," he teased. "But come—" He paused, first to place a cigar in his own mouth, and then, to light both. Presently the car filled with blue, aromatic cigar smoke. "Probably it is too soon to ask, but have you made any fresh discoveries regarding House-on-the-Hill?"

"Several, doctor."

"You have?" The doctor's face lighted with eagerness. "What have you learned, young sir?"

"Apparently the first building to occupy the site of House-on-the-Hill was erected soon after the conquest of England by the Normans. William the Conqueror ordered a keep to be built there, and garrisoned a small force there under one of his Norman followers known as Fitz-Osbern the Bald."

"Of course," Salvaterra interrupted quickly. "The summit of the hill, commanding the countryside for several miles around, was an ideal site for a garrisoned stronghold." He nodded his head several times, as if communing with himself; for several seconds there was silence in the car.

Then Señorita Salvaterra said unexpectedly: "I agree, Vicente; it must have been later." She saw the expression of astonishment which appeared on Terhune's face, and added quickly: "I did not mean to surprise you, señor. I was answering one of the questions my brother asked himself. I did not realise that he had not spoken aloud."

Salvaterra took her left hand within his and patted it. "You have accidentally illustrated to our young friend here the story we were relating to him just now of our telepathic communication." He laughed genially. "You must be more careful; we might unwittingly betray our deepest secrets to him."

Terhune was not aware of any change in Salvaterra's voice or attitude; nevertheless, he noticed a cloud pass across the señorita's eyes, as though his laughing reproof was not quite as caressingly teasing at it had sounded.

"*Si, si. Seré mas cuidadosa*," she said quickly, adding with a laugh which sounded somewhat strained: "I have just promised to take more care, Señor Terhune. You see, my brother is embarrassed lest I should make other people think me—what do you say in English? A little crazy—no? for apparently speaking my thoughts aloud."

Salvaterra nodded his head in confirmation. "That is so, young sir. But the thoughts which my sister answered were these: 'I was asking myself if some dreadful happening could have occurred within the keep which had left its supernatural influence upon the site. Such a happening, for instance, could have been the mass execution of Saxon villagers, condemned to death by the Norman lord, perhaps for conspiracy, perhaps for disobedience to military orders. But, as you may have guessed from my sister's remark, further reflection made me unwilling to subscribe to that theory. Even had such a massacre taken place, I do not believe it would have had a psychic aftermath."

"Why not, doctor?"

"Because, young sir, the souls of those murdered people would not have been influenced by a psychical resentment against their executioners. War, unhappily, can justify, and legalise offences and punishments which, in times of peace, would not be punishments, but crimes. In peace, rape by a civilian is a serious offence. In war, the rape of the female population of a conquered country is, inexcusably, the prerogative of the victorious soldiery, and is not, generally speaking seriously punished. Sometimes, it is encouraged.

"A woman raped in peace becomes a woman consigned by her own outraged pride and modesty to the blackest pit of horror. But a woman raped in war shares the scars of war with her male folk, whose blood has already soaked the battlefield of their defeat.

"So it is with death. A soul murdered in peace is a soul abused, a soul crying soundlessly, restlessly for vengeance. But a people overtaken by war is a people prepared for death, however and whenever it may come. If death come, though it be not the more welcome, yet a murdered soul, being resigned to its fate, seeks oblivion, not vengeance; and the chains which fetter it to this earth are struck from it by a merciful agent of Heaven who guides it to its last abode." Salvaterra glanced questioningly at his guest.

"I think I understand," Terhune assured the little man.

The doctor smiled easily as though he had not expected any other answer. "Suppose, therefore, that the Saxons living around the keep revolted, or perhaps only conspired to revolt. In taking either course, they would have done so in the full knowledge that their lives were in peril, either in battle or by execution. Suppose that their plans miscarried, and, in consequence, many of them were dragged inside the keep, and there hanged or killed by other means, their souls—I use non-technical words to make my meaning clearer—would have departed to that happier world reserved for brave people; they would not have remained chained to the site of their execution in an everlasting torment which can influence, and often does, the sensitive subconsciousness of living people afterwards inhabiting that supernatural prison of unhappy spirits. Come, young sir, have you learned what happened next to the site of that Norman keep?"

"More than a hundred years later a hermit by the name of Robert built himself a hermitage there, and constructed a grotto which became a place of pilgrimage for barren wives."

Salvaterra made the end of his cigar glow redly. "A hermitage and grotto! Interesting. Very interesting. But I do not think that the hermit's occupancy of the site can have any significance on its psychical history."

Terhune's eyes twinkled. He believed that he was going to surprise the little man. His voice became eager with anticipation.

"Within seven years or so of the grotto's becoming famed as a shrine, Robert the Hermit was accused by the villagers of certain malpractices. Before the Rector could investigate the charges, the hermit vanished, and there is no record of his having been seen or heard of again."

"*Santa Maria!*" For the first time since meeting Terhune, the Panamanian's voice became sharp and shrill. He sat bolt upright, and snatched the cigar from the corner of his mouth, which it had occupied without pause from the moment of being lighted.

"What practices, young sir?" he demanded brusquely. "Were they of a religious or secular nature?"

"They were, I gather, of the—the earth, earthy."

"Ah!" Salvaterra's eagerness relaxed, as he chuckled loudly. "A profaned shrine! Need one look farther, I wonder, for an explanation to account for the superstitious fear with which House-on-the-Hill is regarded? When Robert profaned that shrine which prayers had made holy, be sure that he caused the place to be forever accursed, unless its haunting evilness be exorcised by Mother Church, and its cleanliness and purity restored by the Lord's Blessing."

Terhune shook his head doubtfully.

"Do you disagree?" the little man asked sharply.

"I know nothing of psychology, and little of the mysteries of religion, doctor, but records show that the original House-on-the-Hill was occupied, by successive generations, from the end of the sixteenth century to at least the middle of the eighteenth. If the place is cursed, I do not think the curse began to operate much before seventeen ninety-three."

"Why do you specifically name that year?"

"In that year a Lord Kenelm Chisswell stayed there for Christmas. Some days later he committed suicide. So far, I have not discovered his reason."

"Ah! Continue, young sir, continue."

"Some fifty years later, after a succession of trifling incidents, the house was bought by an American citizen, who spent a small fortune in rebuilding and enlarging the place. Shortly afterwards he moved in—and vanished."

"Vanished!"

"Like Robert the Hermit, he vanished, and was never heard of again."

Salvaterra placed his slender, narrow hands one on each side of his head, and gently rocked it to and fro in a comical manner.

"Aie! Aie! Aie! Praise be to God for bringing us to this neighbourhood!" he muttered in a voice hoarse with excitement. "And there it is!" he exclaimed loudly. "House-on-the-Hill, the House with Crooked Walls, the house of profanity, disappearances and suicides!"

And House-on-the-Hill, looming up just ahead of them, appeared to curse them for disturbing its selfish, melancholy solitude.

Chapter Eight

Although he had seen it from a distance a thousand times, and close at hand possibly a dozen times, Terhune inspected with eager eyes the house in which he had come to have such an absorbing interest. And because of this interest he noticed details which he had not, consciously, observed before.

The house was less one building than a squat, sprawling edifice comprising at least seven distinct, though not separate structures—these were apparent from the front; there were others, facing north, which were invisible from the road by which they were approaching the house.

The main structure was roughly the heart and centre of the house, and was an oblong building. Its length formed the façade, faced south, and was about one hundred feet in all. Its width was not discernible from the front, due to the presence, on either side, of flanking buildings, but, to judge by that part of the centre structure which had an outer wall, the depth was possibly seventy feet or more.

The lower half of the walls of this main building consisted of rough-hewn irregular blocks of stone, which must have required considerable skill and artistry to arrange—and where the builder had found it awkward to use the square or oblong-shaped blocks he had filled in gaps with rag-stones or even large, smooth, rubble stones obviously transported from the sea-shore; all spaces were filled in with a concrete-like mortar. The portion of the walls above was of brick and timber.

It was obvious, even without the use of a spirit-level or plumb line, that this part of the house had been built exactly on the summit of the hill, so exactly, indeed, that either end of the main wing was below the main level, though whether the original builder had deliberately followed the sloping lie of the land, or whether the foundations had sunk less in the middle than at the ends, it was difficult for a layman to determine. Whichever the cause, the effect of roof and walls sloping downwards from the middle was heightened by the existence of a chimney stack half-way along the roof, and a porch half-way along the wall.

Even the ridge of the roof was not level. Looking up from ground level, one gathered the impression that here and there king-posts had either rotted away or had been removed, for the ridge dipped perceptibly in several places, while the tiled roofs were so dented in parts that one was tempted to imagine that a giant hand had once pressed on the roof and had bent it haphazardly. The chimney stack was equally eccentric. Originally it was of elegant design, and surely must have been erected by an artist. But at some period during its existence the stack had been struck by lightning, and the upper part twisted awry, so that it overbalanced its base at a precarious angle, giving one the impression that the first gale must inevitably topple it over. The chimney pots, of fanciful corkscrew design, pointed skywards at all angles.

The walls were crazier than the roof. Not only did they sink at either end, not only did the half-timbered upper-story parts bulge outwards, but in between some of the windows the wall was supported by fair-sized buttresses which, slight beneath the gable, broadened out considerably at the base. Why these buttresses had not prevented the upper bulge was yet another strange freak. Lastly, adding to these several peculiarities, was the capricious arrangement of the windows, of which scarcely any two matched, for they were at varying heights, of dissimilar design, and of different sizes.

Attached to the west wall of the main building was a wing, consisting of three cottages built (apparently without reason) in the form of a right angle. Perhaps these cottages had once been separate entities, but now all three formed an east wing. Time and weather had dealt hardly with these cottages. But they had been patched and repatched; their roofs tiled and retiled; their stone walls studded with a succession of angle irons. With the help of man, they still looked capable of defying the ravages of time and weather; for all that, they sadly resembled three senile centenarians, weary and forlorn, who had crept close together for warmth, while patiently but hopefully waiting for the Grim Reaper to claim their worn-out bodies. These cottages, Terhune reckoned, were what remained of the three cottages built by Sir Godfrey d'Angillon.

Attached to the west wall of the third cottage, but roughly at right-angles to it, was still another building—a long, narrow stone-built affair this, its style of architecture immediately proclaiming the stables. It looked—and undoubtedly was—of far more recent date than the cottages which it flanked. In spite of that fact, it, too, was unlevel, for its builder, as though infected by the centre building, had countered the effect of the sloping ground on which it was built, not by heightening the foundations of the lower end, but by building the stables, sectionally, in the form of unequal steps, each step being lower than its neighbour.

The east wing was even more fantastic than the west. In his anxiety to increase the existing accommodation, one of the past owners had enlarged House-on-the-Hill by adding to it a long, narrow structure, half the width of the main building, but built more in the form of an extension than a wing. Had the front wall of this extension remained flush with the front wall of the house, the effect might have been that of enhancing the appearance of the south façade. But no! The addition had been built flush with the back of the house, so that the structure extended some thirty feet behind the building line. As if further to exaggerate the incongruity of this architectural fantasy, the height of the extension was some five feet less than its parent structure; the walls were of red brick, its roof was at a different angle, and its one chimney stack was of plain design, with four square chimney-pots. Nor was the wall buttressed.

Lastly, yet one more addition had been made to the front of the house. The extension had its own extension, but this time in the form of a wing, at right angles to the extension. This wing was, at a rough estimate, between eighty and one hundred feet in length. In consequence, its southern end protruded beyond the building line by some fifty feet. Had this wing been in harmony with the rest, its extraordinary situation might have helped to make the house, as a whole, picturesque if unusual. Instead, while stressing the oddness, it had completely robbed the house of any suggestion of the picturesque by introducing yet another style of architecture. The roof, out of harmony with any other roofs, descended steeply from its ridge, higher than that of the main building, to rather less than six feet above ground level. In consequence, all windows facing west were either small and low or else were gable windows, built in, thus marring the broad expanse of roof. And, as in the case of its companion structures, this out-flung wing appeared to have been erected without recourse to plumb line or spirit level.

At a signal from Salvaterra, the chauffeur—his name, apparently, was Moore—brought the car to a stop a hundred yards from the front porch. Upon signifying his desire to alight, Terhune stepped out, and was immediately joined by the doctor and his sister—who, Terhune was now able to confirm, was indeed the same height as her brother, if allowance were made for her high, slender heels.

Standing in line, the three people stared at House-on-the-Hill. As Terhune's gaze slowly travelled along the front aspect of the straggling house, his first reflection was of astonishment that any one person, still less several, could have been so incredibly devoid of artistry as to have designed, or allowed to be built, so many irreconcilable additions to a main building already sufficiently peculiar. It was not the first time the same thought had occurred to him, but previously it had been impersonal, a casual reflection. Now, it had become a matter of absorbing interest.

Because of this interest, astonishment was succeeded by perplexity. Whether the time of day was unhelpful, or whether his disbelief in the supernatural made him less receptive to psychic influences, he could see nothing about House-on-the-Hill to inspire him with horror or fear. He could think of a dozen other adjectives which he was prepared to agree justifiably described the house—it might rightly be called grotesque, fantastic, extraordinary, unusual, almost ugly. He went further; he could appreciate the feeling which had prompted the author-artist to etch the house as cursing the interloper for disturbing "its selfish, melancholy solitude." The house did seem to leer at one; it did give one the impression of being gloomy. It did make one depressed to see it decayed for want of care and attention—not one square inch of paintwork could be seen; many of the window panes were broken; many roof tiles were missing; two chimney pots were cracked, two of them smashed. But it did not make his heart beat quicker to look at the place. Nor did his mouth become dry, his spine chill, or his scalp tingle. The only real effect the house had upon him was the thought that the world would not sustain a great loss if House-on-the-Hill fell into complete ruin.

"Well, young sir, what effect has the place upon you this afternoon?" Salvaterra asked eagerly.

"I feel no different towards it now than I did upon the last occasion I visited this spot. My principal impression is one of regret that so much money has been wasted in building a place that has no real beauty."

"Then your discoveries of this morning have not affected you?"

Terhune smiled his negative reply, but the Panamanian did not appear to be disappointed. He chuckled deep in his throat, and as he glanced quickly at his sister an expression revealed itself on his face that was partly tolerant amusement, partly eager anticipation.

"Evidently you are not an impressionable young man? Perhaps you have no belief in the supernatural?"

"I am not qualified to believe or disbelieve; I have never studied the subject."

"I doubt whether many of the local inhabitants have studied psychical research, but they have, nevertheless, become unpleasantly aware of the psychic influences radiated by the house in front of us. But no matter!" Salvaterra continued pleasantly. "We came here to inspect the interior, not the exterior. I have a key to the front door, though, with so many broken windows within reach, it is scarcely necessary."

He led the way towards the house; closely followed by his sister. Terhune hung back a little; in doing so he was amused to notice the short, quick paces taken by the two foreigners—compared with his, he was sure they took one-third as many.

Upon reaching the porch, Salvaterra inserted a rusty, old-fashioned key in the lock. At first he had some difficulty in turning it, but as Terhune was about to offer his help, the key turned. The Panamanian pushed at the large twin doors; they swung inwards, stiffly, with a shrill protesting squeal. Salvaterra stood aside, and courteously waved his sister, and afterwards Terhune, to precede him.

Terhune found himself in a large-sized hall, of the type which he associated with the Elizabethan period. He looked about him with eager curiosity. The wood-panelled walls stretched upwards the entire height of the house to the ceiling, which was of massive, carved oak beams and plaster. This height created an impression, not only of size, but also of elegance and grace, an impression that was aided by a gallery which occupied three sides of the hall some fifteen feet above ground level. The gallery opened on to a handsome staircase which descended, immediately opposite the door, and spread out with each stair to a graceful semicircle, eventually joining the floor about half-way across the hall.

Terhune's glance next travelled round the lower part of the hall. Immediately to his left was a closed door. Farther along the wall was an immense ingle-nook fireplace, surrounded by sculptured stone. Between the fireplace and the north wall was another door-way, but the door had broken away from its hinges, and had toppled on to the floor, where it remained, almost hidden by an accumulation of filth.

The north wall, the whole of which was shadowed by the gallery above, was split in two by the staircase, but, beyond having two doors, one on either side of the staircase, there was nothing about it to interest Terhune, so his glance travelled round to the east wall. But this, with its two doors, and another ingle-nook fireplace, was the facsimile of the west wall, so his gaze ascended the stairs to the gallery. In all, seven doors opened inwards from the gallery; three from the north, and two each from the east and west.

These general observations prompted Terhune's imagination: a mental picture painted itself of the hall as it might have been in the time of the first Mulholland to own it; or might be now, in better circumstances. He saw the walls above the gallery lined with sombre portraits, he saw the oak beams gleaming and the plaster work white and unbroken. Opposite the staircase, and above the door behind him he saw the walls decorated with tapestries and Mediæval arms. In the fireplaces he saw log fires glowing red, with oaken armchairs before them, and thick rugs. On either side of the bottom stair he saw a shining suit of armour.

The vividness of this imaginative scene was not of long duration. The youthful vision of what the hall might be was dissolved by the chilling reality of what it was. Instead of colourful rugs upon the floor, he saw only a thick layer of dust; instead of polished boards, he saw the yellow powder of dryrot; instead of crackling fires in the twin fireplaces, he saw only pieces of chimney pots, broken bricks, and dead leaves; instead of plaster work, he saw broken laths and daylight. He saw gaps in the floorboards, gaps in the carved wooden balustrade of the gallery, gaps in the stairboards, gaps in the two large windows which gave the hall its light. He saw, in fact, only decay, and desolation, and gloom, and unexpectedly he regretted having entered the house.

Having allowed Terhune these few moments to observe the hall, Salvaterra resumed his rapid chatter.

"Can you see this hall, young sir, as it will be when the builders have finished?" he demanded gaily. "No more broken floor-boards or dangerous stairs. No more broken windows to let in the dust and dirt." With a flamboyant gesture, he waved his arm at the two windows. "In these windows there will be stained glass, to soften the bright glare of the daylight, and make this hall a place of mellow tints and shadowed corners. Up there, in the gallery, there will be exotic plants and sweet-smelling flowers. And there, and there, and there, tapestries from the Continent. And there and there, portraits of my ancestors. And there and there, furniture from the antique shops. And in the fireplace, blazing fires and massive fire-irons."

Salvaterra's joyous enthusiasm irritated Terhune. Though the Panamanian had done no more than to put into words much the same picture as he, Terhune, had visualised not half a minute pre-viously, his mood was no longer receptive to such light-hearted impressions. He was conscious of a feeling of depression which he could not shake off, and which grew steadily more intense. It was easy enough to paint rosy pictures, it was easy enough—for one who had it to spare—to spend hundreds of pounds on renovating the house. But would the mere expenditure of money suffice to dispel the atmosphere of gloom which filled the hall, and restore to it a sense of homeliness?

With burning, eager eyes, Salvaterra watched the changing expressions which crossed and recrossed Terhune's face. "But I do not have to paint a picture for you to see it, young sir, for you are a young man with imagination, well able, I am sure, to see what could be made of this house. But come, before you give me your impressions of it, you must see all of it, for this hall is but a tiny part of the whole. Which way shall we take our young friend, Inez, my dear?"

"To the west wing, Vicente, which I am anxious to see again. Already I have decided what to make of those cottages."

"Lead the way, my dear. We will surrender ourselves into your hands, and follow whither you lead."

She pointed to the doorway from which the door had fallen. "I want to go that way, brother, for I want to have a second inspection of the kitchen quarters."

Señorita Salvaterra led the way across the hall with an enthusiasm which matched her brother's. Her tiny feet seemed to twinkle as she walked, and the hollow tapping of her high heels upon the bare floorboards was accompanied by the soft rustling of her black silk dress and the silk petticoat beneath.

She picked her way with care round broken gaps in the floor boards, from which ascended a damp, earthy smell, and round other boards which, though still whole, were worm-eaten and crumbling. When she reached the fallen door, she carefully lifted her skirts above her ankles, and stepped over the obstacle with the graceful caution of a cat avoiding wet puddles. Upon reaching the far side of the doorway she glanced backwards for one moment, and Terhune saw the same burning gleam in her eyes that he had previously observed in her brother's.

Then followed a thirty-minute period which was to leave an indelible impression upon Terhune. Sometimes in a group, sometimes in Indian file, the three people proceeded from room to room, from passage to passage, from wing to wing, and everywhere they went there was only neglect and decay to be seen. Thick layers of dust hid everything that was not swept by the wind or washed by gale-driven rain. This dust filled the air as they moved; it settled on their clothes, in their hair, entered their noses. Such ceilings as had not already crumbled, were stained with mildew. Walls were disfigured by green-slimy streaks of moisture. Floors were rotten and dangerous. Windows were loose or broken. Doors hung by a single screw or had fallen on the floor, like the one in the main hall.

Spiders' webs were everywhere festooned in incalculable numbers. They curtained windows and doors; they draped the walls; they hung from the ceilings, revoltingly obscene. It was impossible to move without disturbing them. Their sticky, dirty threads clung to eyebrows and eyelids, to hair and ears, to shoulders and arms and hands, until Terhune felt unclean.

The floors were littered with the mummified carcases of insects—flies, cockroaches, beetles—and birds—sparrows, finches, young starlings—and filthy with the droppings of vermin. Every corner, every nook and cranny was filled with decayed, and decaying, leaves. Walls were fungus-covered.

Before he had proceeded far, Terhune was filled with repugnance, and would gladly have left the place by the first available exit. Not so the two Panamanians. Apparently regardless of the dust, the filth, the spiders' webs, the fungus, the decay, their tiny feet pattered through room after room; they laughed gaily, and spoke cheerfully to each other of what this room was to be, or how that room was to be decorated; or what furniture to put here, and what colour scheme to use there. Their voices and hands, alike expressive of their enthusiasm and delight, were never still. No two schoolchildren, on their first visit to a fair, could have revealed more naïve pleasure in their outing.

The tour continued. They passed through room after room, of which no two seemed alike. Some, like the hall, had panelled walls, some had walls of bare bricks, some had plastered walls. Some had beamed ceilings, others had lath and plaster ceilings. Two rooms had wood-panelled ceilings; three others had plain oak boards. No room was of any considerable size, but some were ridiculously tiny. Most were dark and gloomy from lack of window space. None had a floor completely level or corners completely square. And everywhere there were dark, mysterious nooks and crannies, half-concealed alcoves, unsuspected doors and passages, dangerous steps.

These things Terhune presently ceased consciously to observe. One fact, and one fact only was paramount in his thoughts. Everything about the house—the dank, musty smell which permeated every room, no matter how violent the draught which blew through it; the gloomy corridors and rooms; the uneven floors; the crooked, bulging walls—everything about the House with Crooked Walls was sinister and evil—obscene...

Chapter Nine

I

As Terhune arrived at the front door of Willingham Manor, he heard the grandfather clock inside strike seven. He grinned cheerfully as he pulled the wrought iron bell handle; his timing was punctuality *par excellence*.

Phillips opened the door, and gave him a polite smile. "Good evening, Mr. Terhune. Would you please enter the Long Room? Miss Julia told me to tell you that she will join you shortly."

"Shortly!" Terhune repeated as he handed his outer clothes to the butler.

"Yes, sir. Miss Julia preceded you by no more than two minutes." Phillips deposited the clothes inside the closet, and unhurriedly led the way towards the Long Room. "May I bring you a dry sherry, sir?" he asked, as he opened the door of the Long Room and switched on the lights.

"Thanks."

Terhune entered the long, narrow and invariably draughty drawing-room which Mrs. MacMunn had been pleased to call the Long Room. Making his devious way round the massive Victorian furniture, Terhune drew up an armchair before the fire—recently stoked up by the look of it—and settled himself with the familiarity of a welcome visitor.

Phillips was not long in returning. "Your sherry, sir." he

announced in his even voice as he handed a glass to Terhune. "Can I find you a magazine or book, sir, or would you prefer that I switched on the radio?"

"Does that mean that Mrs. MacMunn is out, Phillips?"

A suspicion of a smile crossed the butler's face. "I have neither seen nor heard anything of madam since she left the house within an hour of Miss Julia's leaving it this morning."

Terhune refused both magazine and radio music, and chuckled to himself as Phillips left. This household of two women, served by a staff of five servants, was a queer *ménage*. Alicia and Julia MacMunn were more like two guests residing at the same private hotel than mother and daughter. Friendly enough in a curiously detached manner, each went her own way without reference to the other. With one exception—that Alicia MacMunn insisted upon Julia's living with her in the same house. She would not allow her daughter to be away for more than a week-end, even though she was perfectly aware that Julia's one ambition in life was to travel; a form of recreation and pleasure which she, Alicia, loathed and detested. And because she had sole control of the family exchequer, and because, also, Julia was unexpectedly pliant in matters of filial duty, Alicia had her way, and Julia continued to live at Willingham.

Perhaps it was fortunate that the two women could behave so impersonally, for no two other members of one family could have been more dissimilar in temperament. Julia was intelligent, cynical, reserved and, when she wished to be, mulishly obstinate. Alicia, on the contrary, had a delightful and charming personality, that was offset only by the fact that she was utterly and entirely feather-brained, and possessed a tongue that was inactive only when she was asleep.

With nobody to exert authority upon them, the movements of these two women were, in consequence, completely unpredictable. Terhune pondered upon the strangeness of their lives as he dug his back deeply into the chair and tried to manœuvre his feet into a position where they would suffer least from the draught. Poor Phillips could not lead an easy existence, never knowing from hour to hour what might happen next, and having to remain constantly on the alert to handle any and every contingency. No doubt, early in the morning he had made every preparation to serve lunch for both Alicia and Julia. But both, it seemed, had left the house soon after breakfast, and, without a word to him, had lunched elsewhere—Julia, at the "Almond Tree" in all probability, and Alicia, Heaven alone knew where. As if that were not enough to tax anyone's patience, Julia had returned home at five minutes to seven with the information that she had a guest for dinner (unless she had telephoned Phillips, which was unlikely, he thought) and, later on, as likely as not, Alicia would come along maybe with guests of her own—one, two, three, any number up to six. Nevertheless, as Phillips had served Alicia MacMunn for more than twelve years, it seemed that his shoulders were broad enough to carry these troubles.

While Terhune was thus ruminating, he heard the front-door bell tinkle; a minute later Alica swept majestically into the Long Room, her hand outstretched, her face welcoming.

"What a pleasant surprise, Mr. Terhune, to find you here awaiting my return. You are positively our first visitor since our return from those terrible Canary Islands. Why Julia should have wished to go there for a holiday I really do not know. Do you know, only a few of the natives were able to speak English? Can you imagine that there exists in the world a place where only one person in a hundred can speak our language? I should have thought that, by now, everybody everywhere would have taken the trouble to have learned our language. What a lazy people they must be, those inhabitants of the Canaries." She laughed insincerely. "I must let Julia know you are here, Mr. Terhune. I am sure she would like to come down and talk to you."

"I have already met Julie, Mrs. MacMunn. She asked me to come along to-night and have dinner."

"Did she? How delightful! I am glad you have met her already. Do you know, Mr. Terhune, I do not mind confessing to you now that I was afraid that Julia would never want to speak to you again after—after—well, you know what I mean." She paused, agitated by a reference which she evidently considered indelicate. In a futile effort to relieve the situation, she continued flusteringly: "I must ring for Phillips to bring you a drink, Mr. Terhune." She moved towards the bell.

"I have one already," he informed her quickly, adding gratuitously: "A dry sherry."

"Dear me! How thoughtful Phillips is!" she murmured vaguely. "Where is Julia, I wonder? Why isn't she down here with you? I must go and fetch her…"

Julia saved her mother that trouble by entering the room at that moment.

"Hullo, Mother," she greeted carelessly.

Alicia was obviously relieved. "So there you are, my dear. I was just speaking to Mr. Terhune of your rudeness, leaving him alone."

"It is his own fault. He should not make such a fetish of punctuality. Have you told Mother that you are staying for dinner?"

"He has, which means that I must change in a rush, and you know how much I hate having to do things in a rush," she complained in a plaintive voice. "You should have warned me, Julia; I could have come home sooner, and have been ready by now."

"As nobody knew where you went to, or where you have been all day, I do not see how I could have warned you. Now run upstairs like a good soul, and be down just as soon as you can."

"Very well, my dear." She turned towards Terhune. "I am glad you have come to dinner. I want to talk to you about a book for my nephew in Africa…"

"Theo has not come here to talk shop," Julia interrupted firmly. "At least, not that kind of shop." A wicked twinkle made her dark eyes gleam with mischief. "Theo has come to talk to us about House-on-the-Hill."

"House-on-the-Hill!" Alicia repeated in amazement. She became of a sudden intensely curious and eager. "Then the rumour I heard this afternoon, is true. Somebody is going to buy that horrible place." She placed her gloved fingers on his arm. "What do you want to talk about, Mr. Terhune?" she asked breathlessly. "Do tell me..."

"When you come down, Mother dear. Not a word before then. So the quicker you are—"

Alicia took the hint. With a friendly but impatient smile at Terhune, she bustled out of the room.

Julia waited only for the door to close behind her mother before turning eagerly to Terhune.

"Well, Theo?"

"Not a word before Mother dear comes down."

"Don't be silly," she exclaimed impatiently. "What happened?"

"You laid down the conditions, not me."

"Theo, you are a pig," she asserted viciously. Her angry eyes tried to subjugate him and force compliance with her demands. She failed. Terhune was in no mood to tell the same story twice in one hour, which he knew he would have to do if he gave way. At last she gave up the attempt and testily poured out a drink for herself.

I I

The subsequent meal, like most meals at Willingham Manor when a guest was present, was a long-drawn-out business. Not because of the number of courses served—in actual fact, only three—but because Alicia could not both talk and eat at the same time, and as conversation was, to Alicia, more important than food, it was usually the meal which suffered.

No sooner had Alicia rejoined Julia and Terhune in the Long Room than Phillips announced that dinner was served, so she led the way into the dining-room, sat down and, waiting only for Terhune to do the same, said impetuously: "I cannot wait another minute before hearing all about House-on-the-Hill, Mr. Terhune. Do you know whether it is true that it is to be sold? I have had it on absolute authority, from Diana Pearson, that an Indian Prince has made an offer for the property."

That was the beginning. A fresh question followed as quickly as one was answered, until Terhune despaired of finishing his soup before it was stone cold. Fortunately, Julia came to his rescue, and insisted upon his finishing the course before answering one more question. This he did, but as he swallowed the last spoonful Alicia impatiently put another question at him.

So, item by item, Terhune related the events of the day in chronological order—to Julia's annoyance, for her anxiety was to hear of his impressions of the house itself. At last, with the serving of the sweet, she had her wish.

"But what were your impressions of the interior?" she slipped in, taking advantage of one of her mother's rare pauses.

Alicia did not allow him to answer the question. "You have seen inside, Mr. Terhune? When? Recently?"

"To-day"

"To-day!" Alicia raised her voice in a slight scream of excitement. "You must tell me what the inside of that terrible house is like? Is it really as terrifying as everyone makes out? Is it"—her voice became hushed—"is it—ghostly?"

"He did not reply immediately, but played with the fragile stem of his wine glass, turning it round and round in an absent-minded manner. Presently he looked up at Julia.

"Have you ever been inside House-on-the-Hill, Julie?"

"Not since I was a small girl. Several of us were picnicking there, and somebody dared me to climb in through a broken window. I did so, but I was so frightened that I climbed out again at once. Of course, I was only a child, and as I had heard so many strange stories of the house it was rather natural for me to have been alarmed. Whether it would have the same effect upon me now I cannot say."

He turned, and looked at Alicia. "And you, Mrs. MacMunn?"

She shuddered theatrically. "I would not enter that house if you paid me a king's ransom to do so."

"Yet Dr. Salvaterra and his sister are willing to pay money for the privilege of living there permanently," he pointed out.

"You haven't answered my question, Theo," Julia interrupted quietly. "What effect had the house upon *you* when you entered?"

"I can answer that best by telling you first of my impressions as I inspected the house from a hundred yards' distance."

"Well?"

"I thought that all the people who have had anything to do with the building and designing of it must have been either crazy, or blind, or devoid of any sense of artistry. Beyond that reaction, was no more affected than at any time in the past."

"Didn't the mere sight of it make you positively shiver?" asked Alicia anxiously.

"I am afraid it did not."

Alicia was obviously disappointed, "I thought that you, as an author, possessed a vivid imagination."

"Why do you keep on interrupting, Mother dear?" Julia protested testily. "Why don't you let Theo tell his story in his own way?"

"I was only asking Mr. Terhune what he thought of the House with Crooked Walls."

"Isn't that what he is trying to tell us? Go on, my pet. So the exterior of the house did not affect you."

"Not in the slightest. I went inside convinced that people had allowed themselves to be unduly influenced by their own foolish imaginations."

"What nonsense, Mr. Terhune! Do you think that I should have allowed myself to be so influenced?"

"Theo was not talking personalities, Mother. Well, Theo, did you change your opinion?"

He nodded. "Yes, Julie. I did. Salvaterra took me through every room, every attic, and every cellar in the place. There isn't a room in the place which doesn't reek with mildew and decay, which isn't in some way open to the weather, which isn't filthy with dirt, spiders' webs and dead insects."

"Almost any house which has been unoccupied for so long would be the same," Julia commented shrewdly.

"I know. That is what I kept on telling myself at the time," he admitted sombrely. "I have seen mildew, and decay, and filth and dead insects before now. But House-on-the-Hill is different. There is something about the place which gives one the creeps, and makes one want to run from the neighbourhood as far and as fast as possible."

His voice became strained and husky as he continued: "It is no use my trying to explain why, Julie. Ever since my return, I have been trying to discover any one good reason for feeling like that, but I haven't succeeded as yet. I came away convinced that the place is obscene, evil, but, damn it all! I saw nothing there more obscene than spider's webs, nothing more evil than mummified beetles and flies."

Julia gazed with bewilderment at her guest. Owing mainly to his horn-rimmed glasses Terhune's countenance appeared severe, but she knew that closer inspection usually revealed the ingenuous, likeable face of an overgrown schoolboy; the type of face which every woman instinctively wanted to mother, a face in which quiet (and sometimes not so quiet) humour was predominant;

an expression that was apt to crinkle and twinkle at the slightest provocation.

This evening she found herself facing a different Terhune; a Terhune whose expression was drawn. A metaphorical shadow had fallen upon his face, concealing even the smallest glimmer of light-hearted relief. Had she not seen for herself, she would, cheerfully have wagered that the circumstances were not invented which could rob him of that ingenuous joy of living which was so great a part of his charm, but, even more than his words, his expression convinced her that there was indeed something vile about House-on-the-Hill.

Having commenced to speak of his impression of the house, Terhune continued, deliberately, as if obtaining a measure of relief from voicing mental reactions which had worried him during the past few hours:

"I am not impressionable, nor am I susceptible to psychic influences, but this afternoon I was conscious of sensations which I hope never to experience again. Although we were constantly moving during the thirty minutes we were in the house, I had not been there long before I became so cold I could cheerfully have worn a second overcoat, although the cold was the kind which no amount of clothing seems ever to check." Unexpectedly he shrugged his shoulders. "Of course, the afternoon wasn't too warm, and, as the house must be damp through and through from years of exposure to the weather, I suppose it was only to be expected that one would feel colder inside than out. I realised this and the fact might not have worried me, but—" His words tailed off.

"But what, Theo?"

"Neither Salvaterra nor his sister showed any signs of feeling cold. In fact, Salvaterra became so warm after a while that he took his coat off, and even the Señorita undid the top buttons of her coat."

"Perhaps they were warmed by their own enthusiasm," Julia suggested.

"Exactly, Julie! I had the same thought. But in the name of Heaven! what is there about that place to arouse their enthusiasm?"

"There is no accounting for taste!" Alicia interrupted tritely, a little impatient of having been chased off the centre of the stage.

Terhune grinned feebly. "You've said it, Mrs. MacMunn!" he muttered slangily. "It does not seem possible that any sane person could want to live in House-on-the-Hill."

"I suppose they are sane," Julia suggested suddenly.

"They are deep, but I think they are sane. Salvaterra knows what he is about. He knows that the house affects most people as it affected me. That is his chief reason for proposing to buy it. But the curious part of the phenomenon is that he is not similarly affected. It means no more to him to walk through House-on-the-Hill than for me to enter Edward Pryce's old oast-house. The same applies, as far as I could judge, to his sister."

"Your visit there this afternoon has not made you believe in the supernatural, has it, Theo?"

"Not—not really," he stammered. "And yet—"

"And yet?"

Terhune shook his head abruptly. "I am talking a lot of blithering rot, Julie. Of course, it has not made me believe in the supernatural."

"Then why did you hesitate just now?"

"Because that cursed place bewitches one. There was a moment when I should have found it quite easy to believe I was in a charnel house. Especially when I was in the grotto."

"The grotto!" Julia repeated sharply.

"Haven't I mentioned Robert the Hermit's grotto? It still exists, in the form of a wine cellar."

"How do you know it is the hermit's grotto?"

"I am taking Salvaterra's word for that," Terhune confessed, with a somewhat sheepish grin. "Archæology seems to be another of the many subjects with which the old bird has more than a speaking acquaintance. What happened was this. He was showing me the cellars, and presently arrived at one in which there were a few remains of some old wine bins. Just as I was thinking that the cellar was peculiarly shaped, Salvaterra yelled out with excitement, made a dash for the walls, and began examining them with the aid of his torch. Presently he called his sister and me over, and pointing to the stones which formed the walls, tried to prove to me that they were identical in shape and nature with those found in the ruins of Norman buildings in Kent. Then he referred to the design of the cellar as a whole, and informed us that, in all probability, we were standing in the remains of the original grotto of Robert the Hermit. I must admit that the cellar looks as though it might once have been a grotto."

"It is the first time that I have heard that the grotto still exists."

"To-day is the first day you knew anything at all about the grotto, isn't it, Julie?"

"Yes," she agreed. "But it is funny that none of the books you have consulted to-day has mentioned it. Surely, the grotto would have been a matter of real interest to one or another of the writers?"

"Perhaps Salvaterra is the first man to possess both the necessary archæological experience, and the knowledge that a grotto once occupied the site of House-on-the-Hill."

"Perhaps," she admitted doubtfully. "But what were you saying about a charnel house and the—the grotto?"

"You will not laugh at me if I answer that question?" He glanced doubtfully at the two women in turn.

"Of course not, Mr. Terhune," Alicia promised skittishly. "I should not dream of being so rude. Besides, I am sure there is nothing laughable about House-on-the-Hill."

Julia said more simply: "I promise."

Terhune stared down at the white tablecloth. "On one occasion during the War I passed through a village which had changed hands four times in as many days. During a lull the Huns had piled all their dead in the cellar of one of the ruined houses, preparatory to disposing of them at a convenient moment. That moment never arrived. When the village fell, for the last time, into the hands of the British, those bodies were still there. The—the smell from them was not—pleasant. It took me the rest of the day to forget it.

"This afternoon, while I was standing in the wine cellar, the stench of that house came back to me..."

Alicia emitted a delighted shriek. "You are not suggesting that dead bodies are buried there?" she demanded breathlessly.

"No, Mrs. MacMunn. I don't suppose the smell even faintly resembles that of a charnel house. But for a few moments I imagined it did. In those same moments I seemed to sense evil spirits surrounding me; to hear Robert the Hermit piously murmuring prayers to his Maker, to see his leering face as he rose from his knees, and approached his unsuspecting victims—"

"For Heaven's sake stop, Mr. Terhune," Alicia demanded gaspingly. "If you say much more I shall not dare to go to sleep to-night for fear of dreaming."

Julia rose abruptly to her feet and held out her hand to Terhune. "I think it is time for us to go into the library and consult Grandfather's book," she announced. "When Mother has one of her dreaming fits she is unbearable all the next day. Are you ready?"

He nodded.

Chapter Ten

Terhune handled Lord Fulchester's book with caressing fingers, for it was a handsome volume; a representative product of British craftsmanship which gave him pride and pleasure to behold and touch. No expense had been spared in its preparation. The vellum which comprised its pages was of beautiful quality and texture; the rich leather binding was exquisitely tooled, and decorated with a delicate pattern of gold leaf and royal purple.

The literary quality of its contents was of equal merit and artistry. True, the book throughout was in manuscript, but the writing, although small, was so beautifully formed that it was as legible as type, and almost as easy to read. Further, wherever necessary, the biographies had been illustrated by exquisite little water colours of heraldic devices and armorial bearings.

"Where shall we start?" Julia asked, as Terhune carefully laid the large volume down upon the library table.

"At House-on-the-Hill."

She shook her head. "Grandfather only dealt with personalities, not with buildings. You can look, but I doubt whether an entry under the name of the house will say much more than: 'See So-and-So.'"

Terhune carefully turned over the pages, to find that Julia was not mistaken. Beneath the Gothic heading: "House-on-the-Hill Parish of Willingham," Lord Fulchester had written: 'See:

Winstanley, Family of; Winstanley, James Algernon Spencer: "Pickthall, Family of; Pickthall, Silvester Alaric.'

"Pickthall! I don't know the name, Julie. Do you?"

She nodded. "Vaguely. I believe they used to live in a house about half-way between Bray and Great Hinton. I cannot remember the name, but the house I mean was bombed."

"You mean Chartings."

"That is the place. I recollect visiting there when I was about seven or eight for a church bazaar, or some such fête. A Mrs. Pickthall was living there at that time. She was a very old lady. She kissed me on the forehead. I have never forgotten that moment, because I was particularly impressed by the fragrance of lavender which clung to her. Isn't it funny how curious little trifles of that sort remain in one's mind, although far more important matters completely disappear."

"Speaking of little trifles—" he murmured. "What about ye olde family of Pickthall?"

"Sometimes I think you are a perfect pig," she informed him serenely. "Instead of asking me so many questions, why don't you look for yourself?"

He turned over the pages. "I was testing your memory."

"It does not need testing, thank you. My memory is quite good. I think you will find that the Mrs. Pickthall I have just described was the last of her line. When she died all her property, including Chartings, went to distant relations in Burma, or Singapore, or some place out East. They did not want the house, so they gave instructions for it to be sold. It was bought by some people by the name of MacAdam, who returned to Scotland when war was declared—fortunately for them, perhaps, otherwise they might have lost their lives when Chartings was bombed. As far as I know, they are still in Scotland. Now, Mr. Clever Dick, have I a memory, or have I not?"

By this time Terhune had found the Pickthalls. He looked up, and grinned. "You have not," he told her with relish.

"Why do you say that?"

"According to your father, Chartings was purchased by a Mr. MacAllan."

She was sport enough to echo his laughter. "What does it say about the Pickthalls, Theo?" she asked eagerly.

Five Pickthalls were listed, including Susannah, the last of that name; widow of John Henry Pickthall. Terhune turned to Silvester Alaric.

"Here we are, Julie. Silvester Alaric, second son of Julian Henry, Born 1801; died 1853. Married Mary Anne, daughter of the Rev. Edmund Clouston of Weymouth, Dorset—" His voice sank to a whispering murmur as he skipped the unimportant details of Silvester Pickthall's life. "Two sons—three daughters—educated—called to the Bar—travels through Europe—spendthrift and gambler—friendship with Spencer Winstanley. Ah! Here is the milk in the coconut, Julie." His words died completely away.

"What does it say?" Julia prompted impatiently, trying in vain to peer over his shoulder.

For some seconds Terhune did not reply, but when he did so his voice was tinged with disappointment:

"Your grandfather hasn't helped us much. Silvester Pickthall purchased House-on-the-Hill for four hundred and sixty-five pounds, at an auction sale held by Phillips, Son and Neale. Apparently he was tight at the time, and didn't know what he was doing. When he came to, and realised that he had bought House-on-the-Hill he tried to back out, but the auctioneers were up to his tricks. They forced him to pay up, but then offered to put the place up again at their next auction. They did so, but couldn't get an offer, and it was left on Silvester's hands. It remained his until that night in 1840, when he played *écarté* with Spencer Winstanley.

"According to your grandfather, Silvester lost a packet that night. Winstanley had the devil's luck. First he won all Pickthall's cash and then his IOUs. At last all Pickthall had left to wager was House-on-the-Hill, so Winstanley, as a sporting gesture, and believing that the luck had to change sooner or later, offered to back half the IOUs he had won against the deeds of House-on-the-Hill. You know what happened. Winstanley won again, and found himself the owner of the house, which, soon afterwards, he exchanged for the famous mare."

"Grandfather doesn't say who put the house up for sale?" Julia asked in a pessimistic voice.

"No such luck."

For a short time there was silence in the library, while the two people stared at the manuscript pages as if by the sheer force of their will they would compel the neat writing to yield up more secrets.

Julia was the first to speak. In a hesitant voice she said: "I do not know whether this affair has affected my imagination, Theo, but I cannot help feeling that the name Phillips, Son and Neale is familiar."

"The same thought was in my mind. I have heard of, or read that name very recently."

"In one of the books you consulted?" she suggested.

He shook his head. "I don't think so. It was in small print." Suddenly he whooped with excitement. "I remember, Julie. It was in the advertisement columns of one of the daily papers. The *Daily Telegraph*, I believe. That was it. It was while I was reading the *Telegraph* at breakfast this morning. They were announcing the sale of some castle or other."

She placed her hand on his arm. "Theo, Phillips, Son and Neale must still be holding auction sales?"

"Obviously."

"In that case——" She choked; the words would not form themselves quickly enough for her. "In that case, Theo, if they have kept their records intact, might it not be just possible that they could inform you who put House-on-the-Hill up for sale in 1840?"

"They might."

"Then shall we call at their office when we go up to town next Tuesday?"

"*We?*"

"Yes, *we.*"

"It's an idea," he agreed enthusiastically.

11

Apart from the information about Silvester Pickthall, and one other possible "clue" (the mention of Phillips, Son and Neale), Lord Fulchester's manuscript yielded up nothing more of value. Having exhausted Pickthall, Terhune turned to the end pages, in the hope of learning something from the Spencer Winstanley biography which the contemporary Winstanley might have forgotten to mention, or perhaps did not know.

Alas! He had forgotten that the history stopped at the letter T, owing to Lord Fulchester's death. He turned back, but not hopefully, to the M's——but no Mulhollands were listed. Thence to the I's, but the result was the same. At Julia's suggestion, he turned to one name after another, just in case he might accidentally come across a lead. His efforts met with no success; presently they decided to waste no further time. They replaced the volume in its honoured place among the hundreds of books which had once comprised Lord Fulchester's library (some of the books Terhune had himself sold to his Lordship), and then rejoined Alicia MacMunn in the Long Room for the rest of the evening.

During the next six days, Terhune spent every spare moment in trying to learn more of the past history of House-on-the-Hill, but he had no luck. Not one item of any significance did he find during all those six days, though he searched diligently in the most unlikely books.

During that time he saw nothing more of the two Panamanians. This did not surprise him. Nor did he see anything of Julia, which did; he had expected that her curiosity would urge her to make at least one appearance at the shop in order to find out what progress he was making. But she neither appeared at the shop nor troubled to telephone him. By the time Monday morning arrived, he had almost reached the conclusion that her interest in House-on-the-Hill had been transitory, and that she had subsequently regretted having acted against her principles in mixing herself with matters of no personal concern to her.

That afternoon he learned, gladly, that he had misjudged her. She phoned at last, to confirm the time of their meeting the following day. Her voice, far from expressing regret, was excited and eager.

Early the next morning Julia's car drew up in Market Square. Several toots on the horn warned him that she had arrived, and was impatient to get going—for she had insisted upon going to Town by car. He gave last hurried instructions to Mrs. Mann about leaving something for his supper that night, and to Miss Amelia about some books which he had chosen and put aside for various people who were to call in for them during the day. Then he joined Julia in the car, which started off Londonwards.

Their first visit was to the office of Phillips, Son and Neale. There they were interviewed by a sleek-haired, pleasant-mannered young man who asked them cheerfully what he could do for them.

"We have rather an unusual request to make," Terhune warned him.

The young man appeared undismayed. "We are used to unusual requests, sir," he lied gracefully.

"In eighteen hundred and forty, or perhaps a year or two previously, your firm sold a property entitled House-on-the-Hill, situated at Willingham, Kent, to a Mr. Silvester Pickthall. At a subsequent sale you again put the property up for sale, this time on Mr. Pickthall's behalf. Apparently you were unable to sell it the second time. Would it be causing you too much trouble to tell us whether you still possess records of the first sale, and if so, the name of the client on whose behalf you sold the property to Mr. Pickthall?"

The other man's expression did not change. "You did say *eighteen* hundred and forty, sir?"

"I did."

The young man nodded his head reflectively. "For the moment I do not recollect that particular sale," he asserted seriously. Then he was foolish enough to glance at Terhune's twinkling eyes and was unable to maintain his composure. "Your request certainly is a little unusual, sir," he admitted presently. "But it might be possible to give you the information you require. We have some old records which could be consulted, although I do not promise that the sale in question will be among them. At the same time, sir, before I can do anything about turning up the old records I must consult our Mr. Lansdowne, who is not in at the moment. Would it be convenient for you to call back again later on in the day?"

Terhune glanced enquiringly at Julia. "Yes," she confirmed instantly, giving the young man one of her rare smiles.

He was delighted. "In that case, sir, you can rely upon my doing my best to oblige you."

They thanked him and left, this time for the Reading Room of the British Museum.

During the next hour Terhune initiated Julia into the mysteries of literary research. As soon as he was satisfied that she had grasped the first principles of the task, he left her, to proceed about the usual business which took him up to Town on the last Tuesday of each month—the business of buying books.

As soon as he had finished, he returned to the Museum. There he found Julia, tired, irritable, and frowning with a nagging headache, but gamely carrying on. She had had no luck, so she returned the books, some to the open shelves, and some to the centre desk from which they had been issued to her. Then they returned to the car, and drove off in the direction of the auctioneers' office.

"Well?" Terhune asked.

"Now nothing ever will make me love books."

"I warned you—"

"I know you did, my pet," she interrupted with asperity. "I do not regret having made the offer"

"But you do not want to repeat the dose?"

"Indeed I do. I am coming up again on Friday."

"No, Julie. There is no need for you to. I love the work, and there is no urgent hurry—"

"I am coming up on Friday," she repeated firmly.

He knew it was useless to argue with Julia once she had made up her mind to any particular course of action. He relapsed into silence, and marvelled again at her dexterity in directing the heavy, powerful car through the unceasing stream of traffic which flowed through the streets.

Within a few minutes they were back again at the offices of Phillips, Son and Neale. The same young man attended to them, his face beaming.

"I have the information you want, sir," he told them.

"You have?"

"Yes, sir. House-on-the-Hill was put up for sale in the February of eighteen hundred and thirty-eight, and was sold to Mr. Silvester Pickthall of Bray-in-the-Marsh for the sum of four hundred and sixty-five pounds—a ridiculously cheap price, I should imagine, even allowing for the difference in the money values."

"Yes, yes. But for whom did you sell the property?"

"For a Mr, Rupert Drummond, sir."

"Rupert Drummond!" Terhune turned to his companion. "Is the name of Drummond familiar to you, Julia?"

"Not in connection with Willingham."

"A letter to us was addressed from Willingham," the young man interrupted eagerly. "It was headed: 'By the courtesy of Mr. Ebenezer Hocking, Care of Peartree Farm, Willingham, Kent.' "

This name was familiar to them both. A Bram Hocking still lived at Peartree Farm. But Terhune was more interested in Drummond.

"If Drummond was living in Willingham at the time of the sale, we might find him in your grandfather's book, Julie," he began.

But Julia shook her head sadly, and Terhune remembered that the earlier pages of Lord Fulchester's book were missing, having been stolen by the murderer of Jasper Belcher's heir: unfortunately, all biographies up to, and including those from A to D were among those pages.

He turned to the young man. "Many thanks for your trouble."

"It was no trouble at all," was the assurance given, sincerely, but with an undercurrent of wistfulness, which Terhune rightly interpreted.

"I am writing the history of the house for its new owner," he explained.

The explanation did more than suffice; the young man was exceedingly gratified to know that he had contributed, however humbly, to the making of a book. Before they left, he made Julia and Terhune feel that they had done him a favour, rather than the other way about.

III

Upon his return to the shop that evening the flustered Miss Amelia welcomed Terhune with a diverting piece of news. Workmen had that day begun on their task of renovating House-on-the-Hill.

Chapter Eleven

I

Days became weeks; the weeks, months. During that period a large company of men were employed at House-on-the-Hill, transforming it from a derelict building, fit only for the rats and the beetles which had inhabited it for so long, into a luxuriously appointed home at which some began to look with envy.

Into this work of renovation and rehabilitation, money flowed in a seemingly unending stream. Among the inhabitants of Bray-in-the-Marsh, Wickford and Willingham, anything and everything about House-on-the-Hill became the principal topic of conversation. Rumours circulated with amazing speed; the fact that nine-tenths of them proved unfounded in no way deterred the gossips.

Apart from the traditional and understandable interest of rural communities in new or prospective arrivals in their neighbourhood, there was every reason for their unabated curiosity in House-on-the-Hill. In the first place, the number of men employed was a matter for astonishment. Naturally, local estimates varied from slight exaggeration to fantastic distortion, but even to the sober-minded the number still seemed high. From miles around it could be seen that the eminence upon which the house was so arrogantly situated was covered with a number of temporary erections, ranging from the night-watchman's tarpaulin tent to three second-hand motor caravans in which some of the workmen slept at night.

Sunday morning excursions to the house became a regular feature. People walked there, cycled there, motored there, to stare, with wondering eyes, at the supply of bricks which had been stacked up in one spot, the quantity of timber piled up in another. It was particularly noted by the more observant of these sightseers that of these bricks, although some were new, the greater proportion of them were already weathered, and appeared to have been taken from demolished buildings. So with the timber, most of which was oak. The countrymen could see, by the rough-hewn surface, the shape, and the age, that most of the bigger beams had come from old houses or even old barns. In the light of this discovery, it was concluded that the work of renovation was being carefully done so as not to detract from the indisputable age of the existing structure.

Evidence of the work being done at House-on-the-Hill was to be adduced by carefully observing the traffic passing through Bray. For several weeks not a working day went by which did not see a lorry load of materials going through, apparently *en route* for the house. One day a number of cast-iron pipes were to be seen, piled high in a five-ton lorry—so House-on-the-Hill was to be connected with the water-main, more than a mile away. That would cost the new owner a pretty penny! Another day a small van was seen heading in that direction with a number of baths and water-closet cisterns aboard—so House-on-the-Hill was to have modern sanitation. Yet another day, hot-water radiators. That probably meant central heating. And a dynamo, with fifty or so of the latest type accumulators—House-on-the-Hill was to have its own electrical supply. And the familiar Post Office telephone vans were seen making for there. And a supply of telegraph poles. And so on. It was small wonder that, with little else at the moment to argue about, the local people talked of House-on-the-Hill.

Discussion was not confined to the house. If the superstition of burning ears had any basis of fact, Salvaterra's ears can rarely have been cool during the summer months. Not more than half a dozen people, either locally or in town (which meant Ashford to the people of Bray and Willingham) had actually seen Salvaterra and his sister. So hearsay and guesswork played its part in any conversation which concerned Salvaterra; although people listened eagerly to any "authentic" description of the mysterious foreigner, none paid any real attention (and rightly so!) to the extravagant word pictures which circulated. Consequently, curiosity upon the part of many increased with each day that brought nearer the eventual arrival of Dr. Salvaterra.

Terhune, meanwhile, had heard little from the Panamanian. About six weeks after Salvaterra's departure from England, Terhune received a letter, addressed from New York. This contained a cheque for £50, which the doctor considered Terhune had already earned. Then Salvaterra went on to put a further proposition before Terhune—namely, to write a twenty thousand word manuscript of the history of House-on-the-Hill, incorporating all the information and interesting details he had so far discovered. For this manuscript Salvaterra offered to pay a further sum of £100. There was one condition: he was to cable his reply to the Waldorf Astoria, New York.

Terhune duly cabled. In the affirmative.

Notwithstanding this added inducement, neither he nor Julia unearthed any further information of significance. Minor details came to light. For instance, Julia—who proved herself a real brick—personally approached the present Marquess of Hamble, and received permission to consult the family's private papers. From these Julia was able to throw fresh light upon the suicide of Lord Kenelm in 1794. Lord Kenelm, it appeared, had been passionately in love with Caroline Drummond, to whom he was affianced. Late in 1793 Caroline had died in tragic circumstances, the news of which, reaching her heartbroken lover, had caused him to take his own life.

At first this commonplace explanation of Lord Kenelm's death had disappointed Julia, who had romanticised and made a mystery of it. But, when she tried to learn the nature of the tragic circumstances in which Caroline had met her death, it was only to come up against defeat. Nothing in the family papers even hinted at the cause—it appeared, indeed, as though the family had viewed the engagement as something in the nature of a *mésalliance*, and had deliberately conspired to conceal all reference to it. Perhaps this was why a letter, written in 1837 by Lady Hamble, and addressed to her daughter Matilda, related only briefly the news of the impending departure for Australia of "The *Drummond* family, Victor Drummond having stated to George Beauchamp his intention of settling permanently in a new country."

Although it was by no means certain that Lord Kenelm's *fiancée*, Caroline Drummond, was necessarily the "Caroline" of House-on-the-Hill, the chances were, Terhune thought (and Julia agreed), a million to one in favour of that theory. What more natural than that Lord Kenelm should spend his Christmas with the girl to whom he was engaged to be married? Moreover, the acceptance of that theory helped to close the gap of years between 1782 (the year of Sir Constant Fitzwilliam's death at House-on-the-Hill) and the acquiring of the property by Silvester Pickthall in 1838. It looked as though, subsequent to the death of Sir Constant, the place had come into the possession of the Drummond family some time before 1793, when Lord Kenelm had visited there. In 1838 the then Victor Drummond, having decided to emigrate to Australia, put the place up for auction in February, when it was bought, in a moment of alcoholic exuberance, by the unfortunate Silvester Pickthall.

Although Julia met a check in trying to learn the cause of Caroline's death, she continued her enquiries by writing to friends of hers in Sydney, asking them whether they would employ a private detective agency to try to investigate the arrival, about 1838, of the Drummond family, and if there were descendants living, to ascertain, if possible, the cause of Caroline Drummond's death in 1792.

Terhune was sceptical as to the result of the enquiry. Not every family could produce family documents dating back a century and a half—not by a long chalk, he added, with a grin. His own, for example. But it was worth trying.

One other item which Julia discovered by accident—this time at the British Museum—referred to the fire at House-on-the-Hill in the year 1763. The reference was a slight one, and appeared in the diary of Lady Anne Hepworth. On the 1st of December, wrote Lady Anne, she was awakened in the early dawn by a clamour of voices. Upon making enquiries, she learned that a house nearby, called House-on-the-Hill, was on fire. "Some damage done, I learned the next day, but not irreparable." This was in the year 1763. She was staying at that time with her friend, Mrs. Willoughby, at Wickford. But within a week she had moved on to Folkestone, and there was no further reference in her diary to House-on-the-Hill.

11

One Sunday morning in late August, Terhune's telephone bell rang. He answered the call, and was greeted by "Is that Mr. Terhune?" in a deep, rich voice. Despite the months which had passed since he had last heard the voice, there was no mistaking it.

"Good morning, Dr. Salvaterra."

The Panamanian laughed. "You are quick to recognise my voice, young sir. You are quite well, I trust?"

"Yes, thank you. And you?"

"In the best of health, and happy to be back in England again: this time, I pray, for always. How is the story of House-on-the-Hill progressing?"

"Completed, as far as all the information I have been able to discover is concerned."

"Excellent! Excellent!" Salvaterra complimented with satisfaction. "Is the manuscript available for me to read?"

"I can hand it to you any time you wish."

"This morning, for instance? Or are you otherwise engaged?"

"I am doing nothing this morning."

"Then would you do me the honour of calling upon me, young sir, so that we can drink a toast to its completion?"

"I should be glad to do so. Where shall I call?"

"At House-on-the-Hill."

Terhune was astonished. "I did not know the work was completed."

"It is not. I am told that the workmen will be here for at least another three weeks. But part of the house is fit for habitation, so, in my impatience, I am sleeping for a long week-end in Ashford, and spending the days here." Salvaterra laughed. "I think my architect is sorry to see me back in England. Already I have suggested alterations which will delay completion. But why not? I propose spending the rest of my life here, so why should I not have the house to my satisfaction?"

"Naturally," Terhune murmured.

"I shall send the car for you, young sir. What time is most convenient to you?"

"There is no need to send the car, Dr. Salvaterra. I shall cycle."

"But I cannot put you to that trouble—"

"I always walk or cycle on Sunday mornings. I should miss the exercise."

"If you insist—At what time may I expect you?"

"About eleven-thirty."

"An excellent time. One word in your ear, young sir. You would oblige me by not mentioning a word to anyone of the manuscript you have written for me."

"I am sorry, Dr. Salvaterra—"

"Well?" the other man interrupted sharply.

"One person already knows of it. She has assisted me with the research work."

"Of no matter. But if she will say nothing of it for the time being—I have my reasons—"

"I will mention it to her. I am sure I can speak for her discretion."

"Good! Good! Then I shall expect you about eleven-thirty."

III

As Terhune cycled along the road leading to House-on-the-Hill he found it hard not to keep glancing at the building which stood out so boldly on the hilltop before him. From a distance, only the outline was clearly visible, and this did not appear to have altered in the slightest. Yet, for the first time, it seemed to him that the distant outline of the squat, indefinite structure bore an uncanny resemblance to an outsize toad, bloated and loathsome, crouched for a spring. He stared at the house again and again, but with every glance the simile seemed to become more apparent.

Obviously his imagination was being influenced by the contents of the manuscript he carried with him—else why had the same notion not occurred to him before? This annoyed him, for he felt that it betrayed a weakness of character to discover evil in something which he had previously thought of as merely commonplace. Determined not to allow himself to remain a victim of a psychologically inspired optical illusion, he tried deliberately not to see the ridiculous similarity. The effort was completely unsuccessful. Outlined against a sky that was grey with approaching rain-clouds, the dark silhouette of House-on-the-Hill continued, in his eyes, to resemble a large toad.

Presently the road curved, and Terhune saw the house from a different aspect. At once the previous illusion vanished, destroyed by the outline of the stables, which had come into view. The road continued to curve as it skirted the lower slope of the hill below House-on-the-Hill. Consequently, the stables again disappeared from view, and the house once more became seemingly a compact mass, now more of a toadstool than a toad.

Terhune had to exert more pressure on the pedals to maintain consistent speed. Soon he was in sight of the "Hare and Hounds," and Keppel's Farm, beyond. As he progressed, the work done to the house during the past few months became apparent. The roof—or, rather, roofs—were now variegated, for the many bright patches of new tiles were in sharp contrast to the dull, weathered brown of the original slates. The walls were less of a patchwork, because of the supply of used bricks which the builders had been able to obtain, but even so it was possible to see where the walls had been rebuilt, or new walls added. The new paint-work gleamed brightly, almost vulgarly, in fact, reminded Terhune of the effect of a too liberal application of cosmetics to the face of a woman past her prime. This reflection was succeeded by another—surely there were more windows than before? Or had some been substituted by others of a different design? Or both. At any rate, there was one arch window immediately above the porch which was different. To judge by its black appearance, this was the stained glass window which Salvaterra mentioned.

For a minute or so Terhune was too interested in noting the minor changes to the structure of the house to gain any impression of its general appearance, but as he passed Keppel's Farm and began to breast the steepest part of the hill, he was suddenly and acutely conscious that the new trimmings had not banished the inexplicable suggestion of malevolence with which the house seemed to curse anyone who dared to disturb its solitude. If the face of the house had changed at all, that change was not for the better. If it still jealously guarded its solitude, it did so no longer with melancholy, but with unholy arrogance.

Then the house was temporarily hidden from view by the copse which once had been the paltry object of litigation between two claimants for its freehold. No sooner had he reached the far end of it than House-on-the-Hill seemed to spring up before him, like a released Jack-in-the-box, stark, leering, and huge.

He had no opportunity to inspect the house at his leisure; outside, on the porch, was the tiny figure of the Panamanian, standing in an attitude which suggested that he was awaiting Terhune.

By his first words Salvaterra confirmed that this was so.

"I saw you coming," he said as he greeted Terhune with outstretched hand. "As a matter of fact I have been watching you for the past fifteen minutes. I have a pair of powerful field glasses." He waved his hand gracefully towards the south where, four miles off, the sea lay, sullen and gloomy. "I am having a telescope installed so that I shall be able to see the ships going by." He laughed. "If the sun should ever blaze with heat, and the sky become really blue, I shall be able to imagine myself back in Panama. I lived not far from the Canal, and spent thousands of hours looking at the ships through my telescope. Shall we go inside? Just leave your bicycle where it is."

As Terhune followed his host into the house, for the first time in his life he became fully conscious of the power of money. The hall was altered beyond all recognition; although his own imagination, and Salvaterra's previous disclosure, had warned him of more or less what he might expect, the reality was quite beyond anything he had anticipated.

First impressions were of magnificence. The hall was magnificent. That word, and that word alone, seemed, to Terhune, adequately to describe it. No matter in which direction he looked, the hall had been restored to something more than its original glory. To begin with, the floor. Every rotten, every doubtful board had been replaced by one in good condition; the older boards (if there were any left; it was impossible to distinguish them) had evidently been relaid; the entire floor had been levelled, planed, stained and highly polished.

The staircase had been similarly restored; all the missing banisters had been exactly matched and replaced, and it was possible to see how handsome they were. The plaster work of the ceiling had been more than repaired; it had been hand-painted with a bold colourful design. The panelled walls had been restained and polished. An immense electric chandelier, of delicate iron scrollwork, and quite obviously of genuine antiquity, was suspended from the ceiling by a strong chain. Electrified lanterns were attached to the walls above and below the balcony. Two complete suits of gleaming armour stood on each side of the lowest, curving stairs. Lances with pennons, shields and broadswords decorated the walls below the balcony; large portraits in oils, the walls above.

It was not easy to appreciate all this elegance in one, comprehensive glance, but even as his glance moved slowly from object to object, Terhune was conscious of a carping note of criticism in his mental verdict. Furniture and decorations appeared to be genuinely period pieces, and to have been hung or arranged with obvious artistry. For all that, considered not as separate items, but as parts of a composite whole, they produced a dimensionless picture; an artificial picture, a picture produced with studied effect. The floorboards were polished too highly; they gleamed so brightly one hesitated to risk scratching them with one's everyday shoes. The suits of armour sparkled a little too brightly; the painted ceiling was somewhat too bold in design and tints; the stair-carpeting and rugs were rather too colourful; the chandelier too large, the stained-glass window too handsome.

The hall, in fact, was not the hall of a rural Kentish home. It was an exhibition piece; a small edition of some baronial hall in a Mediæval castle. Better still it was not a hall at all, but a piece of cleverly painted scenery which needed only the noise of hammering in the distance, a series of brilliant carbon lamps above, coils of insulated electric cable underfoot, a cameraman, and a number of busily idling men in shirtsleeves, to confirm the impression that one was inside a typical film studio.

Salvaterra waved a graceful hand towards the far door on the right. "My study is over there. We can talk in peace." He led the way across the hall, then courteously opened the heavy, carved oak door for his guest to precede him.

Terhune entered the study; a small room not unlike his own at Bray. But the books which occupied the shelves were mostly companion sets in ornate binding, the table-desk was highly polished, the floor likewise. The chairs, two in number, were business-like. Everything about the room was scrupulously clean; meticulously tidy—it provided Terhune with a slight, ironical shock to see a burned match-end on the rug beneath the table.

Salvaterra took the chair behind the table, indicating to Terhune that he take the other. This Terhune did, with an uncomfortable feeling of embarrassment comparable to that felt by a schoolboy summoned to his headmaster's study, or an applicant for staff employment being interviewed by the manager. To recover from this sensation, he made a show of extracting the manuscript from his despatch case and passing it over to the Panamanian.

Salvaterra glanced casually through the manuscript, but soon put it away in a drawer of the table, which he carefully locked.

"I will look through the manuscript at my leisure. Tell me now, shortly, what you have discovered about House-on-the-Hill during my absence abroad."

Terhune began his brief recital which pleased the Panamanian, whose eyes brightened with each successive item related by his guest.

"I congratulate you, young sir," he said enthusiastically, as Terhune finished speaking. "I wish my sister had been here while you were talking, but she is busy elsewhere in the house. However, I shall have all the more pleasure in telling her myself. Perhaps I shall read your story aloud to her. Inez is always happiest when I read aloud to her. But I want to speak to you on another matter, young sir, if you will be so kind as to give me the benefit of your advice. My English is good, is it not?"

"It is excellent, señor."

"Thank you. And my manners? Are they—"

The last word remained unspoken, for Salvaterra sharply closed his mouth as the door opened. Two people entered; one was a dark-haired, olive-complexioned woman of medium height; the other an equally dark-complexioned young man, of slight stature and sleek appearance.

Salvaterra rose to his feet, Terhune also.

"What is it?" he asked sharply.

"I did not know you were engaged. I will go, Vicente," she replied flatly, turning.

"One moment, my dear. As you are here, I shall take advantage of the opportunity to introduce my young friend to you. Dolores, my dear, this is my friend, Mr. Terhune, of Bray-in-the Marsh. Mr. Terhune, Señora Salvaterra, my wife, and Andrés, my son."

Wife... Son... With difficulty, Terhune concealed his astonishment.

Chapter Twelve

Terhune's astonishment was not lessened by his surreptitious inspection of the two people to whom he had just been introduced. Señora Salvaterra was unmistakably foreign. Her blue-black hair was no darker than Julia's, yet it certainly had that appearance, possibly because of its coarse profusion, possibly because of the blatant lustre of its oiled sheen. The pupils of her eyes were dark brown; the eye-ball had a dusky tinge rather than that quality of blueness which marks the Anglo-Saxon. Her face was long; her cheek-bones high; her flesh a rich olive. Her figure, too, conveyed a suggestion of svelteness seldom seen among women of British nationality. Her style of dressing, also, was conspicuously foreign.

Her appearance alone was not responsible for provoking his further bewilderment. Her age was not easy to guess, for there was a dryness about her flesh which made him think that the fierce heat of Panama was probably more responsible than her years for the lines at the corners of her eyes. Even if one made no allowance for the ageing qualities of a tropical climate, she looked no more than half her husband's age—that is, if Terhune were justified in estimating Salvaterra's age at sixty-five or so.

A fact which riled Terhune was that, not for one moment had he thought of the Panamanian as a married man. Everything about Salvaterra had been subtly suggestive of bachelorhood. Never once had he mentioned a wife or family. His demeanour, his attitude to life, had been that of a man who had no interests other than his own to consider.

This impression had not been contradicted by the close companionship which obviously existed between him and his sister. Their deep affection for each other was unmistakable—the way they looked at each other, spoke to each other; their mutual interests. Such affection was explainable in a brother and sister, both unmarried; also their mutual interests. But was it so easily understood when one of the two was married? Terhune could not believe that it was. Recollecting the few conversations he had had with Salvaterra, he remembered that the sister, not the wife, had helped to choose the house: the sister had fixed where the kitchen quarters were to be; the sister had decided which bedroom was to be Vicente's; the sister who travelled everywhere with him; the sister who played cards with him.

To Terhune it appeared that this extraordinary situation was further complicated by the comparative youthfulness of Salvaterra's wife. If the wife had been approximately of Salvaterra's own age, then the husband's attitude towards his sister might have been understandable, while not, perhaps, being justifiable. One might have been tempted to conclude that he turned to the love of his sister as a relief from, perhaps, the cantankerous nagging of his wife. But Dolores Salvaterra was young enough to be capable, in normal circumstances, of holding her husband's affections; she was not startlingly pretty, but her looks were by no means displeasing; they were certainly not those of a cantankerous woman.

Perhaps these flashing reflections sharpened Terhune's critical faculties. Normally he was an unobservant man where personalities were concerned: he was content to accept people as they were, and not to try to penetrate the outer shell in order to pry into the inner ego. But in Señora Salvaterra's case he did this subconsciously, and so became aware of a complex character which he found hard to analyse. There was, for instance, an expression in her eyes which provoked his curiosity, for it seemed to him that it was one of agony and resignation. An expression, indeed, such as one might surprise in the eyes of an invalid suffering from an incurable, and painful, disease.

He rejected this solution as soon as it occurred to him. Señora Salvaterra's face was drawn, but she looked too well to be suffering from a painful malady. The cause of that secondary expression was, he thought, mental rather than physical.

He did not have time to complete his inspection. With a formal murmur: "I am happy to meet you, Mr. Terhune," she indicated her son with a deeply affectionate glance. "Andrés is anxious to meet you. My husband was rash enough to tell him you are a writer."

Terhune glanced at Andrés. Andrés was a slim-built youth of medium height. His hair was as dark as his mother's, as heavily oiled, and brushed well back from his high forehead. The dark shadow of an embryo moustache was beginning to reveal itself above his upper lip; his sloping chin was spotty. Terhune guessed the boy's age to be about nineteen or twenty.

"Good—good morning, señor. Are you real—really—a writer? I would like to be a writer, like Ibáñez or Julio Camba, and write ma—many bo—bo—books." Andrés spoke haltingly, in an unnaturally high-pitched voice, and picked each word with care, as if uncertain of the English tongue. His accent was not good, but it sufficed to make his conversation intelligible.

Terhune answered the youth's remark by some formal words on the subject of books—fortunately he had read translations of Ibáñez, and knew something of Julio Camba's work. He had, in fact, a copy of Camba's *La Rana Viajera* on his bookshelves, where it had been for some months, awaiting a buyer. While he did so he closely inspected Andrés, for there was something abnormal about the young man's appearance which provoked his curiosity.

At first, Terhune was unable to define precisely what gave him this impression, but presently he came to the conclusion that Andrés's eyes were responsible. They were not shifty, but nor were they steady or consistent in expression. At one moment they appeared to stare with an embarrassing glare; the next, they were jumpy and nervous, like the eyes of a jungle animal who has just sniffed danger in the wind.

It was evident to Terhune that Andrés was suffering from a severe nervous strain, a conclusion which seemed to be confirmed by a number of irritating gestures and affectations. His hands were never still; they fidgeted with one or the other of his ears, or with the lowest of the three buttons of his jacket (never with one of the other buttons, Terhune noticed), or with his tie, which he had straightened and re-straightened so often that the tie was stained by his fingertips. Another gesture was an irregular twitch of his mouth—every now and again he sucked in the left corner of his lips with a slight sissing noise. Sometimes his eyelids were still, as when his eyes glared; at other times they blinked incessantly.

"What should I d—do to make myself a writer?" he asked presently. "S—sometimes I s—sit for hours trying to think of words to p—p—put down, but sometimes—*nada! Nada! Nada!*" he repeated shrilly. "Nothing! The words they no come to *mi pluma*—my—p—pen. They are here"—he tapped his skull with his nervous finger—"but they will not write themselves. *Comprende usted; señor?* D—do you understand what I m—m—mean?"

Terhune nodded understandingly. "Sometimes even the most fluent and experienced of writers find it difficult to put their thoughts into words—satisfactory words," he qualified.

"Are you—what you say—a—fl—fluent writer, señor?"

Terhune grinned. "I am *not*. Not nearly fluent enough to please me."

"But do you no sometimes find it hard to—to start?"

"Yes."

For a moment Andrés looked almost happy, but before he could continue the conversation Salvaterra interrupted:

"That is enough, Andrés. Some other time, perhaps. Just now Señor Terhune and I are busy."

"Come, my Andrés," Señora Salvaterra said in an expressionless voice. "Come. You hear what your father says."

The spark of enthusiasm in Andrés's eyes quickly vanished. "*Sí*. I hear," he muttered tonelessly. He held out a limp hand to Terhune. "*Adiós, señor*. Perhaps you will permit that I call upon you when we mo—move into this h—h—house." With these words he accompanied his mother to the door.

Salvaterra waited for the door to close behind his wife and son, before saying: "He is a dear lad, Andrés. I took the liberty of telling him of your literary abilities because of his interest in that art. I trust I may be excused."

"Of course, señor, but I doubt whether I am capable of being of much assistance to him. I am little better than a beginner myself."

The Panamanian waved away the objection with an eloquent, expressive gesture. "You are being too modest, young sir." He smiled drily. "You forget that I have a sample of your work in this drawer to disprove your statement. But come, let us continue our interrupted conversation. I was about to tell you of myself. I am the kind of man who, in your language, might be described as companionable. I like to be friendly with people, to receive my neighbours, and be received, by them."

He paused, glanced quickly round the room, then fixed his glance upon the door—there was a happy light in his eyes which convinced Terhune that the little man opposite him was basking in the warmth of pleasure which came of his possession of House-on-the-Hill.

"Nothing will give me greater happiness than for this house to become a 'Liberty Hall'—you say that, no? In the winter, dances for the younger folk—for Andrés—and for me, and Inez, intimate dinner parties, and card parties. In the summer, tennis parties and bowls tournaments. Perhaps croquet parties. Why not? I am too old to play energetic games, but croquet pleases me. I play it well."

He laughed softly. "Am I a dreamer, young sir? No doubt, you will be thinking to yourself: 'Indeed he is a dreamer, that Señor Salvaterra. He does not know the etiquette to be observed in a small English village, nor the insularity of the local inhabitants.' But I do. I do. I believe it to be more than a fable that one must reside in a neighbourhood—how many years?—before one is recognised as being a resident and admitted to its many friendly circles. I am not criticising, young sir. That insularity, that proud conservatism, is the heritage of the Briton, and perhaps his strength. But it is so—no?"

"I am afraid so, señor."

"And especially to foreigners, no?" Salvaterra laughed at Terhune's embarrassment. "But I come from the New World, where people are less reserved, and I am too elderly, too impatient, to wait so many years before making friends of my neighbours, and my neighbours, friends. I seek a short cut to that friendship, and that is why I am asking you for the privilege of your advice and assistance."

Terhune was bewildered. "Any help I can give, señor, I will give gladly. But I am not among that circle—"

"Are you not?" Salvaterra interrupted blandly. "Are you once again being too modest, young sir? Perhaps I know more about you than you suspect. I have learned, for instance, that you have won your own particular niche in local society. You would like to convince me that you are only a shopkeeper. But I know better. I am aware that you are now a personal friend of Lady Kylstone, of the Hon. Mrs.MacMunn, and her daughter, Julia, of that charming character, Mr. Winstanley—but I will not continue. I am embarrassing you, and I have no wish to do that."

He paused to offer a small casket of cigarettes to his visitor, and to light one of his usual thin cigars. Presently the atmosphere of the small room was blue and fragrant.

"I will be frank with you, my young friend. When I move into House-on-the-Hill I should like to hold a house-warming party, to which I should like to ask all the people of this neighbourhood whom I wish to make my friends. But if I were to do that, would they accept my invitation?"

Terhune glanced despondently at his host. Darn the man for asking a question of that nature! How on earth was it to be answered without giving offence?

He overlooked the Panamanian's facility for reading one's more obvious thoughts. Salvaterra laughed ironically. "You do not have to reply; I can see the answer written in that too expressive face of yours, my young friend. But, of course, that answer was already known to me." His dark eyes twinkled. "I have an obstinate nature; I am not easily defeated. I also possess imagination. That is why I believe that you could ensure the success of my house-warming party."

"I?" Terhune stared at the other man, and, in case his expression should again be rightly interpreted, tried hard not to wonder whether Salvaterra was a trifle mad.

"You, young sir," Salvaterra confirmed with emphasis. "If Lady Kylstone and Mrs. MacMunn were to accept my invitation, is it not likely that many others would be glad to satisfy their curiosity about me, and about this house, by following the example of two ladies who are recognised as being more or less leaders of local society?"

"Probably."

"Then, Señor Terhune, will you place me in everlasting debt to you by persuading those two ladies to come to my party?" He hurried on, as if afraid he might be interrupted before finishing what he had to say. "I beg you not to be insulted by my unusual request," he pleaded. "I would not dare to put it to you, but—" He shrugged his shoulders, and with his tapering fingers ruffled his thick mane of snowy-white hair. "You see, the years left to me are not many," he explained with unexpected pathos. "I do not want to waste half of them before I have the opportunity of enjoying to the full this England of yours which I have come to love so much."

Salvaterra's appeal helped to dispel Terhune's feeling of resentment. Having recently experienced the friendliness and hospitality freely offered to a stranger by the people of the New World, he could readily sympathise with the Panamanian's desire to make friends quickly. For a person fond of being surrounded by gay company, it could mean little to occupy a reasonably large and not unlovely house, situated in a beautiful corner of Kent, and yet be deprived of that sincere, happy companionship which makes life in the country so joyfully different from the more worldly friendships of town and city.

As though the frank plea for friendship had robbed Salvaterra of his normal, outer gloss of sophistication, Terhune saw the foreigner in a new guise. Instead of the polished cosmopolitan, instead of the brilliant dabbler in psychology, he saw a little, frail man, nearing the end of his allotted span of life, pathetically anxious to become friendly with the people among whom he proposed to spend the rest of his days.

The role which Salvaterra was asking him to play was not a pleasant one. Nor was it likely to prove a difficult one, for the foreigner had not exaggerated the situation. Many of the members of local society were intensely curious to hear more of the mysterious, and seemingly very rich stranger who was proposing to reside among them: they were equally anxious to see how House-on-the-Hill looked as the result of so much expenditure. Given the right circumstances they would welcome the opportunity of satisfying their curiosity.

The trouble was, that the circumstances were not right. The receipt of an invitation to a house-warming party was likely to be regarded by many as a breach of etiquette, committed by a bumptious intruder anxious to force himself upon them before they had had the chance of judging for themselves whether or no he was a man whom they would be willing to admit to their restricted circle of friends. To be asked to House-on-the-Hill before a voluntary, formal visit there...

On the other hand, if once it became known that Lady Kylstone and Alicia MacMunn had promised to accept the invitation to House-on-the-Hill, it was likely, as Salvaterra had suggested, that the example would prompt others to overlook the normal conventions and do the same. It was equally possible that Terhune might influence this result by intervening with the two people on Salvaterra's behalf. Julia, for instance, undoubtedly would be his ally; because of having helped him to write the history of House-on-the-Hill, she was interested and anxious to see more of both the house and its new owner. It was certain that, if she wanted to accept the invitation, her mother would eventually do likewise, for Julia's persistence was notoriously effective. As for Lady Kylstone, it was probable that she, also, would accept, if only as a favour to him—for he was not so modest as to be blind to the fact that Lady Kylstone was very fond of him, notwithstanding the existence of two sons of her own.

Should he oblige Salvaterra as suggested? He gazed surreptitiously at the Panamanian, whose attention was fixed, as before, on the door, as though, beyond it, Salvaterra could visualise the hall as it might be on the night of the house-warming. Poor little man! There was something rather sad about his wistfulness.

"I will do what I can, señor," Terhune announced abruptly.

Salvaterra's expression radiated his joy. "You will not find me wanting in gratitude, dear friend. You have filled my cup of happiness to the brim. I know that Andrés will be equally delighted. He is anxious to meet young people of his own age. He is a fine tennis player. I have hopes of seeing him play at Wimbledon before many years have passed."

He leaned forward—his eager, vivacious face so changed from what it had been a few seconds previously that he seemed almost to be a different man. "Will you do me yet another favour, dear friend? Will you suggest to me the names and addresses of people likely to accept my invitation?"

Terhune felt that, having gone so far, it would not be easy now to withdraw. He nodded shortly.

"You will?" Salvaterra revealed his beautifully white, even teeth in a smile of gratitude, and hastily produced a pad of paper, and pen, from one of the desk-table drawers. "Lady Kylstone—" he began suggestively.

"Timberlands, Willingham," Terhune supplied. "And if I may suggest another name, señor—"

"Of course. Of course."

"Miss Helena Armstrong, at the same address."

Salvaterra's white eyebrows lifted slightly. "Miss Armstrong?" he hinted.

"Lady Kylstone's companion and secretary."

The Panamanian's lips parted in a slyly significant smile. "Ah!" he murmured.

Terhune's recently aroused sympathy for the other man was immediately dispelled. Damn the old man, jumping to conclusion he thought angrily. He resolved to give Salvaterra further food for thought.

"The Hon. Mrs. MacMunn, and her daughter Julia," he went on quickly, emphasising particularly, he hoped, Julia's name.

He achieved the wanted effect. The smile vanished, to be substituted by an expression of perplexity.

Terhune was delighted. "Julia was the girl I mentioned to you over the telephone," he explained, with deliberately laboured casualness.

All Salvaterra said was: "And the address, young sir?"

"Willingham Manor, Willingham."

Salvaterra wrote down the address.

"Sir George and Lady Brereton, Ten Chimneys, Bracken Hill; Everard Winstanley, three Seaview Road, Bray-in-the-Marsh..."

The list was a long one—Dr. Harris, the Rev. Ellis, Mr. Justice Pemberton, Major Blye, Colonel Hamblin, Isabel Shelley, Edward Pryce...

Willingham, Wickford, Bracken Hill. All three villages supplied their quota, to say nothing of Bray-in-the-Marsh, which served as a market town to the surrounding villages.

The compilation of the list occupied time, for Salvaterra was not a quick writer, and there was an interval between each name, taken up by Terhune in satisfying the other man's curiosity as to the why and wherefore of each person mentioned. But, like all things, it came at last to an end. After a longer pause than usual, Salvaterra prompted:

"And the next?"

Terhune shook his head. "You have them all, señor. At least, all I can remember just now. If I remember any names I have forgotten I will telephone them."

Salvaterra shook his head. "There is one name you have forgotten, my young friend."

Terhune could not think of it. "Who?" he asked, at last.

"Your own," Salvaterra answered with a sly chuckle.

Chapter Thirteen

I

Another month passed. During that time local interest in House-on-the-Hill and its new owner grew ever greater. Rumours spread with greater frequency as this person, or that, caught a glimpse of one or another of the Salvaterra family, or had occasion to enter the house, and see for himself or herself something of the transformation that was taking place.

The grounds slowly altered as the work neared completion. Temporary buildings began to disappear, as different groups of workmen completed their tasks and moved elsewhere to their next job.

At length the last erection disappeared, and then the last pile of unused building material, the last mound of rubbish, the last workmen. Hot on the heels of the workmen followed the landscape gardeners. Mysterious things happened, almost overnight. Freshly turfed lawns took the place of the rough fields of noxious weeds which had grown up unchecked for so many years. Two tennis courts appeared, one grass, one hard. A bowling green was laid down. Shrubberies of flowering, evergreen and deciduous bushes were set out in decorative plantations. A rose garden was sunk; a rock garden constructed; a slimy pond transformed miraculously into an ornamental lake, with water-lilies, magnificent goldfish, a canoe, and an island pergola.

All these hastening events were, in themselves, enough to cause an excited fluttering in the dovecotes of local society. But one day a late post changed this fluttering into a commotion...

I I

It so happened that Terhune was dining with Lady Kylstone that night. No sooner had he greeted his hostess and Helena than Lady Kylstone announced calmly:

"It has come, Theodore."

The reference mystified him. "What has come?" he asked in perplexity.

"The invitation from your friend Señor Salvaterra. Have you received yours yet?"

The question reminded him that he had seen a square, stiff-looking envelope in his letter box which he had not troubled to open.

"A letter arrived earlier on which I have not opened."

"Not opened? Why not?"

"I never open letters at night. If they contain good news, the news is not likely to become bad by waiting until the morning. If they contain bad news, I am better able to face it after a good night's sleep."

"An excellent plan which many would do well to follow." She turned to Helena. "What did I do with my invitation, my dear?"

"I think it is in your bag, Lady Kylstone."

Lady Kylstone opened her bag, and produced an envelope, which she handed to Terhune.

"Open it, Theodore."

He did so. Inside was a square of gold-rimmed, white pasteboard, intimating that Señor and Señora Salvaterra requested the honour of Lady Kylstone's company at a house-warming to be held at House-on-the-Hill on Saturday, the 15th of October.

"Helena received hers by the same post. So did Diana Pearson and Olive Brereton."

He grinned. "Have they already telephoned?"

"They have," Lady Kylstone replied dryly. "The local telephone exchange must have had a busy time during the past few hours. Everybody appears to be telephoning everybody else."

"What did Lady Brereton have to say? Are she and Sir George accepting?"

"Young man, if I dared to repeat to you some of the things Olive Brereton said over the telephone your dear, foolish notions on womanhood would be irretrievably destroyed, and I do not want that to happen. There are too few men like you about. Broadly speaking, Olive thought that the foreign—er—*gentleman* must be either mad, or an utterly impossible person, to think that *she* would accept an invitation to attend a boring dance in that ghastly house, from some terrible Brazilian halfcaste she hadn't even met."

"Panama," he corrected.

"So I told her, Theodore, but you know Olive. A mere few thousand miles means nothing to her. Brazil, Panama, and the United States are all but the same, except in name. Having said that, she continued: 'Of course, my dear, as a sort of fellow countrywoman, as it were, I am sure *you* have received an invitation.'"

Terhune chuckled. "Was she very disappointed on hearing you had?"

"She did her best to conceal the fact. Then she asked me whether I intended to send my regrets or ignore the invitation entirely—which latter course she felt should, in the circumstances, be followed." Lady Kylstone smiled. In her quiet, undemonstrative way she appeared to be enjoying herself.

"When I said, 'On the contrary, Olive dear, I intend to accept the invitation,' I thought I had caused her to have a choking fit. As soon as she had recovered from her shock, she gasped out: 'You are going to do *what*, Kathleen?' So I pointed out to her, most diplomatically I hope, that my curiosity to meet the mysterious Señor Salvaterra, and to see what changes had been made to House-on-the-Hill, was stronger than my concern over matters of etiquette."

"Did she rise to the bait?"

Lady Kylstone nodded her head. "I must confess that she did," she admitted sadly. "She said that if I were going there was no reason why George and she should not share in the fun." Really, there are times when I wonder what has happened to our womanly pride. Had you not asked me to accept the invitation, Theodore, I should have refused, in spite of my curiosity to see the mysterious Señor Salvaterra."

"Not because of convention?" Helena asked.

"Of course not, my child. No. I should have refused because I have no wish to visit that horrible house, however much a lavish expenditure of money may have changed its external appearance. To me no amount of make-up will disguise the face beneath. House-on-the-Hill possesses a power for evil which central heating and electric light are not likely to dispel."

"How can a house possess a power for evil?"

Lady Kylstone smiled. "That is not really what you mean, is it, Helena? Is not the question you really want to ask me this: how can *I*—a prosaic, unimaginative woman at all times—believe that a house can possess a power for evil?"

Helena nodded.

"I cannot answer that question, because I do not know the answer," Lady Kylstone went on. "But I will tell you of something I heard on the radio some years ago. During the war, at one of the sessions of the Brains Trust, the question was asked: Does the Brains

Trust believe in black magic? I cannot recollect all the arguments for and against the possible existence and practice of black magic, but one of the visitors present, a prominent priest of the Church of England, spoke of his early experiences in Africa. He went to that continent, he said, as a young man, believing only in God, and regarding the manifestations of evil as no more than a superstitious hallucination. On several occasions, however, he passed by reputedly evil places, and took advantage of the opportunity to visit those places in order to disprove the physical existence of evil. He admitted quite frankly that his experiments failed. In spite of his deep and sincere faith in goodness as opposed to evil, he was oppressed by an overpowering consciousness of evil.

"He did not attempt to offer any explanation for those manifestations. His only conclusion was that, just as there are places in the world dedicated to goodness, such as Christian churches, where even the unbeliever is influenced by a feeling of spiritual benediction, so, also, there are other places in the world dedicated to evil, where even the true Christian is not proof against the influences of evil.

"Such a place I believe House-on-the-Hill to be. Years ago, my child, I visited House-on-the-Hill. I went there because my brother had the intention of moving to this neighbourhood, and had written to me from the United States asking me to find a suitable home. I visited the house with an open mind, but I had not been there many minutes before, like the priest in Africa, I was overwhelmed by a feeling of evil. I did not trouble to see over all the house. I left it as quickly as I could escape from the charming but persistent estate agent who had conducted me there. I confess to you two children that, since I have been told the story of Robert the Hermit, I have come to believe that he was the miscreant who was responsible for that atmosphere of evil which pervades House-on-the-Hill, either because of a curse laid upon the grotto by a shocked priest or because of Robert's own wicked depravity. Perhaps both."

This speech considerably surprised Lady Kylstone's tiny audience, both on account of its length—for she was often abrupt in her conversation, and, normally, never used two words where one sufficed—and because of its underlying sentiment. There was no doubting her sincerity—she was invariably sincere—but neither had ever known her to be other than severely practical; consequently they were amazed to discover that she could be equally emotional.

Possibly she was instinctively aware of their reaction, for she laughed lightly, as though to dispel the momentary tension for which she was responsible.

"But there, Theodore, I have promised to attend your Señor Salvaterra's party. No doubt I shall enjoy it just as much as Olive, and all the others who attend."

"Is Diana Pearson also going?"

"She is."

The conversation was interrupted by the telephone. They heard Briggs's slow even step out in the hall, as he made his way towards the telephone.

"Probably someone else to say how annoyed she is to receive an invitation," Lady Kylstone murmured drily.

She was right. A few moments later Briggs entered, to report that Colonel Hamblin wished to speak to her ladyship.

She nodded, as she rose from her seat, and moved nearer to the telephone. "Put the Colonel through, Briggs," she ordered.

"Very good, my lady."

Lady Kylstone lifted the receiver. "Yes, Alec."

There was a long pause. Lady Kylstone looked across at the younger people, and smiled.

"Yes, Alec, I have. So has Helena. They arrived by the last post," she said presently. "I think Señor Salvaterra has sent to quite a number of our friends—names and addresses? Perhaps a little bird whispered them—my dear Alec!—as a matter of fact Olive Brereton is going to accept. So is Diana Pearson—"

From where they sat Helena and Terhune heard Colonel Hamblin's exclamation of astonishment. "I'll be damned!" said the hollow echo of his voice. Terhune chuckled loudly.

"But, Alec, my dear, I *am* going to accept. Yes, that is what I said—curiosity, Alec. A woman's curiosity, if you like—it is nice of you to pay those compliments, Alec, but, after all, Señor Salvaterra comes from the same continent—"

Whatever reply Alec Hamblin made to that remark, it caused Lady Kylstone to laugh. "Well, perhaps you are right, but, nevertheless, I am still going... I know I do not go out much, but is that a good reason why I should not go out when I choose? He may be a bounder, as you describe him, Alec, but I think that remains to be proved, don't you? After all, none of us have yet seen him in order to judge for ourselves... Why not, Alec? You might find the señor extremely interesting... Very well, my dear—yes, next Friday—good night."

"Cousin Alec is accepting," Lady Kylstone said as she returned to her chair. "The good doctor proved himself an excellent psychologist when he prophesied that, given the slightest excuse, we should all accept his invitation. Curiosity! What deeds are done in thy name! Theodore, I think it is time for you to pour out some sherries."

III

On the night of Salvaterra's house-warming party, Lady Kylstone and Helena called for Terhune. He was all ready by the door as the car drew up opposite, so he hurried out, and had opened the rear door before Gibbons had time to leave the driving seat to open it for him.

"Good evening, Theodore," Lady Kylstone greeted as he seated himself upon one of the tip-up seats. "You see before you two very excited women. By the way we have both been behaving all day, we might be on our way to our first party, instead of—well, I haven't enough fingers to count the years."

"You are not the only people to feel excited."

"Not *you*, too, Theodore."

He grinned sheepishly. "Silly, isn't it, but I ate a miserable lunch, and no tea at all. I think the reason is, that I am just as curious as anyone else to revisit the House with Crooked Walls."

"But you have seen it since its renovation, Tommy," Helena pointed out.

"I saw only the hall and Salvaterra's study. But I am not anxious to go there again to *see* the house, Helena, but rather to sense its atmosphere in the different circumstances of to-night's visit. I wonder whether I shall experience the same aversion towards it when I see it brightly lighted, beautifully furnished, and filled with people enjoying themselves? Or were my previous feelings not truly of supernatural origin, but caused merely by seeing it empty, desolate, and dirty?"

"I think many of us are asking the same question," Lady Kylstone told him drily. "As I have said previously, if House-on-the-Hill is really evil, then all the luxurious decorations and modern amenities will not suffice to dispel that aversion which every person of sensibility automatically experiences upon passing within its crooked walls."

He laughed shortly. "If all the guests become subject to feelings of that nature, the evening is not likely to be very jolly."

"I agree," Lady Kylstone said thoughtfully. "That was my first thought upon receiving the invitation."

"If I had realised that, Lady Kylstone, I should not have asked you, on Salvaterra's behalf—"He paused unhappily.

"I know, Theodore. That is why I said nothing of my fears. I did not want to ruin the party even before the invitations were sent out. After all, we may be making a mountain out of a molehill. Perhaps you are right; perhaps people have allowed themselves to be prejudiced by their eyes into experiencing strange fancies which have no justification whatever."

Helena looked distressed. "It will be horrible if everyone wants to leave almost as soon as they arrive."

Affected by this miserable prospect, the three people lapsed into an uneasy silence, which was not broken until the car had left the outskirts of the town behind, and was passing dark fields in which the only lights to be seen were those of scattered farmhouses and cottages.

Suddenly Helena called out: "Look."

Her companions followed the direction of her gaze. Twinkling far off in the darkness ahead of them, they saw a cluster of tiny lights, high above them, seemingly afloat in a velvet sea of blackness.

"House-on-the-Hill!" Lady Kylstone exclaimed.

"It looks more like a fairy palace than an ogre's dungeon."

Helena's employer laughed softly. "If all the younger people agree with you, the party is certain to be a success. It will put them all in the right mood." She continued to stare at the lights. "But I must agree with you, my child. From here the lights look very pretty. Maybe——"She stopped abruptly.

"Maybe——" Helena prompted.

"I was about to add that, maybe those lights resemble a symbol—the power of light over darkness; the power of good over evil; the conquest of thirteenth century superstition by twentieth century worldliness." She smiled drily. "See how quickly a woman changes her mind, Theodore. A moment ago I was sure that no amount of beautifying was likely to exorcise the spirit of evil which has haunted House-on-the-Hill for so many years, and now the sight of those twinkling lights has already caused a change of opinion."

As the car drew nearer to its destination, the lights of House-on-the-Hill sorted themselves out from the confused mass of shimmering, twinkling fairy lights, and became separate entities. In doing so, something of their romantic, fairy-like quality was lost; on the other hand, the more distinguishable they became, the more fantastic became the theory that House-on-the-Hill was defiled by evil.

In every part of the house windows blazed with light: big windows, little windows, arched windows, round windows, dormer windows, oriel windows—and specially, the stained glass windows, startling, multi-coloured, romantic. Lights pink-tinted, green-tinted, yellow-tinted, blue-tinted, according to the shade of the curtains reflecting it or the colour of the lamp-shade above. White lights from the open door of the porch, golden-tinted lights from half a dozen miniature lamp-posts which lined the gravel drive in the immediate vicinity of the house. And even red lights, through the open door of the engine-house, in which the dynamos were humming with the effort of supplying the necessary electric current. And more red lights, too, from the small line of cars which were lined up along the drive, waiting to deliver their occupants at the porch.

Gibbons took his place at the end of this slow moving line, and throttled down. Above the noise of the several automobile engines they heard the loud-pitched whine of the dynamo and the monotonous chug-chug-chug of the stationary engine driving the dynamo. And above all other noises, they heard, too, the faint echo of dance music.

The three people in the Kylstone car gazed at one another in amazement. How could it be possible for House-on-the-Hill to be so transformed? A year ago—six months ago, indeed—a decaying house had stood upon this site—a dirty, disreputable house, infested by vermin and noxious insects, and regarded by everyone around with repugnance.

And now? Now, the house was bustling with life and movement, gay with music, cheerful with light—the destination of all local society, there to welcome the newcomer in their midst.

One by one the cars moved nearer to the porch, while those which had already deposited their occupants turned and were parked by their chauffeurs in or near the long narrow building which once had been the stables, but was now a commodious garage.

Light! Music! Laughter! The mood of the night was infectious. Whatever aura House-on-the-Hill might have diffused for many years past, to-night—for the time being, at least—the spirit of happiness and gaiety was predominant.

Helena laughed aloud as she saw the Pemberton brothers alight from their sports car and enter the porch. Lady Kylstone smiled. Gibbons exchanged a wink with Butler, the Blyes' chauffeur, who was driving his empty car towards the parking place.

Terhune, alone, was unaffected by the general animation. A moment previously he had been as cheerful as the others. Unfortunately, he had glanced upwards at the stained-glass window, and so, for the first time had become aware of its subject.

With a sense of humour, which impressed Terhune as being somewhat perverted, Salvaterra had had there reconstructed a representation of Robert the Hermit in his unholy, infamous grotto.

Chapter Fourteen

I

The three people from Lady Kylstone's car passed into House-on-the-Hill immediately behind Dr. and Mrs. Edwards, and thus were given the opportunity for a hasty glance around while they waited a few moments for the doctor and his wife to advance towards their host and hostess.

Even for Terhune, who had seen the hall not many weeks previously, the scene was unforgettable, and one that far excelled anything which his imagination had anticipated. Once again his immediate reaction was to associate the picture before him with the ostentatious resplendence of the film studios. How often had he seen comparable receptions depicted on one of the Folkestone cinema screens? Times without number. One week, the scene was that of the Long Island home of an American millionaire; another week, of the European Embassy of a Great Power; another, of the lounge of Grand Hotel; another, of the lounge of a Transatlantic liner. There were innumerable variations, of which the Hollywood and Denham scenic designers made the most, but the basic principle remained invariable— flamboyant design, a prominent staircase, clusters of exotic flowers, an orchestra, and, above all, people; men and women, dressed and coiffured immaculately, gossiping in groups, drinking cocktails...

Now, for the first time in his life, instead of being merely a spectator, watching the finished scene being enacted on a white screen some distance before his eyes, he felt as though he were watching the actual filming of one such scene. As if an unseen director had already given the order for the cameras to "roll 'em," each minor character in the scene was playing his or her allotted role. From the ceiling, and from all sides, a strong but mellow light played upon the guests, who moved slowly about on the floor below, or stood in groups upon the stairs, or wandered in and out of one or another of the doors opening out on to the gallery.

The gallery itself was, for once, in truth a minstrels' gallery, for one corner of it was occupied by a small orchestra of six musicians, playing light music. Their faces were bored; their playing, too, for they played with impatience, as though anxiously waiting for the chance to crash into a livelier dance tempo.

Flowers were everywhere in profusion. In massive banks, blossom concealed the entire length of the gallery banisters, and also bordered the stairs—the air, although already blue with cigarette smoke, was sweet with their cloying fragrance.

In and out of this scene moved a constant succession of waiters; some carried trays of cocktails in variety, others, trays containing an assortment of cocktail delicacies. They had sharp eyes, those waiters: no sooner was a glass emptied than it was deftly collected and a filled glass substituted. In consequence, the atmosphere was already cheerfully noisy; excited chatter and laughter almost drowned the instrumental music.

Terhune was still comparing the artificial with the real when Dr. and Mrs. Edwards moved into the body of the hall; so he and his companions advanced towards the small group of people comprising their hosts: Salvaterra, his wife, his twin sister, and his son.

As soon as Salvaterra recognised Terhune, his fixed, formal smile was replaced by a vivid expression of welcome; a curiously mischievous light made his dark eyes gleam. However, he said nothing, but allowed Terhune to proceed with the introductions.

Señora Salvaterra held out a limp hand to Lady Kylstone. "Good evening, Lady Kylstone," she greeted in an emotionless voice. "It gives my husband and me great pleasure to welcome you to our new home," she continued in a manner of repeating a lesson well learned.

Her husband was infinitely less formal. He bent low over Lady Kylstone's hand, and brushed the back of it with his lips. "I shall never be able to express my gratitude sufficiently, dear lady," he murmured, with a significant glance at his guests. "This party is due entirely to your generous kindness."

She dismissed the claim with a determined gesture: "Nonsense, señor. We older residents of the neighbourhood consider it a pleasure to meet you for the first time in such delightful circumstances."

He shook his head in disparagement of her denial, but did not pursue the subject. "I shall look forward to the honour of having the supper dance with you, Lady Kylstone, unless it would embarrass you to partner a man of my small stature."

She laughed warmly. "My dear man, it is many years since last I danced. You would find a sack of potatoes lighter than me. But if you are prepared to take the risk of my dancing on your toes, I am willing to make an exhibition of myself. Señor, this is Miss Helena Armstrong…"

"Ah! The Señorita Armstrong. My dear young friend, Señor Terhune, has several times spoken of you. Señoras, may I introduce my son Andrés, and my sister Inez."

Andrés glanced nervously at the guests. His eyes were strained; there was an unnatural flush in his olive cheeks which made Lady Kylstone look closely at the young man to see if he were suffering from a fever. Only when he saw Terhune facing him did Andrés look a little happier.

"Thank you, señor, for sending me that bo-book. I have read it through twice already. Perhaps, later, you will pe-pe-permit of m-my discussing it wi-with you."

"Andrés," Inez Salvaterra muttered sharply, for other guests were already being greeted by her brother. "Later."

The unhappy expression returned to Andrés's eyes. He nodded his head in mute acknowledgement, and turned away from Terhune, who moved on and joined Lady Kylstone and Helena. As he did so Sir George Brereton approached.

"Hullo! Hullo!" he began jovially, in a loud, booming voice. "Hullo, Kathleen! Hullo, Helena! How d'you do, Terhune? What do you think of House-on-the-Hill now? Rather a change, what, from what it has been for the past half-century? I wouldn't have thought it possible. Are you going to spare me a dance, later on, Helena?"

"Well, really, George—" Lady Kylstone expostulated.

Sir George looked confused. "What have I done wrong? Mayn't I ask Helena to dance with me?"

"Of course you may, my dear George, but I think it would be more polite for you to ask me first."

"Ask you whether I may dance with Helena?"

"No, you stupid man. You are very dense to-night. I am speaking of your first asking me to dance with you."

Sir George's confusion changed to blank amazement. "You, Kathleen—dancing—I haven't seen you dance for years..."

She laughed gaily. "I have just promised our host to have the supper dance with him."

"Well I'll be—"

"George!"

"All right, my dear. I know we have a young lady present. But I mean it. Well, well, well! This place must still be bewitched." He laughed jovially and bowed in a purposely exaggerated manner. "Madame, will you do me the honour of having the first dance with me?"

"If you promise not to tell me one single fishing story."

"I won't, my dear. But speaking of fishing, did I tell you what happened last Thursday week when I fished old Campbell's stream?"

"George, do you remember having tea with me on Tuesday?"

"Yes."

"Then please try to remember that you told me the self same story at least twice in an hour."

"Oh!" Brereton looked glum, and beckoned a passing waiter. "Tom, bring me another of those white, frothy-looking concoctions you gave me some minutes back."

"A White Lady, sir. Certainly, sir. And the ladies?"

I I

During the next fifteen minutes the guests continued to arrive; sometimes one after the other in quick succession, sometimes with a short interval between one party and the next. The hum of conversation steadily grew louder; laughter became more frequent. As every passing minute confirmed the success of the evening, Dr. Salvaterra's expression changed from doubt (well hidden, but still apparent to searching eyes) to confidence, from confidence to overwhelming happiness. His eyes gleamed with a fierce pride, his perfect teeth were revealed in a broad smile which threatened to become perpetual.

His delight was faithfully mirrored on the face of his sister. They exchanged frequent, triumphant, and loving glances. Every time there was a slight pause between the arrival of guests they moved close to each other, and spoke quietly together. After a while they no longer even attempted to maintain a decorous formality, and, like two children at a Christmas party, frankly permitted everyone to know that events were surpassing their most optimistic expectations. Because happiness and excitement are infectious, their guests chuckled at this *naïveté*, and decided that the Salvaterras were going to make delightful neighbours.

Yet there were a few among the guests who were conscious of matters unnoticed by the casual observer. Dr. Edwards, for instance. Dancing was soon to begin; meanwhile the guests, at the urgent invitation of their host, were exploring the house, from east to west, from basement to the two attics, converted by Salvaterra into games-rooms, where one could play darts, table tennis, billiards, shove-halfpenny and other games. At one moment Dr. Edwards found him-self alone with Lady Kylstone in one of the smaller rooms, on the upper floor of the east wing.

"Admiring the room, Lady Kylstone?" he asked her.

She nodded briskly. "I am. This is a charming little afternoon-room, doctor. Cosy in the winter, and in the summer" She pointed to the oriel window, which had been fitted up with a comfortable window seat. "I can imagine what the view must be from that window, doctor. I feel sure it would not be easy to find a grander in this part of the country."

He agreed, adding: "Dr. Salvaterra has made a wonderful job of transforming a derelict old house into a magnificent home. Of course, the result is not above criticism. In my opinion, he has made the place almost too magnificent. But every man to his taste. Meanwhile, he and his sister seem very well content with their party."

"*Their* party?" Lady Kylstone emphasised drily.

The doctor laughed. "I did not mean that literally, but, judging by the attitude of the people concerned, one might believe that his sister had a bigger share than his wife in its organisation and success. Have you glanced at the wife's face, Lady Kylstone?"

"I have," she replied emphatically. "She is not a happy woman."

"That is more or less my own conclusion," he agreed. "She is trying to appear as cheerful as her husband, but, though her face smiles, her eyes do not. As for her voice—" he shrugged his shoulders. "I do not remember ever having heard a voice express less normal human emotion. It is a 'dead' voice; the voice of a human automaton."

"She is not—" Lady Kylstone hesitated to use the word. Not so the doctor.

"Mental," he supplied. "I do not think so. Ann and I were talking to her about five minutes ago. Not for long, I grant, but long enough to convince me that she is as intelligent as the average woman. But, even so, my feeling is that she is not intelligent enough to satisfy the mental demands of her husband. Dr. Salvaterra impresses me as being a man of brilliant intellect."

"Do you think that she is unhappy upon that account?"

"That was more or less my conclusion."

She shook her head. "If you are right, you are only half right, doctor. I think that the cause of Señora Salvaterra's unhappiness is—Inez."

Edwards raised his greying eyebrows enquiringly.

"My dear man, wouldn't any wife resent a husband's giving his sister first place. From one or two 'things which I have heard from various sources, and from what I have seen to-night, I am convinced that his sister has the larger share in managing Salvaterra's household. No, doctor, the son puzzles me more than the wife."

"Andrés?" He nodded. "I agree. There is something decidedly unnatural about that boy."

"Is he ill?"

"Physically? I do not think so. Mentally? Yes. All his symptoms are those of a man on the verge of a mental breakdown. His eyes are strained and restless; his fingers never still for a moment. If he were my son, I should call in a specialist."

Lady Kylstone looked sad. "He looks such a nice boy," she murmured. Her lips tightened.

"There are too many Andrés in the world," Edwards said quietly.

III

Meanwhile, Terhune was escorting Helena and Julia on a tour round House-on-the-Hill. Many, seeing them, discreetly expressed their surprise in their own individual way. For those three people—Terhune, Helena and Julia—represented a problem to local inhabitants which they were eager to have solved. For months now the question had been—which? Some thought Helena, some, Julia. But all were convinced that it would be one or the other. Perhaps the only person who had never given a thought to the problem was Terhune himself. Consequently it caused him no embarrassment to have them both with him. Blithely unconscious of the mutual antagonism which Helena and Julia felt for each other, he gaily discussed House-on-the-Hill with them.

"I take off my hat to the architect who renovated this place," he stated enthusiastically. "You ought to have seen what this passage was like a few months ago. If it were not for remembering that I very nearly cracked my head on that beam over there, I don't think I should recognise it. See the window there. Doesn't it look as if it had been there since the days of Queen Anne at the latest? Well, it hasn't. Six months ago the passage didn't have a window of any kind in it. As for that door—"

He steered them through room after room, from one wing to another, comparing and admiring. Above all, admiring. He was amazed at the changes which money, imagination and toil had wrought. Cleverly, the old and the modern had been combined in such a manner that it was difficult to realise that centuries parted the two styles. Salvaterra had selected the Elizabethan style for the only motif. Fabrics, furniture, decoration—nothing apparently was not in keeping with the selected period. The result was extraordinary; at times it was quite an effort for Terhune to realise that he had not been mysteriously wafted back into the sixteenth century; every time he glanced at Helena or Julia, he half expected to see their dresses change suddenly into jewelled stomachers and wide lace ruffs.

Beneath the surface, however, the modern predominated. The candles on the mantels, in the candelabra, on the tables, were electric. The monk's chest in each room was no monk's chest in reality, but a piece of camouflage cleverly concealing the radiators. The tapestries on the walls looked old and faded, but they were in reality, contemporary with some of the cleverly designed modern furniture.

If criticism were justified, it was on the grounds that the whole scheme was somewhat too true to the past. Too perfect. Again and again a niggling simile presented itself to Terhune and his companions. As they inspected one room after another, they were reminded of former Ideal Homes Exhibitions, where Famous Rooms of Bygone Centuries and other similar tableaux had been exhibited. Any one of the rooms might have been lifted complete from one of those tableaux: Sitting-room, *circa* 1603; or A Bedroom in the time of Queen Elizabeth; or Reproduction of an Elizabethan Antechamber.

Helena was the first to speak of this comparison. She did so on account of a shiver, which Terhune noticed.

"Are you feeling cold, Helena?"

"Good heavens, no! I'm boiling. The central heating system must be working at high pressure."

"I saw you shiver."

"Did I shiver? I did not do so consciously, Tommy; and certainly not from cold. I suppose my thoughts were responsible. Dr. Salvaterra has made a marvellous job of repairing House-on-the-Hill, but I do not feel that he has made a home of it. You have been inside Edward Pryce's house, haven't you, Tommy?"

"Yes."

"And I know you have, Julia. Well, Edward's house is reputed Elizabethan, so it must be about the same age as this part of House-on-the-Hill. One or two of his rooms remind me very much of the one we are in, but his rooms are—are—well, friendly, which is the only word I can think of just now. But this room does not strike me as being friendly. It is too—too" Once more she paused for want of the right word.

"Too museum-like," Julia suggested quietly.

Helena nodded. "That is what I mean, Julia, and now I know why. Your mentioning museums reminds me of a time when I accompanied Lady Kylstone on a tour of the *châteaux* country in France. Some of the *châteaux* were still used by the owners, but whenever they were not in residence the public were allowed through some of the rooms. The fact that they were lived in was obvious merely by walking through, even though everything was precisely in its place; everything was so neat and tidy that I felt almost nervous about stepping on the carpet. I didn't dare touch anything, although I saw some lace which I dearly wanted to examine closely.

"If only there was an ashtray to be seen with a cigarette-end in it, the house might seem like a home," she continued a little breathlessly. "Or if there were a newspaper about, or an open magazine. If only that cushion over there had a dent in it, to convince one that sometimes it was used!"

Terhune grinned. "I have been thinking much the same, Helena, but, after all, we ought to remember that the family hasn't been living here for more than a week or two."

"All houses where a number of servants are employed are apt to resemble museums," Julia pointed out quietly. She turned towards Terhune. "What alterations has Dr. Salvaterra made to the grotto of Robert the Hermit?"

"I don't know."

"Do you know the way down there?"

He nodded. "I do. But you don't want to go down there to-night, do you, Julia?"

"Yes, Theo."

"So do I," Helena added quickly.

"I would rather you did not."

"Why not?" Julia snapped.

He shrugged his shoulders. "It is a depressing sight—"

Julia's lips betrayed her temper; it was apparent to the others that she was rapidly falling into one of her obstinate moods, "I do not propose to leave House-on-the-Hill without seeing its *pièce de résistance*," she told him firmly. "If you will not take me, Theo, I shall ask Dr. Salvaterra personally to escort me there. I am sure that *he* would be delighted to do so."

"He probably would," Terhune muttered. "Well, if you must go—I only hope it doesn't spoil the rest of the evening for us."

Despite his boast that he could lead the way to Robert's grotto, several minutes elapsed before he succeeded. Every time he thought that he was on the right road it was only to find himself in one of the wings away from the grotto, or back at the spot from which he had started, or else down in the basement, where, to his surprise, he was unable to identify the door leading into the wine cellar, although he was sure that when he had previously visited the grotto he had done so via the basement. True, there were several cellars in the basement, now used as either storehouses, larders, pantries, or a dairy. There was even a wine cellar, stocked with an enviable and mouth-watering profusion of wines, properly binned and tagged, but close examination convinced him that this wine cellar was not the one which Salvaterra had identified as the site of the grotto.

Eventually, he discovered the grotto by the simple expedient of opening every door in turn, to find out what lay on the far side. Presently he opened one which he had previously ignored, because its situation was so far from the place where he had believed the grotto to be. As he did so a musty draught of air chilled his face.

The nearest light was towards the far end of the passage. Because of this and the fact also that the door opened into the passage on that side, he could see neither what was on the farther side of the door, nor an electric light switch. He peered into the dark space, and fumbled about for the switch which he could not see. In consequence, his fingers informed him that he was facing a narrow passage, apparently bordered on either side by walls of bare brick.

Unable to find the switch on the right-hand side of the passage, its natural spot, he tried the opposite wall, but with the same result. He struck a match. The flame flickered in the draught and went out. He struck a second match and cupped the flame in his hand. This time the match flared up, but the light only served to reveal a flight of stone steps, and, to intensify the darkness beyond, also to show that the walls of the passage were not of brick, but of ragstone, much of which was green with damp moss.

"Why are you waiting?" Julia questioned impatiently from behind him.

"I was looking for an electric light switch, but I cannot find one. I don't think the electricity extends thus far. We had better give up the search for the grotto and return to the hall. Dancing is due to begin at any moment."

"Have you any matches left?"

"Yes. Why?"

"Is the grotto down there?"

"I cannot be sure…"

"But you think it is, don't you, Theo? I do."

"Why?"

"The draught coming through the door smells horrible—earthy and cold," Julia replied in a voice far less confident than usual. "It is making me shiver. I am sure—in fact, I *know* that the Hermit's grotto is down there, Theo. I know it. I feel it. If you strike some matches, there will be enough light for us to take just a quick glance at the place."

"The walls and floor are damp, Julie. It would be madness for you two to go down there in your thin shoes and dresses; you might catch pneumonia."

"I am going down," she snapped. "What about you, Helena?"

"I—I don't know, Julia. I don't truly want to go down there. It—it smells abominable, revolting. And yet in a funny sort of way I—I do. Please take us, Tommy. We need not stay there long enough to get too cold." Despite her frank doubts and the slight quaver in her voice, Helena sounded as determined as Julia to investigate the grotto.

Terhune was disconcerted. His companions appeared to be victims of a strange fascination for the horrible, the unknown. Helena, even so, might be amenable to persuasion, but he doubted Julia's being so. He realised that to dissuade her from seeing the grotto he would have to be forceful, perhaps rude. That would inevitably spoil their friendship. His best course, he decided, was to defer to them, in the hope that they would be anxious to hurry back to the warmer, purer atmosphere of the hall.

"All right," he agreed grudgingly. "But for Heaven's sake keep still directly a match goes out. If you slip down the steps, you might break a limb. Hold on to my shoulders, and close the door behind us—we don't want a crowd following us down."

From the distance they heard the music of a waltz—the dancing had begun. Having taken a quick glance up and down the passage to make certain that nobody else was approaching, Terhune advanced three steps down. Helena held on to his left shoulder, Julia his right.

"Now close the door."

One of the girls—he was not sure which—did so. A solid, repulsive darkness enveloped them. He hastily lit a match. While it remained alight, he descended three more steps. He lit a second match, and descended a further three. And then three more while the third match flamed. As he puffed out the third match, he became aware of a light to his right. It was faint, but enough to reveal that he had arrived at a kind of half landing, that from it descended, at right angles, a short, gentle slope of hard, beaten earth, at the bottom of which was an open doorway.

Stepping carefully to avoid sliding on one of the slimy patches underfoot, he advanced down the slope, his companions following closely behind him. Twelve paces brought him to the open doorway. One glance beyond confirmed that they had arrived at the grotto of Robert the Hermit.

Chapter Fifteen

I

The same sense of perverted humour which had prompted Salvaterra to select the grotto as the subject for the stained glass window was again apparent. All evidence of the use or uses to which the grotto had been put during the intervening centuries had been carefully removed. There were now no dilapidated wine bins, pieces of broken bottle, old corks, or decaying timber. Instead, the place had been cleverly restored to resemble the grotto as it might have been in the days of the Hermit.

The only doorway was in the form of the cinquefoil arch of the later Norman style; the floor was of hard, beaten earth, covered with rushes; the ceiling, roughly domed, was constructed of hard stone, crudely hewn into square blocks, which were green with damp. The most striking feature of the grotto was the walls. Three of these were composed of ragstone, faced with worn mosaic work, representing crude foliage inset in squares of coarse fret. The fourth wall, facing south, was on the left of the entrance. This, too, was decorated with mosaic-work, but of a more ambitious pattern. Against an una-dorned background of light grey, three subjects were crudely but unmistakably depicted; on the right a representation of the Infant Jesus, on the left, the Holy Mother, and in the centre, a Cross. On the floor in front of the Cross was a three-pronged candelabrum of hewn wood, in each holder of which burned a thick tallow candle.

For many seconds, amid a profound and unexplainable silence, the three people remained in the doorway of the grotto, staring at the scene before them with wordless amazement. Terhune's first reaction was to wonder how much of the grotto was genuine and how much restored. The doorway itself, for instance! He was certain it was new to him. The last time he had entered the grotto he had done so through quite a different doorway, and from a different direction.

In the not-too-good light from the candles he examined the stone-work of the lower part of the doorway, and the sculpture work of the cinquefoil arch. He was quite incompetent to judge the age of the doorway, but as far as mere appearances were concerned, he could find no evidence to suggest that the stone work had not been in position for several centuries.

Terhune turned to the walls. Here again everything looked genuine. The materials which comprised the mosaic-work were undoubtedly old, and the mortar in which the pieces were set crumbled into dust when he scratched it with his finger nail. On the assumption that the mosaic was genuine, why had he not noticed it on the previous occasion? He visualised the grotto as he had last seen it, and came to the conclusion that, as far as the walls were concerned, they had been so covered with an accumulation of dirt and grime and green mildew that everything beneath might well have been hidden to casual observation.

What of the other doorway by which he entered? He looked round more carefully, and this time became aware that one part of the wall opposite the Cross, roughly the size and shape of a square door-way, lacked any suggestion of mosaic-work. Examining that area more closely he saw that, while the ragstones were undoubtedly old, the mortar had the hardness of concrete. It seemed apparent that, during the progress of building work, the original, arched entrance had been uncovered, and the newer entrance had been bricked up—an explanation which fitted in perfectly with his recollection of having reached the grotto by the main basement.

Having solved the mystery to his satisfaction, Terhune relaxed, and allowed his imagination to drift back through the centuries to that brief period when Robert the Hermit had occupied the grotto. He pictured a peasant woman, dressed in the coarse clothing of the century, kneeling upon the floor before the Cross, with Robert standing before her in an attitude of benediction as he interceded with the Mother of Jesus to grant the supplicant the miracle of fertility.

The vision was not a lasting one, for it was succeeded—though not by any volition on his part—by another; a revolting, debasing picture... He shivered as the coldness of the grotto penetrated his evening clothes. The fetid atmosphere filled his nostrils, and a consciousness of evil and of the obscene which he had previously experienced, again manifested itself.

The two girls were similarly affected.

"This is a horrible place!" Helena exclaimed unexpectedly: although she spoke in a voice little higher than a whisper the words had a loud, hollow ring to them as if echoing through a tunnel. "Why does Señor Salvaterra keep those candles alight? To me it is like—like blasphemy to do so."

"I do not think he means it to be blasphemous," Julia commented. "Probably his penchant for the theatrical is to blame, and his exaggerated veneration for the past."

"But there is something about this place—"Helena shuddered, "I cannot explain my feelings, Julia, but—I—I don't want to stay here..."

"Nor do I." Julia turned to Terhune. "I am sorry we came down."

There was a curious expression on both faces which warned Terhune that he should take his companions away from the grotto as soon as possible.

"Come along," he muttered brusquely, not sorry to have an excuse for hurrying away. He ushered them out of the grotto, up the slope and, with the help of his box of matches, up the stone steps to the ground floor of the house. As they opened the door into the passage beyond, a blast of hot air warmed their faces, the sound of dance music cheered their ears.

Both warmth and music were very comforting.

I I

For two hours the band, an excellent one, played almost continuously. The musicians played the latest hits with a verve and a rhythm which made even the non-dancers tap their toes in time.

In consequence, the atmosphere of the party apparently left nothing to be desired—an excellent dance band, a moderately crowded floor, contented faces, laughter, conversation, and a host who had a natural gift, not only for putting his guests at their ease, but also for ingratiating himself. The elder women were enchanted by his courtly, graceful manners; the elder men found him damned intelligent and a witty conversationalist; the younger women considered him a dear, and the younger men: "not at all a bad old stick."

Andrés, too, made himself liked—at least, by the women: by those who were twice his age, because his manners were just as polished and exquisite as those of his father, and because their motherly instincts were aroused by his expression, which they interpreted as tragic. And by the younger women because they soon discovered that he was a superb dancer. The menfolk were less impressed by Andrés. For them he was too sleek, too "nattily" dressed, too slim, too palpably a blasted foreigner.

Inez Salvaterra created less of a definite impression on the critical minds of the guests. They found her personality too complex for a snap judgment. As far as the men were concerned, she was somewhat too intelligent and had too many independent opinions. On their part, the women vaguely resented the obvious affection which existed between brother and sister. Yet this resentment was not aroused on behalf of Señora Salvaterra. Nobody could identify the cause, indeed. But it was instantly apparent that Inez Salvaterra was less acceptable to them than was her brother.

And Dolores Salvaterra? Poor Señora Salvaterra! Scarcely anyone gave her a second thought. She wandered politely among the guests, but exchanged with them no more than a few formal sentences. Throughout, her face remained an expressionless mask unrelieved even by her eyes, which were dull and apathetic, and gave her guests the impression that she was incapable of carrying on a sustained conversation.

Despite the loud, cheerful music and frequent laughter from the younger people, towards the end of the second hour's dancing, the sparkle of genuine enjoyment imperceptibly deteriorated. Conversation ceased to be spontaneous and light-hearted, and became, instead, depressingly stilted. To counteract a feeling of embarrassment, some of the guests drank rather more than they would have s in ordinary circumstances. In consequence, the note of gaiety was once more heard, but it was an unnatural gaiety, which strove to conceal a strained uneasiness.

The restiveness spread from the onlookers to the dancers. Less and less people took to the floor; instead, the majority congregated round one of the two blazing log fires, and talked of cabbages and kings, and of other subjects which bore no relation to a presumably happy dance.

Salvaterra was quick to sense the change. For some time he did nothing to check it, perhaps in the hope that it was merely a temporary lull, which would soon be corrected. But when he realised that it was persisting he ascended the staircase to the gallery, and approached the leader of the band.

The music ceased. Salvaterra advanced to the edge of the gallery.

"*Señores, señoras y señoritas*—ah no! I mean, ladies and gentlemen—but no, why should I be so formal? Perhaps you will permit me the honour of addressing you as—my friends!" The guests politely murmured their permission, and Salvaterra gave one of his dazzling smiles.

"Thank you—my friends. The next dance is to be the supper dance, so shall we all dance, *all* of us, and make it the happiest dance of the evening, no?" Again the guests signified their assent—a very cheerful assent, this time, because many of them hoped that supper might help to dissolve the slight chill which had developed.

"Good! And now, my friends, allow me the privilege of choosing my own favourite tune—an old-fashioned waltz—from *The Merry Widow* for the next dance. For an old fogy like me, that tune contains many happy memories. Am I forgiven by the younger people?" Taking the forgiveness for granted, Salvaterra smiled broadly, and gave a signal to the band leader.

While the opening bars of the music swelled out, the Panamanian trotted down the staircase—his short legs seemed to move at an amazing speed. By the time he reached the dance floor, several couples were already swinging around in quick tempo; dexterously steering clear of them, he proceeded to Lady Kylstone's side.

He bent low over her hand. "Ah, dear señora! How can I describe the pleasure with which I have looked forward to this dance?"

She rose from her seat, and moved forward into his arms. "I have been watching you dance, Dr. Salvaterra. You dance in an old-fashioned but graceful manner. I am sure you were an enthusiastic dancer when *The Merry Widow* first thrilled the world."

"It is true, gracious lady. I was."

"And your sister, too—surely she must have been equally fond of dancing?"

"You are right again. Many a night have we danced through, Inez and myself."

"While your son is superb."

"Dancing is one of his passions in life."

"But Señora Salvaterra, does she not enjoy dancing, doctor? I have not seen her dance once to-night."

"Dolores!" He shrugged his shoulders. "No, gracious lady. Dolores has only one interest in life," he explained carelessly.

"Andrés?"

"Yes, Andrés. If Andrés is happy, Dolores is happy; when Andrés enjoys himself, Dolores enjoys herself. She asks nothing more of life."

"Is Andrés happy to-night?"

"I think so."

"You *think* so, doctor! Do you not know him well enough to be sure whether or no he is enjoying himself?"

"No," the Panamanian confessed. "Andrés is subject to mild neurosis. He is highly strung. Sometimes his nerves work independently of his mental reaction. It is possible for him to appear happy and excited, although, in fact, he is subject to the deepest depression."

"In those circumstances, House-on-the-Hill is the last house in which a neurotic should live," she said sharply.

"But dear lady," Salvaterra expostulated mildly. Why should Andrés not live in House-on-the-Hill?"

The question was an awkward one to answer without being rude, so Lady Kylstone ignored it, and gave herself up to the enjoyment of the dance.

III

Supper had the desired effect—it restored the conviviality of the first hour's dancing. Choice food and exquisite wines made the guests forget the strange sensations of the previous hour. Before long a happy hilarity reigned along the length of the several supper tables, an hilarity which was not lessened when champagne was served.

No sooner was the last champagne glass filled than Sir George Brereton pushed back his chair and stood upright.

"Ladies and gentlemen—" he began in a loud, booming voice.

Laughter and conversation died fitfully away; everyone present turned dutifully towards Sir George.

"Oh, dear!" Lady Kylstone whispered in a low voice to Terhune—she was sitting between Salvaterra and Terhune—"for Heaven's sake tell Helena to pinch him if he remains on his feet too long. I know what George is when he gets up on his feet."

Brereton gazed benignly at his audience. "Ladies and gentlemen or to borrow our host's happy form of address—my friends—"

"Not when you tell your fishing stories," Alec Hamblin interrupted with a guffaw.

A cheer from Brereton's many victims greeted this sally.

"My friends!" Sir George repeated, unperturbed. "During all festive occasions of a private nature, there comes a moment when it is the privilege of one of the guests to rise to his feet in order to propose a toast to the host and hostess."

"Hear! Hear!" Winstanley called out loudly.

"Usually this privilege is claimed by an old friend of the host, but alas among us all to-night Dr. Salvaterra has no old friends, for he has come among us as a total stranger from another country. But I will add this: if none of us present tonight can lay claim to being an old friend of our host and hostess, every one of us can claim, equally and with good reason, to being a *new* friend of Dr. and Señora Salvaterra."

Genuine applause confirmed Brereton's assertion.

"Charming! Charming!" murmured the gratified Salvaterra.

"Our George is in good form to-night," Lady Kylstone whispered in Terhune's ear. "The wines must have suited his palate."

Sir George looked pleased with himself. "In the light of that equality, as it were, you might well ask: Why has George Brereton taken it upon himself to usurp the enviable privilege of proposing the health of our host and hostess? I will tell you why. Because I was the first to think of the idea."

More appreciative laughter.

"This is the first time that that has ever happened to you, George, old boy," Major Blye chuckled.

Which was more or less true, so there was more laughter.

In the consciousness that he was doing well, Brereton was armoured against all sallies.

"So here I am, lad—I mean, my friends, on my feet, charged with; the pleasant duty of asking you to drink the health of our host and hostess." There was a movement among his audience. "But," he said loudly, raising his arm commandingly, "before I do so, I; propose to say a few words of appreciation…"

Lady Kylstone shook her head in disappointment. "I thought George would be unable to avoid spoiling an excellent beginning," she said to Terhune. "Now he will speak for another ten minutes at least."

The estimated time was nearly reached as Sir George began his concluding remarks.

"And so, my friends, I charge you to be upstanding, to drink the health of our host and hostess, coupled with the names of Señor Andrés and Señorita Salvaterra."

The guests drank the toast, after which Winstanley's unsteady voice boomed out: "For they are jolly good fellows—"

They sang the chorus cheerfully, gave three cheers, and sat downs Then Edward Pryce called out: "Speech! Speech!"

The demand was energetically taken up. "Speech! Speech! Speech!" everyone called out. "Dr. Salvaterra. We want Dr, Salvaterra."

Amid a din which threatened to become deafening, the Panamanian rose to his feet. There was a suspicious moisture in his eyes, but otherwise his face was abeam with happiness. No one present could fail to realise that his cup of contentment was full and brimming over.

So, too, was his sister's. Her face was even more expressive than his, for she gazed at her brother with adoring eyes which spoke adequately of her own estimation of the success of the party. Even Andrés looked happier and more lively than heretofore, though this effect might have been caused by the temporary disappearance of the strained, nervous expression from his eyes. Señora Salvaterra alone seemed unmoved by the reception which had been accorded to her land her husband. She looked at her guests in turn with eyes that were timid and dull.

The rising of Salvaterra to his feet was a signal for the noise to cease. "My friends—" he began. "My friends indeed," he repeated emphatically. "It would take too long to express all that I feel in my heart for the sympathetic kindness which you have all shown to me and my family to-night, firstly, by doing us the honour of attending our little party, and now by the wonderful reception you have just accorded us.

"Let me confess, dear friends, that it was with trepidation that my dear wife and I decided to ask you all, our neighbours, to our new home. I am sure it can be no secret to you that, abroad, English people have the reputation for exhibiting a frigid reserve towards strangers which even your own people have difficulty in penetrating.

"To-night, you have proved the falseness of that reputation. With kindly toleration, you have permitted a small family of foreigners—of a nation which might be completely unknown to you but for the happy existence of a world-famous canal—to ride—as you say in your language—roughshod, no?—to ride roughshod over hidebound formalities and finer points of etiquette, and have accepted them in your midst with a welcome which no other people in the world could have made more warm or more sincere. With enthusiasm you have, through your spokesman, Sir George Brereton—with whom I hope to have many future arguments concerning certain piscatorial achievements—opened not only your hearts, but also your homes, to four grateful souls from a distant continent. For that kindhearted and generous gesture, worthy of so great a people, I and my family will owe you, and your fellow countrymen, an undying debt of gratitude, the chance to repay which I pray God may one day be given to us."

The embarrassed guests shifted uncomfortably in their chairs. "The old boy is laying it on a bit thick." Arnold Blye whispered to Julia—but when Winstanley called out loudly; "Bravo!" they applauded warmly, for they were convinced that sincerity underlined the florid speech.

"Wait! If you please!" Salvaterra pleaded quickly. "Have you not in English a saying: 'Give him an inch and he will take an ell'? That is true in my case, dear friends. In matters of etiquette you have given me an inch. Now I beg you to allow me to take the ell. Forgive an old man his whims and impulses, dear people, and accept, in the same spirit as it is given, a memento of this happy, happy occasion."

Amid an astonished silence the guests saw Salvaterra give a signal. Waiters immediately appeared, carrying trays upon which were heaped a quantity of thin packets, tied lip in brightly coloured paper. These packets the waiters began to distribute, one to each guest.

For a few seconds, the guests glanced at one another in awkward embarrassment. What on earth would the strange little man be about next? Then they recollected Salvaterra's plea to accept the memento in the spirit in which it was given. With cheerful laughs, they began to tear off the outer wrapping.

Terhune realised immediately what the package contained. A book of some sort. He had handled too many books in his time not to recognise the feel of one. But what on earth—a book—about what—why—

With eager curiosity, he broke the length of decorated tape, tore off part of the wrapping, and exposed one corner of the book. He had no need to look further to know that he was handling a binding of rare and exquisite workmanship. He caressed the corner with his finger tips, and with tormenting slowness, tore away the remainder of the coloured tissue.

The gold-leaf letters stood out vividly from a crimson background.

HOUSE-ON-THE-HILL

With the exciting realisation of what he might read on the title page, Terhune's heart began to beat with a breath-shortening pitter-pat. With shaky fingers, he opened the book.

He read:

THE STORY OF

HOUSE-ON-THE-HILL

TOLD BY

THEODORE TERHUNE

WITH ILLUSTRATIONS BY

EDWARD PRYCE

His first book! His very first book!

Lifting his head, he glanced at the quaint little man who had done this for him. And Salvaterra smiled happily when he saw the unmistakable gratitude which shone from Terhune's eyes.

Chapter Sixteen

I

Was Salvaterra's house-warming party a success? For days afterwards this question was debated among the guests. All agreed, unhesitatingly, that the party had achieved its object in helping Salvaterra to make a host of friends—for, taken by and large, the inhabitants of Bray, and Willingham, and the surrounding districts, decided that the menfolk of the Salvaterra family were an acquisition to that part of the county; the father for his charm, his intelligence, *and* his bridge (Hamblin, who was a bridge fiend, had succeeded in ascertaining the fact that the Panamanian was a superb player); and the son for his rather exciting manner and his fascinating dancing.

But had the evening been really enjoyable? Certainly, it had had its high lights—the reception, the first hour's dancing, the supper and, above all, the truly handsome memento of the occasion which Salvaterra had presented to his guests. Unfortunately, each high light had been succeeded, as it were, by contrasting shadow, that indefinable sensation of—what?—which had somehow robbed the party of ultimate, unqualified enjoyment. As soon as the stimulation of supper had died away, the vague chill which had preceded the meal returned. In consequence, some of the more susceptible to psychic influence had left earlier than intended, and the retreat quickly became a rout.

Nobody blamed Salvaterra or his family for the part failure of the party. Everybody recognised that the blame rested solely upon the House with Crooked Walls. The house was haunted by evil spirits, as they had always maintained, and these spirits had risen from their tombs of desolation and decay to curse and extinguish the flame of happiness which the Panamanian had sought to ignite.

In the succeeding days, after they had had the opportunity of reading Terhune's book, and digesting the story of House-on-the-Hill, the guests became more convinced than ever that the house was a place of iniquity, and they marvelled that the Panamanian had the courage to live there. Terhune's vivid account of past history touched off the powder of their own imaginations. Alicia MacMunn suddenly remembered having seen a ghostly figure dressed in a friar's habit; Mrs. Edwards spoke of having heard somebody behind her speak with an American accent, but, on turning round, she had been unable to see anyone; Diana Pearson told a highly coloured story of being kissed by a handsome young man, dressed in the clothes of a previous century ("obviously that unfortunate Lord Kenelm, my dear") who had immediately afterwards walked straight through a blank wall.

Yet another consequence of Terhune's book was a revival of interest in the author. For some days afterwards Terhune received many letters of congratulation on the excellence of his style, and telephone calls from this person and that, to say how much he (or more often *she*) had enjoyed reading Terhune's story of House-on-the-Hill, and was he writing any more books? Because, if so, he must advertise the date of publication, and title, and so on, for, naturally, everyone was eager to read everything he wrote. To say nothing of the several people who took the trouble to call at the shop. During the course of his research work on House-on-the-Hill, had he come across any mention of The

Towers—or the White House—or Bower Farm—or Windmill Lodge?...

Terhune himself remained in the highest of spirits. Not because he had become a temporary local lion, from which unenviable role indeed, his natural modesty shrank, but on account of the book. Every time he picked up the book to examine it—which was often—he glowed with an inward warmth. His first book! True, it had been published privately; all criticisms were obviously biased in its favour, it had not been published for its worth, but for its subject—and so on. But no carping thought changed the one basic fact. A book of his had been set up in print and published. And what a publication! He hesitated to estimate what the cost must have been. But even apart from his understandable prejudice in its favour, as a book-lover it gave him infinite pleasure to stroke the leather binding, to feel the fine texture of the paper, to inspect the clear type, and to enthuse over Edward Pryce's illustrations.

Perhaps Pryce had never done better work. At any rate, never more realistic work. The illustrations which dealt with episodes of the past were based on the facts in Terhune's manuscript. Pryce had cleverly captured the atmosphere of the grimmer scenes. He had limned Robert as a saintly character, with sparse figure, gaunt face, and benign expression: only a second, closer inspection shocked the reader into recognising veiled lust in the pale, watery eyes. In another illustration, this time of Lord Kenelm protesting his love for Caroline Drummond, Pryce had further tricked the readers. Looked at from the immediate front, there was nothing in the scene to distinguish it from any other similar scene of that same period. But when looked at from an angle, the background of the scene— which was that of a panelled wall, fireplace and overmantel, with all the usual trappings of the age—appeared to change from a solid substance into something intangible, in which was vaguely to be distinguished the sardonic features of that same Robert, creating an uncanny sensation that the spirit of the Mediæval hermit still lived in the bricks and mortar which had been erected upon the site of his one-time hermitage.

II

One morning Terhune was awakened by the telephone bell. For some time he let it ring, for he could not believe that anyone could possibly be ringing him at so early an hour. But his impatience was not proof against the persistent noise. He slipped reluctantly out of bed, wrapped a dressing gown round him, and padded downstairs.

"Hullo!" he shouted in sharp annoyance.

"Señor Terhune, please forgive my ringing you at this early hour, but I must ask you—is Andrés with you?"

Terhune stared at the curtained windows. What was the matter with the old boy? Was it likely that Andrés would be visiting the shop hours before it was due to open?

"I am only just out of bed—"

"Of course! Of course! But has Andrés stayed the night with you, señor?"

"Good lord, no!"

"*Madre de Dios!* Then I do not know what to do next."

"What has happened, doctor?"

"I do not know, señor. I do not know what to think. I am afraid—"

"Of what?"

"I am afraid that Andrés has—vanished…"

"Good God! Vanished! That is impossible, doctor. How could he vanish?"

"I do not know. I pray that you are right," Salvaterra exclaimed disjointedly in a voice pitched higher in tone than usual. "Will you help me, my friend?"

"Of course," Terhune answered promptly. "What do you wish me to do?"

"Give me the benefit of your advice. As a foreigner, I feel helpless... May I visit you at once?"

"Naturally, doctor. I shall dress immediately."

"You are very kind!" Salvaterra exclaimed in a pathetically distressed voice. "I shall be with you in about thirty minutes' time."

During the ensuing half-hour Terhune hurriedly made preparations to receive Dr. Salvaterra. As soon as he had washed, shaved and dressed, he tidied up his study, lighted the fire, and made coffee. Just as the percolator began to spread its fragrant aroma, a ring below warned Terhune of his guest's arrival.

He hastened down to open the door. The Panamanian entered the shop; his bowed shoulders made him appear smaller than ever, his movements were listless, his face paler than usual.

"You cannot realise what a comfort it is to be able to turn to you at this moment of trouble," he began.

"Will you come upstairs, doctor, to my workroom? It will be warmer there."

Terhune led the way upstairs, and made Salvaterra take a comfortable chair before the fire, which was beginning to burn cheerfully.

"I have made coffee, doctor. Will you have some?"

"Coffee! Ah, my friend! You overwhelm me with your kindness. Coffee may help to steady me."

The coffee was soon poured out. While they waited for it to cool, Salvaterra spoke of Andrés.

"I do not know how to begin my story," he began unhappily. "There is not much to tell. Last night we were all at home, Inez,

Dolores, Andrés and me. We had the evening meal at the usual time. Afterwards, we went in one of my favourite rooms, the lounge in the east wing. We settled ourselves in our own particular chairs; Andrés and I began to read; Inez and Dolores to needlework.

"When I grew tired of reading, I asked Inez whether she would care to play cards. She expressed her willingness, so we prepared to play. Just as I was shuffling the cards for the first game, Andrés rose to his feet, saying: 'I am going to listen to the radio, papa; there is a good programme from Boston.'"

Salvaterra paused, but for no more than three seconds. "Andrés is an enthusiastic radio fan," he explained. "In the main building there is one room set aside for his hobby, where he has several radio sets, and listens-in to the world—perhaps you saw it on the night of the party, no?"

Terhune nodded. The sets had made him envious; there was probably no station in the world which was unobtainable by the largest of the sets. In addition, he had seen a television set, and a work-bench piled up with enough spare parts to build yet another radio set.

"Although Andrés is fond of reading, he is equally fond of music. He is in the habit of spending hours in his radio-room, either listening in or experimenting with his own sets. He was proposing, I believe, to build his own transmitter.

"Last night, therefore, when he proposed going to the radio-room, I was not surprised. I nodded my head, and continued shuffling the cards. Andrés went out; Inez and I began to play. We played until midnight, by which time I was tired and ready for bed. During the intervening time, Andrés had not returned to the lounge, but none of us was surprised. The same thing had frequently happened in the past.

"We went upstairs to our bedrooms. On the way to mine I passed by the door of the room which I have called Andrés's radio-room.

Hearing music within, I opened the door to say good night to the boy. Andrés was not in the room, but the light was on, and one of the sets was working. Beside it was a glass, half filled with sherry. Also—and mark this well, señor—an ash-tray, on which was a half-smoked cigarette, still alight.

"Every indication suggested that Andrés had left only for a matter of seconds, otherwise he would have taken the cigarette with him. I shut the door again, leaving everything as it was, and went on to my bedroom, where I undressed, retired to bed, and quickly fell asleep."

Salvaterra turned away to hide his distress, but he could not conceal his trembling lips from Terhune. But soon, after mastering his emotion, he again faced Terhune, and resumed his story.

"This morning I was awakened by my wife. She was alarmed because Smithson, one of the maids, had just informed her that Andrés was not in his bedroom and that his bed had not been slept in. The news did not have the same effect upon me as upon my wife—I concluded that Andrés might have remained all night in the radio-room, having fallen asleep while listening in. Still, to quieten my wife's frenzy, I slipped into my dressing gown and went along to the radio-room. As I approached, I heard the sound of singing, and on opening the door saw that the light was still on. I was sure, at that moment, that my theory was correct. The next—" Salvaterra's face became agonised. "The next moment, señor, I learned that it was not. Andrés was not there.

"Then I, too, became alarmed. I ordered the house to be searched, I but Andrés was not found. I had the servants assembled, and questioned them, but none of them was able to offer any helpful information; they had already retired to the servants' quarters after the evening meal had been served. The last to leave that part of the house had been Randall, who had gone round the rooms on the lower floor just after eleven, to see that everything was safe for the evening. Afterwards he came to me, and, as there was nothing more I wanted, I told him he could go to bed.

"That is all to tell you," concluded distractedly. "As soon as I realised that Andrés was—missing—I telephoned to you. My dear friend, I do not know what to do next. I am nervous—" He broke off, and, seeing that he had not yet touched his coffee, he lifted it eagerly to his lips and drained it.

"Nervous of what, doctor? Surely you do not seriously believe that Andrés has—has— Confound it! It seems ridiculous even to mention the word."

"What word?" Salvaterra asked agitatedly.

"Vanished! What probably happened was that Andrés, being bored with listening-in, and acting on impulse, went off to a dance somewhere or other."

"But dances do not continue until this hour of the morning. Besides, one does not leave a cigarette burning if one intends going off to a dance. Nor is one of the cars missing, which would have been the case had Andrés acted as you suggest. Lastly, I am sure that Andrés would not have left the house without informing his mother or me. We should not have prevented him. Andrés is free to follow his own desires."

Terhune frowned in perplexity. He had forgotten the lighted cigarette, and had overlooked the question of the car. When one examined the circumstances more closely, the situation began to appear strange…

"Speaking of the cigarette end, doctor, did you happen to notice whether it was still where you had seen it the previous night?"

"It was my first act, upon finding the room empty, to examine the cigarette and the sherry."

"Well?"

"The cigarette had burned right away, dear friend. Neither it nor the sherry had been touched subsequent to my entering the room."

"But—" Terhune stopped short and rose abruptly from his chair. "It is too ridiculous, doctor, to believe that Andrés left the house because of a sudden whim."

"If Andrés did not leave the house, then where is he?"

"He must be somewhere."

"You must believe me when I say that he is not," Salvaterra said with a quiet, convincing dignity.

"If he did not leave by car, he must have left on foot."

"For where?"

"For where!" Terhune repeated. The question was justified. To reach any but one of the houses in the immediate neighbourhood, Andrés would have had to walk several miles at least. "What reason would Andrés have had for leaving the house without a word to anyone, and for not returning all night?"

"No reason at all."

Terhune took off his glasses, and polished the lenses—a mannerism which, in his case, usually accompanied profound reflection. Perhaps it was too early in the morning for coherent thought, but he could make no real sense of what he had just been told. No one circumstance dovetailed with any other. If Andrés was not in the house, then obviously he must have left it just before the hour of midnight (if the burning cigarette was to be accepted as evidence). Assuming that he had done this, possibly because he felt in need of exercise, or fresh air, why had he not returned after satisfying that need? Salvaterra seemed certain that Andrés was not in the house, but maintained, in the next breath, that Andrés was not likely to have left the house, with the intention of staying away for an extended period, without first mentioning the fact to one of his parents.

Again, while one might feel annoyed with a son who coolly left home for the night without having made any previous announcement of that fact, one would not necessarily feel alarmed. But

Salvaterra was undoubtedly alarmed, although he seemed to be doing his best to conceal his fears.

But fears of what? Why had the mother become frenzied on hearing that her son had not slept in his bed?

"Had Andrés any reason for leaving home?"

Salvaterra's distress was temporarily replaced by anger. "Certainly not, señor. His domestic life was as happy as that of any other young man of the same age. By that I do not wish to deny that there were occasions when it was necessary for me to remind him that he was still a very young man—he celebrates his twenty-first birthday next January—but most young men go through a period of adolescence when they feel themselves to be fully capable of conducting their own affairs, and I am quite sure that Andrés did not resent my interference any more than other sons resent parental control. Of course, they chafe at being held in check, but not to the extent of—of leaving their homes without a word. You must accept my sincere conviction that Andrés would not have acted so."

"From my slight knowledge of Andrés, I am in complete agreement with you, doctor," Terhune said quietly. "But there is one question I should like to put to you in reference to your account of what has happened at House-on-the-Hill."

"Well?"

"When Señora Salvaterra told you that Andrés had not slept in his bed you said that, to quieten the Señora's frenzy, you slipped into your dressing gown and went along to the radio-room. Why was the Señora in a frenzy even before she learned that Andrés was not somewhere else in the house?"

"Is the answer to that question not obvious, my young friend? To you, especially."

"Why especially to me?"

"Have you not written the history of the House with Crooked Walls?"

"Yes; but——" Terhune paused, wondering what inference Salvaterra was trying to draw.

"Then you cannot have forgotten so soon that, during its long history, two men have previously vanished from House-on-the-Hill."

"Good Lord!" Terhune exclaimed in an astonished voice. "You are not comparing the——the disappearance of Andrés with——with those of Robert the Hermit and Reuben Douglas?"

"Why not?" Salvaterra asked in a strained voice. "Why not?"

Chapter Seventeen

I

As soon as he had recovered from his surprise, Terhune glanced quickly at Salvaterra's face—the Panamanian's theory, was so preposterous, so fantastic, that he hesitated to take the little man seriously. Besides, had not Salvaterra, from the beginning, discredited any suggestion of a curse in connection with House-on-the-Hill? But there was no hint now, in the other man's expression, that he was anything else but gravely alarmed.

Terhune had an immense respect for Salvaterra's intelligence, but he refused to subscribe to the suggestion that Andrés had vanished into thin air, as it were. If he had vanished, no doubt the disappearance would prove to be merely temporary; maybe the sparkling moonlight of the previous evening had tempted the young man to go for a walk: Terhune himself had long ago discovered the fascination of walking along a quiet country road on a clear, moonlight night, with its solemn stillness, its poetry, its mystery, its frigid beauty—and, having walked himself tired, too tired to return, perhaps he had taken shelter somewhere; an inn, maybe, a haystack... Or, while out walking, he might have met with an accident, and was unconscious in hospital, with no papers in his pockets to identify him. Or, he might rashly have ventured into Hinton Woods, and have become lost. Or (despite Salvaterra's assertions that his son would not leave the house without announcing the fact) he might have gone dancing all night, travelling in somebody else's car, and even now he might be on his way home. Or he might have left a note for his parents, which had become mislaid.

Or—or—or—There were a dozen possible theories—two dozen, more—to account for Andrés's disappearance. True, some of them might be unlikely—but Terhune doubted that any of them could be more unlikely than the one Salvaterra had put forward, which ascribed Andrés's departure from the house to psychical or supernatural causes. For such he took Salvaterra's inference to be—and while it might be amusing to associate the supernatural with Mediæval days, or even with the middle of the nineteenth century, well! as far as he, Terhune, was concerned there was nothing in between the supernatural and the middle years of the twentieth century.

He voiced these feelings, but Salvaterra would not listen to them.

"The supernatural takes no heed of centuries, my young friend," he asserted in a harsh voice. "Conditions may have changed for us, who live in the twentieth century, but not for the unhappy spirits of the other world who are doomed to eternal torment."

"But, doctor, surely—"

Salvaterra gestured his impatience. "You do not have to enlarge upon your previous arguments, señor. You cannot conceive a person's vanishing with no trace. You are young, clean-minded, and as healthily intolerant as you should be of the possible existence of strange forces which are not capable of being seen or weighed or analysed by the scientists of to-day. But I have lived longer than you, and have had opportunities to learn for myself that Shakespeare wrote no truer words than: 'There are more things in Heaven and earth, Horatio, than are dreamt of in your philosophy.' You cannot deny that Robert the Hermit disappeared, and was never heard of nor seen again. Naturally, I would not ask you to consider that fact, on its own, as being worth serious consideration, but when it is added to the later circumstances surrounding the disappearance of Reuben Douglas, can you not understand the reason for my present fear?"

"But what could have happened to Andrés?" Terhune protested.

"What happened to Douglas? Reuben Douglas moved into House-on-the-Hill within a few days of its being enlarged and renovated. Shortly afterwards he vanished, and nothing more was ever heard of him. A few weeks ago I and my family moved into House-on-the-Hill after the house had been enlarged and renovated. Now Andrés has vanished. Can you blame me for drawing a parallel and fearing the worst?"

"Andrés has been missing only a few hours. How can you be sure that he has vanished? I still say that he may be on his way home by now or, at the worst, somewhere where his early discovery is certain."

"*Dios!* I wish I could believe you," Salvaterra murmured bitterly.

"It is not necessary for you to believe me, doctor. Believe yourself."

"Myself?"

"Yes. If previously you had believed that House-on-the-Hill really was lying under some curse or other which made people disappear, you would not have moved into the place."

"But I did believe in the curse, señor. Was not that element of psychic phenomenon one of the reasons which prompted me to buy the house? Did I not tell you that I was hoping to have the opportunity of investigating that phenomenon?"

"Yes," Terhune was forced to admit.

"Unfortunately, like the soldier who marches forward into battle convinced that he will survive it, I, too, was confident that I, and my family, would be immune from the effects of psychic influences. I was wrong. *Madre de Dios!* Too late I realise how wrong I was. I was contemptuous when I should have been respectful, reckless when I should have been cautious."

Terhune fidgeted impatiently. "Granted that the house was cursed, or lying under some psychic—influence—" His words came to a stammering pause as he recollected the consciousness of evil with which he had been afflicted on the two occasions he had approached the grotto of Robert the Hermit. "Yes, granted the existence of an evil, psychic influence," he continued slowly, "neither the curse, nor the influence can disembody a living organism."

"What happened to the bodies of Robert the Hermit and Reuben Douglas?" Salvaterra repeated.

Terhune stared uncomfortably into the red heart of the fire. No doubt the mercurial Latin temperament was to blame, but it did seem that Salvaterra had descended from the twin heights of intelligence and optimism to the depths of fantasy and despair. It was absurd to suggest that a living man could vanish in the middle of the twentieth century on account of something which had happened at the beginning of the thirteenth. It was, indeed, absurd to suggest that a living man could vanish at all—as he had just pointed out. On the other hand, what had caused the local inhabitants to hate and fear House-on-the-Hill?

"Don't you think it will be time enough to—to discuss the reason for Andrés's disappearance when we know for certain that he has disappeared?" he said uneasily.

Salvaterra nodded his snowy white head. "I do," he agreed sombrely. "It was for that purpose that I came to you, my friend, but your sympathy unlocked the floodgates of my fears, which I had been trying to repress. What should I do to find out what has happened to my son?"

"Telephone the police," Terhune answered promptly.

Salvaterra looked sad. "Is that quite necessary?" he queried. "Suppose that, after informing the police of my son's absence, Andrés returns safe and sound? What will he think of my involving him in unwelcome publicity?"

"That is a risk you must take, doctor. After all, a little publicity would be worth the safe return of Andrés, would it not?"

"Dear God! yes," the little man exclaimed earnestly. He glanced appealingly at Terhune. "Would I be presuming upon our friendship to ask your assistance in telephoning the police? In ordinary circumstances, it does not worry me to speak English over the telephone, but it is important that I should not misunderstand or be misunderstood."

"Of course," Terhune replied promptly. "Shall I do so at once?"

"If you would," Salvaterra replied anxiously.

The two men went downstairs to the telephone, where Terhune dialled the Ashford police, and quickly found himself speaking to the station sergeant.

"This is Terhune speaking of Bray—"

"The Mr. Terhune who discovered that Joe Richards had been murdered?" the sergeant interrupted.

"Yes."

"We know all about you, Mr. Terhune," the sergeant continued respectfully. "What do you want, sir? Not another murder, I hope?"

"No, sergeant. I am 'phoning up to report a disappearance—"

"Another disappearance!" The sergeant exclaimed in an astonished voice—for Joe Richards had disappeared from the neighbourhood before being found murdered. "What is happening in your neighbourhood in these days? I have been in the Ashford police for nearly twenty years; in all that time nothing has ever happened round about Bray until last New Year. And now, another! How do you come to smell them out, sir?" the man concluded in an awed voice.

Terhune did not trouble to explain. "Listen, sergeant. I am really speaking on behalf of Dr. Salvaterra—"

"What name, sir? I don't recognise it. I thought I knew all the doctors for twenty miles around."

"He is a doctor of philosophy, not of medicine, sergeant. He lives at House-on-the-Hill…"

"The foreign gentleman? Now I know who you mean, Mr. Terhune. You don't mean to say that the disappearance has anything to do with House-on-the-Hill?"

"I am afraid it has."

"My God!" the sergeant exclaimed deeply. Excitement struggled with official dignity for the control of his voice. "What are the particulars?"

Terhune related briefly the details of Andrés's disappearance, which he followed up by giving the sergeant a description of the missing man. When he had finished, the sergeant said:

"If the young man had lived anywhere else but at House-on-the-Hill, I should have said that the father probably hadn't much to worry about. But that house seems to be a place where almost anything can happen. It was only last night that I finished reading that book of yours, which Mr. Fisher lent me. I will see that enquiries are instituted immediately throughout this part of Kent, to begin with. Can I telephone to you, sir, in case I have any news to report?"

"Bray six-five."

"Right you are, sir. I will get in touch with you later on. And will you let me know if anything turns up your end?"

"I will, sergeant."

Terhune turned away from the telephone, to see Salvaterra's long, thin hand outstretched towards him.

"Once again you put me in your debt, my dear young friend," the Panamanian said deeply, turning away—perhaps to hide the fact that his dark eyes were moist.

I I

All that morning Terhune waited expectantly for the telephone to give him news, either from Salvaterra, to say that Andrés had returned home, or from the police sergeant, to report that the young man had been located. But the bell remained obstinately silent, and actually the first information to reach him came, not through the telephone, but by word of mouth, from Detective-Sergeant Murphy, of the East Kent Constabulary. Murphy called at the shop just after three in the afternoon, to say that he was on his way to House-on-the-Hill to interrogate the members of the household concerning the disappearance of Andrés; before doing so, would Terhune please pass on all possible information respecting Andrés, the rest of the Salvaterra family, and the house.

This Terhune did, and, in return, was informed by Murphy that the police had not yet succeeded in finding any trace of the whereabouts, or even the possible whereabouts, of the missing man. All hospitals within a certain area had been questioned, and reported accidents investigated, and a number of local railway employees and local omnibus employees interviewed. From all these activities nothing pertinent had been elicited.

Soon after Murphy left it came to Terhune's knowledge that the news of Andrés's disappearance had reached Bray. In a flurry of unconcealed animation Miss Amelia entered the shop to ask Terhune whether he had heard what had happened up at House-on-the-Hill. Her disappointment was obvious when she learned that he did know, but, recovering, she eagerly questioned him as to how much he knew. He answered her guardedly, and told her nothing fresh, but she was quite satisfied. With her meek face flushed with excitement, she departed for the Rector's, where she was due to give the children a music lesson.

During the next two hours Terhune was kept busy coping with the stream of people who entered the shop, ostensibly to change a library book or buy a new title from the 6*d*. rack, but actually to pump him for information. He parried the thousand and one questions in his customary good-natured manner, but his patience had worn dangerously thin by the time the shop was due to be closed. It was with a genuine sigh of relief that he bolted the door, pulled down the blinds, and went upstairs to his study. There he turned on the wireless, relaxed into his favourite chair, and stretched out his feet towards the fire. No sooner had he done so than the telephone bell rang.

He grimaced, went downstairs and lifted the receiver, prepared to be curt with the person at the other end if any question were asked referring to Andrés. As he had anticipated, the call was about Andrés, but, as the questioner was Julia, he was less curt than had been his intention. In fact, he was not curt at all.

III

During the night the news of the disappearance of Andrés Salvaterra spread from Bray-in-the-Marsh to Fleet Street. In the morning the *Daily Mail* scooped its rivals with a half-column exclusive story of the strange disappearance of a Señor Salvaterra from a house in Kent from which, during its long history, two other residents had previously disappeared.

This was a heaven-sent opportunity for an evening Press temporarily deprived of other current sensations. When the evening papers appeared some time before the luncheon hour, the half column had grown to two columns, with a double column heading set in 30 pt. type.

Meanwhile, reporters from the morning Press were converging on Bray and district.

The first Fleet Street man had not been in Bray half an hour before the Press made the discovery that a book had recently been written about House-on-the-Hill by a certain Theodore Terhune. That discovery destroyed Terhune's peace for the rest of the afternoon and evening, and for many days to follow. Reporters and Press photographers descended upon him in a flock; he was interviewed, photographed, re-interviewed and photographed again. Before that ordeal was over for him, a new one began. One of the Pressmen was foolish enough to make him an offer for the newspaper serial rights of his story of House-on-the-Hill.

The offer was a fair one, but Terhune rejected it, pointing out that, in his opinion, the copyright of the story had passed to Dr. Salvaterra by virtue of his having commissioned the story. The reporter wasted no time: barely was the explanation given than he was chasing out of the shop, *en route* to House-on-the-Hill, to make a similar offer to Salvaterra.

One of the mysteries of the world is that which surrounds the means by which news spreads from one coast of Africa to the other. Whatever that means may be, it is not more extraordinary than that used by Fleet Street reporters to divine the thoughts and anticipate the intentions of their rivals. Perhaps the answer lies in telepathy. Perhaps in bribery. Perhaps in spying. But let one reporter conceive a brilliant idea, before he has had the opportunity of putting it into operation, his friendly but unscrupulous contemporaries have robbed him of the initiative, and have made the first move.

Before the reporter who made the first offer for the newspaper rights of Terhune's story had had time to teach House-on-the-Hill, Terhune was answering a call from London—would he consider an offer for the newspaper serialisation of his book about the House with Crooked Walls? To this second enquiry, Terhune gave the same reply as he had given to the first. He was then asked if he knew Salvaterra's telephone number. Upon his giving it, the man at the other end of the wire hastily thanked him and hung up. Fifteen minutes later Terhune had to answer the same man again. Dr. Salvaterra had stated that the copyright of the story belonged exclusively to Mr. Terhune—so would Mr. Terhune consider the sum of £150 adequate? And could he oblige by giving Edward Pryce's telephone number?

Terhune said "No" to both questions, and rang off. Twenty minutes later, the reporter who had made the first enquiry was back again in the shop—Dr. Salvaterra had said that the newspaper serial rights belonged to the author, who was free to make his own arrangements. Would £100 tempt him to transfer those rights? When Terhune reported that somebody had already telephoned an offer of £150, the reporter's astonishment was amusing to behold. But he quickly recovered his composure, and increased his offer to £175.

Again Terhune refused. Not easily, it was true, for the sum was equal to six months' nett earnings from the shop, but the idea of reaping financial benefit from Salvaterra's personal tribulation was far too distasteful to him to be contemplated for one moment. He rid himself of the reporter with difficulty, and then not before the man had first increased the offer to £200, and then pleaded for permission to telephone his Editor there and then for authority to bid even higher.

Within five minutes of the reporter's departure, the telephone rang once more. Terhune had a notion that the London man was back on the line again; on the way to the telephone, he quickly prepared a cutting little speech on the sanctity of the home, which the Press preached without practising, but he had no opportunity of airing his satire, for it was Salvaterra's voice which he heard in the earphone—a voice pregnant with anxiety and distress.

"My dear friend, the London newspapers are pestering me for the right to publish the contents of your book…"

"I am terribly sorry, doctor. I can assure you that it is no fault of, mine."

"You do not have to give me that assurance. I have informed all enquirers that you own the rights."

"It was generous of you to do that, doctor. I have already received two offers…"

"For how much?"

"One for one hundred and fifty pounds, the other for two hundred."

"You did not accept either?"

"No, doctor."

"Why not?"

"Because—because of the—the circumstances—"

"You did not want my feelings to be hurt by further publicity?"

"Yes," Terhune admitted awkwardly.

"Ah! señor! How right I was to put my trust in your honesty and loyalty! But it would not hurt my feelings to see the story published in a London newspaper. I feel that the disappearance of my dear son should have every possible publicity; feeling that the more the attention of the public is focused upon the mystery the greater chance there will be of my son being found. For that reason I have accepted, on your behalf, an offer of three hundred pounds, and on behalf of Edward Pryce, another one hundred pounds for the right to reproduce the illustrations. Publication will begin to-morrow…"

Salvaterra refused to listen to Terhune's thanks. "Thank me when the dear boy is found," he said in a weary voice. "Meanwhile, I have given to the Press what I fear to be the true explanation of Andrés's disappearance. I have explained that he was a young man with highly-strung nerves and a vivid imagination, upon which the strange history of House-on-the-Hill reacted with unfortunate results. You see, my dear young friend, I have had time to give thought to the problem, and have reached the conclusion that Andrés must have been so affected by your vivid history that he began to brood upon the fact that the house was supposedly cursed. His nerves sagged beneath the stress of fear: acting upon a subconscious impulse, he walked into the night, anxious to put as great a distance as possible between him and the house.

"My sincere belief is that he is still alive. Somewhere in England, the young man may be travelling as far north or as far west as he can. Probably his actions are those of a hunted animal, for, doubtless, he is suffering from what is known to psycho-analysts as a persecution complex—the persecution being that of the curse. Because of that delusion, he may be acting with a cunning of which his conscious mind would be incapable. He may even have forgotten his name and address. Probably his only thoughts are that he must keep moving on, away from the source of that unknown fear, at the same time taking precautions not to be caught. Those precautions may be elementary, such as avoiding people and sleeping in hay-stacks, stables—anywhere, in fact, where his temporarily deranged mind believes he is not likely to be seen and recognised. Or they may be more advanced, to the extent of inventing another personality, changing his style of dress, growing a moustache and beard, or trying to disguise himself.

"I am sure he had money in his pockets when he left the house—probably thirty pounds or more. He would be able to live many weeks on that amount. So you see, dear friend, publication of your story, side by side with the publication of Andrés's photograph and description, may help in bringing him back to his family sooner than I dare hope. Am I forgiven, therefore, for acting in your name?"

Terhune readily admitted that he forgave the strange little man. After all, three hundred pounds…

I V

The publication in one of the more popular daily newspapers of the past history of House-on-the-Hill, side by side with Salvaterra's theory of Andrés's disappearance, created a sensational interest throughout the country, which culminated, as far as Terhune was concerned, on the following Sunday morning. Precisely as the church clock chimed the hour of ten a.m. Terhune was summoned, by the ringing of the electric bell, to the private door of his flat.

Opening it, he recognised the saturnine features of Detective-Inspector Sampson of the C.I.D.

Chapter Eighteen

I

"Well, well, well!" Sampson exclaimed cheerfully. "Didn't I prophesy that it would not take long for you to become mixed up in another mystery?"

"You did." Terhune grinned. "But did you seriously expect that to happen?"

The inspector took a quick glance at Market Square. There were two people, one stationary car, one dog and two pigeons to be seen.

"No," he admitted. "I didn't think it possible that Bray could produce more than one sensation per century." He passed inside the door, which Terhune was holding open for him. "If the newpapers have not been exaggerating, this Salvaterra affair is extraordinary."

"Would you like to hear about it?"

Sampson chuckled. "What do you think I have come for?" he confessed frankly. "After all, isn't it natural for a master to be interested in his pupil's activity?"

Soon the two men were closeted in the study before a blazing fire. Two columns of tobacco smoke eddied up to the ceiling, one from Sampson's pipe, the other from Terhune's cigarette.

The detective wasted no time in preliminaries. "How long have you known the Salvaterras?" he asked briskly.

"I have known two of them—Dr. Salvaterra, and his twin sister,

Inez—for about eight months. The other two; the wife and the son, I have known for approximately six weeks."

"When you mention the son, do you mean Andrés, the missing man?"

"Yes. He is the only son: the only child, in fact."

"How did you come to meet Salvaterra? Did he hear of the book you were writing about House-on-the-Hill?"

"No. I wrote the book for him; he commissioned it. I met him through his calling upon me to know whether I would undertake the work of finding out the past history of the house. At that time he had almost decided to buy the place."

"What made him think you would or could obtain such information?"

"Howard had spun him some yarn about my having a wonderful collection of books on Kentish history, and then added the information that I was by way of being an—an amateur detective."

Sampson chuckled loudly, as Terhune had anticipated he would—the inspector was intolerant where amateur detectives were concerned, although it was true that he had once urged Terhune to adopt that role, and had even gone so far as to promise some coaching and advice.

"Howard, the Ashford solicitor?"

"Yes."

"I remember him. How did he come to meet Salvaterra?"

"Salvaterra was wanting to buy a house in one of the Southern counties. He sent a letter to several of the bigger estate agents asking for particulars of properties for sale. Among those he received was one referring to House-on-the-Hill. He was attracted by its description, viewed it, and opened negotiations for its purchase. That brought him into touch with Howard, who was acting for the previous owner.

"In the meantime, Salvaterra had learned that House-on-the-Hill had a bad reputation among local people. He made enquiries as to the reason of this reputation, and failed entirely to discover one. Everybody said that he would not own the place even if it were a gift, but nobody could say why—or perhaps I should say, nobody could give a reasoned explanation for disliking the place to that extent."

Sampson's scarred face lost something of its usual, intimidating expression as he took the pipe from between his thin, hard lips. "You are beginning to interest me. So, being a cautious man, Salvaterra thought he would find out more about the house before completing its purchase and, hearing that you were an amateur detective "—his white teeth flashed as he drawled out the last two words—"he hoped that you might be able to give him the required information?"

Terhune shook his head. "Hold hard, inspector. His visit to me was not the result of caution, but of curiosity. He had already decided to complete the purchase, not in spite of the house's reputation, but because of it."

"I don't understand."

"Salvaterra is a doctor of philosophy. Because there was apparently no reasonable explanation to account for the repugnance which everybody feels towards the House with Crooked Walls, the place appealed to him as a subject for what I suppose was a type of psycho-analysis, but of a building, instead of a person."

"I follow you." Sampson's hard, penetrating glance turned upon Terhune. "I suppose he is quite sane?"

"I know nothing of insanity; he might be insane, but from what I have seen of him, I should judge him to be saner than most people I know. At any rate, I have rarely met a more erudite man."

"I am interested in hearing that, Terhune. Tell me about House-on-the-Hill as it was before Salvaterra bought it—I mean, as a common or garden house, and leaving out the stuff and nonsense about its being cursed, or, as one of the newspapers put it, 'the aura of evil which emanated from every brick of that age-old pile.' The piffle that some of the newspapers publish!"

"As a house, it has one of the finest pastoral vistas to be found anywhere in England. From the front of the house the ground slopes gradually away for five or six miles, to the seashore. On a clear day there is a wonderful view of the Channel. The view is almost as good from all parts of the house, because it stands immediately on the summit of the highest hill for miles around.

"As for the house itself, architecturally, it is crazy. Its walls really are crooked. But haven't you seen one of the illustrations?"

"Yes. Several, in fact. It wasn't its looks which interested me. What I want to know is, was it otherwise sound?"

"I think so."

"What about the purchase price? Was it high?"

"The past owner was willing almost to give it away."

"Then, damn it all! Terhune, why was it empty for so many years?"

"Because of its reputation."

"Surely you are not being serious? Cute business men, always on the hunt for real bargains, don't let tommy rot of that sort influence, them in spotting a good thing when it is offered to them."

"I was a sceptic, too, inspector, until I entered the house."

Sampson stared at Terhune. "Surely you do not *believe* all the stuff you have written about the House with Crooked Walls?" he demanded incredulously.

"The first time I entered the place I did, so with an open mind, inspector. In less than half an hour I was ready to run a mile to get away from it."

"My God!" For a few seconds Sampson's amazement was complete, but he quickly recovered his composure. "I respect your opinions, Terhune, because you have a damn sight more acumen and common sense than your modesty gives you credit for. If you were affected by the house, I am beginning to realise why it remained empty for so long. On the other hand, your reaction makes the affair more interesting than ever. Tell me, didn't Salvaterra experience the same feelings as you?"

"I don't know. He has never told me, one way or the other. I should say that either he did not or, if he did, then the fact of his doing so was the predominant factor in making him buy the house."

"And you say he is quite sane!"

"Haven't you heard of ghost-hunters deliberately staying all night in a haunted house in order to meet the visitation at first hand?"

"Yes," Sampson agreed slowly. "I see what you mean. All right, let's pass over that for the moment. Now be a good chap and take me into your confidence. How much of the history of House-on-the-Hill which is being published in the Press is true, and how much of it comes from that fertile imagination of yours?"

"Not one word of that history was born in my imagination, inspector,"

"What!" Sampson looked startled, but the expression quickly vanished, and was replaced by a broad, incredulous grin. "Now you are pulling my leg. Or aren't you willing to divulge trade secrets?"

"I am not joking. Naturally, I cannot guarantee that some of the sources from which I obtained my facts are entirely above suspicion, but that is a risk one has always to take in dealing with the past. At the same time, many of the stories are confirmed from other sources."

The answer appeared to embarrass Sampson. With the tips of his right-hand fingers, he gently rubbed the scar which distorted his hard, sharp face into something akin to malevolence—an unconscious, nervous gesture in which Terhune had not previously noticed the inspector indulging.

"You have taken most of the wind out of my sails," he confessed somewhat naively. "I came here this morning believing that all the newspaper stuff about Robert the Hermit and that American chap, Reuben Douglas, was all me eye and Betty Martin. Damned interesting stuff, I grant you, and manna from Heaven for the newspapers. But not for the police charged to investigate the disappearance of that young chap, Andrés Salvaterra. Nor for a certain Theodore Terhune, who, I believed, was probably anxious to stick his fingers in the pie." He recovered his composure; his steady glance held Terhune's. "To what extent is your judgment affected by past history, Terhune? Are you, like me, an out-and-out man of the twentieth century? Or are you being disturbed by that wriggling maggot which some spell—belief in the supernatural?"

Terhune realised that it was necessary to give an honest, frank answer to the question; anything less than that might destroy, if not the friendliness which Sampson felt towards him, at least the god-fatherly interest, which had come into being as a result of Terhune's interest in the affair of the Kylstone family burial vault.

"Here and there, inspector, I am as ready as you to jeer at the supernatural, but the moment I enter House-on-the-Hill—well, I almost begin to agree with Dr. Salvaterra and Shakespeare."

"'There are more things in Heaven and earth—'"

"Yes."

"Shakespeare brought a lot of unnecessary trouble into the world when he penned those lines. Now listen to me, young fellow-me-lad! You are still a young man; you live in a world of books, and you have a writer's imagination. All right. Why shouldn't you believe some-times that there are more things in Heaven and earth than most of us dream of in our philosophy? I am none of those things. I am a hard-bitten man of the world. I live all my moments now, in the middle of the twentieth century. And what is more, I don't step mentally backwards one single day. Still less into a dim, historical past.

"When I see a dead body before me, the obvious victim of an attack, lying in a room of which every door and every window is locked on the inside, I don't start a ghost-hunt. I tell myself that the bullet which killed the poor devil is a very real bullet, fired from a very real gun, held by a very real person. And I start looking for that person. Pronto! If you hope to be any good as a detective, amateur or otherwise— All right! All right! I know you don't wish to become an amateur detective: you just hope you may be pushed head first into a case every now and again! But *if* you do, Terhune, you have got to convince yourself that you damn well live in the twentieth century, that you live in this damned old twentieth century, and that you damn well live in this damned old twentieth century. And then you have got to add this: that the twentieth century is a century of radio, of aeroplanes, of tommy-guns, of poison-gas, and God knows what else to be invented before the century finishes. Radios and aeroplanes and tommy-guns make poor company for ghosts and goblins, and the quicker that is realised the sooner this business of Andrés Salvaterra's disappearance is likely to be solved.

"If you ask my opinion, there has already been too much talk of hobgoblins, and banshees, and curses, and what not. Why, even Murphy, of the East Kent police, started babbling about psychic influences working upon the subconscious when I telephoned him last night. Murphy is an old friend of mine, by the way. I am glad I am not in on this case in an official capacity. I should have something to say. But if you are interested, Terhune, and you would care to have the benefit of my advice, as you did once before, then for the good Lord's sake, remember what I say about this damned old twentieth century."

He paused abruptly, and his manner became almost apologetic. "See how you had me all worked up, Terhune. I have not made as long a speech as that since the day I was chairman at one of Foyle's luncheons."

Terhune's eyes twinkled. "I wonder if you would remain quite so dogmatic after a visit to House-on-the-Hill?" he murmured.

Sampson rose to the bait. "Of course I should," he snapped. "I have defied every superstition that has ever been invented—and I am still here. If I should enter that house convinced that there might possibly be something in sixteenth-century sorcery, necromancy and the like, I might change my mind. But I should go, knowing that I was living in the twentieth century; consequently, the house wouldn't seem to me any different from any other house of that period and style."

"Is that a bet, inspector?"

"Can you take me to House-on-the-Hill?" Sampson asked sharply, "In an unofficial capacity, naturally."

"Yes. Salvaterra would welcome any help in finding his son."

"Then I'll bet a dinner and theatre in town."

Sampson held out his hand, which Terhune clasped, sealing the bet.

I I

On their way to House-on-the-Hill in the inspector's car, Sampson revealed the information that he had already had from Murphy and an outline of the course which police enquiries had taken.

"As long as you do not construe my words into meaning that I hold with this supernatural business, I will admit that young Salvaterra's disappearance is a deuced strange affair. I take it that you already know the main details?"

"I think so. Salvaterra gave them to me early the next morning. After dinner the family retired to one of the sitting-rooms, the servants to their own quarters. Later, Andrés went up to a room fitted up as a radio-room-cum-workshop. About midnight the family retired to bed. On his way to the bedroom, Salvaterra looked in at the radio room. One of the sets was working, the light was on, a cigarette was burning in the ashtray, a glass half full of wine stood on the table. Being convinced that Andrés had gone out of the room for only a minute or so, Salvaterra went to bed, and fell asleep. But, apparently, Andrés never returned to the radio-room. Instead, he just vanished."

The inspector nodded. "They are the main facts. Murphy has confirmed them. He has interrogated separately every person in the house. It seems that the family finished their meal just before eight p.m. All four went from the dining-room to a sitting-room in the east wing. The servants cleared away the dirty crockery, tidied up, washed up, and retired to their own quarters in the north wing.

"Here, possibly, is an important fact. With one exception, every servant in the house remained in one room, their joint sitting-room, until twelve forty a.m. A late hour, but it seems that Andrés is not the only radio fan in the house; Randall, the butler, has an all-waves set. That night, just after eleven he tuned in to a play that was being radiated from one of the American stations. It proved to be so exciting that all voted to remain up until it was finished.

"Between eight twenty p.m. and twelve forty a.m. not one of the servants was out of sight of the others, with the exception of Randall. At ten forty-five he went round the house to see that everything was locked up for the night. While doing so, he heard the sound of music from Andrés's room and looked in…"

"Salvaterra did not tell me that."

"Perhaps he did not know; Randall let it out while he was answering one of Murphy's questions. Anyway, he saw Andrés, and asked if there was anything he wanted. Andrés asked for a glass of sherry, which Randall fetched. Afterwards, as Randall was saying good night, Andrés told him that a good play was due to be radiated from Philadelphia. From Andrés Randall went to Salvaterra, was told he was free to go to bed, and returned to the servants' sitting-room, where he tuned his set to Philadelphia, and listened in with the others, as I have already said, to well after midnight."

"So Andrés disappeared between eleven o'clock and midnight?"

"If we accept the evidence of the lighted cigarette, the time can be narrowed down to between five minutes before to five minutes after midnight."

"Were any doors or windows found open the following morning?"

"No doors were found open, but that is of no significance, because two of the doors had Yale locks, and were not otherwise bolted or barred—Andrés could have gone out by way of one of them, and slammed the door behind him. The same applies to the windows. None of the downstairs windows was open, and all had their catches properly fastened the next morning. On the other hand, many of the upper-floor windows were not fastened, and from some of them it would have been an easy matter for Andrés to jump down to the ground."

"Then Murphy has no definite evidence to prove that Andrés left the house?"

"What more evidence is needed than the fact of Andrés's not being found in the house?" Sampson asked, giving a quick, shrewd glance at Terhune's face. "What puzzles me most is, motive! If Andrés, voluntarily and consciously, left the house—why? Have you any theories, Terhune?"

"Only the one suggested by Salvaterra."

"What was that? The one about the atmosphere of the house working upon the boy's highly strung nervous system?"

"Yes."

Sampson shook his head. "For me to agree that that theory is feasible would mean my acknowledging that there is something spooky about the house—and we have a bet about that already. But even if I grant you that a spooky atmosphere might work upon a highly strung individual to the extent of making him flee from it, the evidence of the family is to the effect that, during the four or five days previous to his disappearance, he was in better spirits than he had been since their arrival at the house."

"Do the servants confirm that fact?" Terhune asked suddenly.

"As a matter of fact, they don't. None of them was conscious of any difference in the lad. But why did you ask?"

"Because I saw him the day before he disappeared, and his manner did not suggest to me that he was any less highly strung than usual. His fidgeting about got on *my* nerves. Bear left," he added.

Sampson bore left. "Was he inclined to shyness and timidity?"

"Yes," Terhune agreed. "Yes, I think I could say that he was."

"That may be the explanation. As long as he was in the presence of the family, he remained in better spirits, but directly the servants entered, or he came into contact with people not part of the family, he relapsed into his old—or perhaps his more usual— nervous mood. Anyway, whether he had changed or whether he had not makes little difference. The point is that Murphy has not yet come across any likely motive to account for his leaving home. If I were you, trying to help Salvaterra find his son, I should keep that assumption in mind."

"You mean the assumption that he has not left House-on-the-Hill?"

"Yes."

"But he has left it," Terhune expostulated. "The house has been searched from top to bottom."

"From top to bottom, maybe. But has it been turned inside out?"

"Inside out!" Terhune began. "What on earth——" But at that moment the inspector's inference became plain. "Good Lord!" he exclaimed in an awed voice. "A priest's hole!"

"Exactly!" Sampson said drily.

Chapter Nineteen

A priest's hole! Terhune gazed with sombre eyes at House-on-the-Hill—the crooked chimneys of which were starkly outlined against a depressing background of grey cloud—and experienced a feeling of gloomy dejection. So much for amateur detection! So much for his overrated intelligence! So much for his literary imagination! For days he had given profound thought to the disappearance of Andrés Salvaterra, had considered it from every angle, had worked out and rejected a dozen theories of what had happened to Andrés, and why, and how. But the one feasible theory had escaped him, mainly because he had unhesitatingly looked to the past to supply a solution. The materialistic, unimaginative Sampson, on the other hand, had insisted upon viewing the mystery from the prosaic present. In consequence, it had taken him less than an hour to deduce an equally prosaic answer to the perplexing problem.

The answer might not be the right one, but at least it was within the bounds of possibility. With its crooked walls, its sloping floors, its odd levels, and its complete absence of any architectural symmetry, it was more than likely that a secret hiding place was concealed within its crooked walls. It was more than likely that Andrés had, by accident, stumbled across this hiding place, and, in a moment of rashness, had investigated—only to find himself trapped and unable to escape.

"Poor devil!" he exclaimed feelingly, moved at the thought of the fate which might possibly have overtaken Andrés.

Sampson smiled thinly. "Aye! Poor devil indeed, if he were trapped. But I shouldn't jump to conclusions too soon," he advised. "After all, I have only offered a suggestion."

"I know, but the suggestion is too damned feasible. House-on-the-Hill is crazy enough to have half a dozen priest's holes. Besides, the known facts coincide with your theory—his apparent intention of returning to the radio-room, the absence of any apparent motive for disappearing, the closed doors, the failure of the police to find a clue leading to his present whereabouts... Oh, God!"

"What is wrong?"

"If, when Salvaterra first told me of Andrés's disappearance, I had thought of the possibility of his having found a priest's hole, he might have been found within a few hours..."

"If! If! If!" the inspector ejaculated swiftly. "Don't you start if-ing, young fellow-me-lad, for it won't do anyone any good. There was no particular reason for you to think-up that possibility, was there? There were plenty of other people in the house with a greater interest than yours in finding the boy. Besides, as I have just told you, it will be time enough for recriminations when we have learned for certain that Andrés was trapped in a priest's hole. There are as many arguments against that possibility as for."

Terhune was ready to snatch at any straw which might ease the burden of self-reproach.

"What are they?" he asked eagerly.

"First: there may be no secret hiding place at House-on-the-Hill. Second: if there is, and Andrés found it, that does not mean, automatically, that he was stupid enough to allow himself to be trapped inside. Third: even if that had happened, wouldn't he have kicked up such a racket that somebody was certain to hear and release him?"

"By that time everyone was probably in bed."

"Yes," the inspector agreed slowly. "But sound travels through some of the old houses. Surely someone would have heard the noise of thumping, especially when they put an ear down on a pillow." He nodded in the direction of House-on-the-Hill. "Is that our house?"

"Yes."

"It can't be too warm in the winter when the wind howls round it. I wonder if that is why the place got a reputation for being spooky—because of the wind, I mean?" He laughed shortly. "Even from this distance I can see that its chimneys are crooked..."

"Wait until you see the rest of the place more clearly."

Little more was said until the two men were passing Keppel's Farm. At that point the inspector exclaimed violently: "Ye gods! What a monstrosity! The damn place appears to jeer at me."

Terhune chuckled unkindly. "You ought to have seen it before it was repaired."

"Still, appearances aren't everything," Sampson consoled himself. He glanced to his right, at the distant sea. "Especially with a view like that to make up for any shortcomings."

A minute later the inspector brought his car to a stop along the drive which ran past the main porch. The two men alighted and approached the door. Their ring was answered by Randall.

"Is Dr. Salvaterra in?"

"Yes, Mr. Terhune. Will you please enter?"

They entered, and advanced towards the left-hand fireplace, in which a huge fire was cheerfully blazing. Randall departed to inform his master of the arrival of visitors, but he had moved no more than four paces when Salvaterra appeared on the gallery, and came down the staircase.

"I saw you step out of the car, my dear friend," he announced in a tired voice. "Do you bring me news?"

The question reminded Terhune of the little man's uncanny facility for interpreting shades of expression. "Yes and no," he acknowledged, trying not to betray his feelings at the sight of the Panamanian's face. In the short time which had passed since

Salvaterra's visit to the shop with the news of Andrés's disappear-ance he had changed. Although his small, plump, round face had always been excessively pale, that paleness had hitherto suggested neither ill-health nor frailty. Now the paleness had changed to a sickly hue, his face looked smaller than ever, for it had lost much of its plumpness, and also something of its roundness.

Salvaterra sighed. "But not good news?"

"I am afraid not, doctor. But first allow me to introduce a friend of mine, Detective-Inspector Sampson of the C.I.D., New Scotland Yard. Inspector Sampson is not here officially, but he will willingly help in any way he can."

"I am extremely grateful for your offer, inspector. I only wish could hope that it might lead to a happy result. But alas! I have lost hope. The Kent police have been admirable; they have worked unceasingly, but have found nothing. Nothing whatever. *Madre de Dios!* The suspense has been terrible. My wife has collapsed; only the loving care of my dear sister has prevented my doing the same. I am no longer a young man able to bear my sorrows bravely, señores."

Salvaterra turned and looked at the fire, perhaps to hide his emotion. There followed an awkward silence of some seconds.

"Dr. Salvaterra, Inspector Sampson has a—a suggestion—"

The Panamanian swung round abruptly, and faced the Scotland Yard man. "What is it, señor? What is it? I beg you to tell me quickly."

"Well, doctor, it is only an idea, but I was wondering whether it was possible for your son to have accidentally found a priest's hole—"

"A priest's hole! *No comprendo*—I do not understand what is a priest's hole."

"A secret hiding place, doctor."

"A secret hiding place! *Dios mio!*" A strange light flared in the Panamanian's eyes.

"What is the matter?" Sampson demanded sharply.

"*Dios mio!*" Salvaterra repeated, and closed his eyes as if to shut put an unpleasant vision. Then he opened them again, and his visitors believed they recognised an expression of horror in their depths. "Señores," he began in a whispering voice. "Only two days before he vanished Andrés spoke to me of a secret hiding place."

"What! He had found one?"

"No, no, Señor Sampson. No. Andrés had not found one—not then! He had been reading Señor Terhune's story of House-on-the-Hill—you have read extracts of it in the newspapers, no?"

"Yes."

"Then you know something of the history of this unhappy house. That morning Andrés came to me and said in an eager voice: 'Papa, do you know of any secret hiding places in this house?' I asked him the reason for his, strange question. His explanation was, that he wondered if the disappearance of Reuben Douglas could be accounted for by the American's having discovered such a hiding place, and being accidentally trapped in it while investigating."

Terhune and Sampson exchanged glances. The inspector's thin lips parted in a mirthless grin, as much as to say: "Douglas too!" As for Terhune, his dejection increased, not only on account of the unfortunate Andrés, but also because of his own lack of perception. Why had that explanation never occurred to him when writing of Douglas's disappearance? The explanation was so damnably feasible, so stupidly simple!

Salvaterra continued breathlessly: "I informed Andrés that I knew nothing of any secret hiding place. My answer appeared to disappoint him, but later on that day I found him measuring some walls with a rule. When I questioned him he told me he was measuring up all the rooms in the hope of finding a space not accounted for."

"Did he find anything?"

"Not to my knowledge, señor. I do not think he did that day."

"Why do you think that?"

"Again the following afternoon I found him measuring the walls. I laughed, and told him not to be too imaginative, but he refused to agree. He said that many of the bigger houses built in the time of your Queen Elizabeth had secret hiding places so that the priests could elude their enemies. Ah! now I understand why you call them priest's holes."

"Your son was right, señor."

"Some of the smaller houses in Kent had secret hiding places, too," Terhune added. "But for smugglers and smuggled goods rather than for priests."

"Señores, I cannot wait to test your theory," Salvaterra said anxiously. "What should I do to try and find one of these priest's holes? Where should I start? Downstairs?—" He paused abruptly, and gazed eagerly at both his visitors in turn.

"You have already done so much for me, señores," he murmured slowly. "I dare not ask—"

"Ask what?" Sampson demanded crisply.

Again the black eyes of the Panamanian uneasily scrutinised the faces of his two visitors. "Are you in any hurry?" he asked Sampson uneasily.

"Not particularly. This is my day off."

"And what about you, my dear friend? Can you spare me yet a few more hours of your time?"

"Willingly, doctor. I had nothing else planned for this morning."

"Then will you give me the benefit of your help and advice? You would recognise more quickly than I the most likely places to investigate. Perhaps you would also do me the honour of staying to lunch…"

His pleading was hard to refuse. "I am afraid I don't know the first thing about looking for secret hiding places, Señor Salvaterra, but I don't mind staying to give what help I can."

"And you, my dear young friend?"

"I shall be glad to do anything I can to help find Andrés, doctor."

"If you will excuse me for a few minutes, señores, I will leave you to make the necessary arrangements." Salvaterra trotted off, looking rather less harassed than he had some minutes previously.

"A queer sort of bloke!" Sampson commented in a low voice. "What do you make of him?"

"I don't know that I can make anything of him, Terhune. Which rather puzzles me. As a rule, my reaction to people is quick and very definite; what is more, my first impressions have never yet been proved wrong. But this chap, Salvaterra—" Sampson angrily shrugged his shoulders as he glanced round the hall. "I don't know what this hall looked like before Salvaterra had it redecorated, but he seems to have done a pretty good job of work." He nodded his head towards the stained-glass window. "Is that johnny in monk's clothes meant to be Robert the Hermit?"

"Yes, Edward Pryce the artist designed it. He lives round here, too."

"Personally, I like a stained-glass window or so in some of these old houses; it helps to give them atmosphere."

Terhune's eyes twinkled. "So even twentieth-century Inspector Sampson likes stepping back into the past on occasion?"

"That's where you are wrong, young fellow-me-lad. Plain Mr. John Henry Sampson may have his sentimental moments, but not Detective-Inspector Sampson. And, speaking of the past, this place doesn't cause me to feel the slightest suspicion of spookiness. On the contrary, it gives me the impression of being a darned comfortable house. Bit on the large side, of course, but otherwise, if I had had the chance, I shouldn't have had the slightest objection to buying it for a song as a place to come to for my old age."

"You haven't been here long enough." Terhune stepped closer to the fire.

Sampson glanced strangely at his companion. "Cold?"

"A bit."

"Funny!" the inspector exclaimed. "To me the place seems confoundedly stuffy, what with the central heating and this damned great fire."

Further conversation between the two men was ended by the reappearance of Salvaterra. As he approached them, the two men noticed that the drawn expression had returned to his face.

"I am sorry to say that Señora Salvaterra will not be present with us during the meal; she is prostrate with grief," he explained in a worried voice. "And now, señores, if you are ready, we will begin our search. I have brought a surveyor's measure to help us." He looked at Terhune. "You know the house, dear friend. Where would you suggest starting?"

Terhune pointed to the door on the right-hand side of the fireplace. "I suggest we start there, doctor, and investigate each room in rotation, wing by wing; the ground floors first, then the basement, and lastly the upper floors."

Salvaterra nodded his head in agreement. "Of course. We must be systematic," he muttered. With his short legs moving at a rapid pace, he led the way to the suggested room, and threw open the door. The three men entered. In a group they advanced towards the centre of the room, where they came to a stop, and began looking about them with perplexed eyes.

The room was a small one, particularly in comparison with the hall outside, the size of which was out of proportion with the rest of the house. The ceiling, like the majority of the rooms, had its oak beams exposed, and though these had recently been treated with a rot-preventative stain, their odd shapes and uneven lines bore witness to having been hewn with the crude tools of the Tudor period. For the most part, the walls were concealed by tapestries, but here and there one could detect bare plaster, colour-washed a daffodil yellow. There was no fireplace in the room: consequently three of the walls, including the outside wall, were as straight as any wall in the House with Crooked Walls could be. The fourth wall—the one dividing the room and the hall, was not, at first sight, above suspicion, for fully half of it formed part of the chimney buttress.

Both Sampson and Terhune appreciated this fact, for both began to speak simultaneously.

Terhune broke off and grinned self-consciously. "You first, inspector."

Sampson did not argue. "I was about to say that, from what little I remember reading about priest's holes, they have often been found behind, inside, or beside the old, wide fireplaces. It might be worth having a quick look at that part of the wall."

He stepped close to the wall and lifted the tapestry which concealed it. The plaster work was new and solid; nowhere was there to be seen any break in the smooth surface, even where the buttress joined the wall or below where the bottom of the buttress was hidden by a skirting.

The inspector shook his head doubtfully. "I can't see how this buttress could possibly conceal a hiding place—at least, not one that has recently been opened. You see, señor, the plaster is unbroken, which couldn't be if any part of the wall hereabouts opened inwards or outwards."

"Entrances into some priest's holes are so small that it would be a tight squeeze to get past," Terhune pointed out. "Some years ago I had an illustrated book on the subject. I remember some of the pictures; one was of a hinged skirting board. To get into the hole one had to lie flat upon the floor, and wriggle under the skirting, which opened inwards."

"The skirting would have to be an inch or two higher than this one," Sampson pointed out. Nevertheless, he knelt down upon one knee, and tapped upon the skirting with his knuckles. The sound which he made was dull and muffled; it conveyed no suggestion of there being anything but solid brickwork behind He tried in several places, but the hollow echo which they hoped to hear was not forthcoming.

"I don't think we need waste much time in this room," the inspector said as he rose to his feet. "But we will take the measurements. Señor, if Terhune and I do the measuring, would you write the totals down? I suggest we measure all walls in the same order—north, south, east and west. When we have finished we can draw a rough plan of the house—"

"I have the surveyor's plan of the house—" Salvaterra interrupted.

"Excellent! Then we can mark down our measurements on that, señor, and if we find, for instance, that the total width of two or more rooms, plus thickness of walls and any passage between, does not agree with the width of the house, we shall know some space is unaccounted for. Then we can do the same with the length and the height."

"Wait a minute, inspector. Surely the surveyor would have measured up the rooms when making his plan of the house. Wouldn't he have noticed any discrepancy?"

"I hadn't thought of that." Sampson frowned, but almost immediately his face brightened again. "Seeing that the surveyor was not looking for a priest's hole, he might not have troubled to check up the total measurements of all the rooms with the total width or length of the house as the case might be."

"That is quite true," Salvaterra agreed. "Shall we consult the surveyor's plans before proceeding further?"

Taking his companions' consent for granted, Salvaterra led the way back into the hall, and so to his study on the far side. He produced a set of plans from one of the drawers of the desk table, and spread the first one out upon the table. The three men eagerly pored over the sheet for a minute or so. Then Sampson seized hold of pencil and paper, and began making calculations.

He checked off all the measurements noted down on the first sheet—which was that of the ground floor of the south east wing, but the figures of the width and length of the wing agreed with the total widths and lengths of the various rooms and passages. So they unrolled the next sheet, and began to examine that. This was of the upper floor of the north east wing, where the servants were housed. Again they found no discrepancy.

One by one they checked off the surveyor's plans for a long time without success. They were, in fact, beginning to despair when Sampson called out excitedly: "Give me those figures again, Terhune."

Terhune repeated the measurements, which were those of two opposite rooms and a passage on the upper floor of the main building. Then followed a few tense moments as Sampson rechecked his calculations.

"I believe there is something wrong here. The measurements don't agree in one corner by a matter of one foot four and a quarter inches."

Salvaterra peered at the plan. "Which room does not agree, señor?" he asked in a strained voice. "The south room or the north?"

"The south, doctor."

"*Dios mio!*"

"What is it, señor?" Sampson snapped.

"That room, señores, is the one used by my son for his radio experiments," Salvaterra whispered hoarsely.

Chapter Twenty

Once again Terhune and the inspector exchanged glances as the significance of Salvaterra's words became apparent. On the assumption that Andrés had found the entrance to a priest's hole in the radio-room, the closed door, the light, the radio, the unfinished glass of sherry, the still burning cigarette all could be explained. Only a few moments previous to Salvaterra's entry to bid his son good night, Andrés might have discovered and entered the hiding place which he had been seeking for the past thirty-six hours. Scarcely could he have stepped inside and have closed the entrance behind him before his father had entered the room; believing his son's absence to be only temporary, he had gone to bed, leaving the radio still connected.

"Will you take us to that room, doctor?" Sampson asked sombrely.

Salvaterra was too moved to speak. He nodded his head, and led the way out of his study, up the staircase to the gallery, and a short distance along a passage leading to the west side of the main building. He stopped opposite the first door on the left, which he threw open.

"Will you enter, señores?" he suggested in a voice so charged with apprehension as to be almost unrecognisable.

The other two men entered; Salvaterra hesitated a few moments before following their example, as though afraid of what tragedy the ensuing minutes might produce. When he did finally enter he closed the door behind him, and turned the key in its lock.

"In case, señores——" he whispered.

The two visitors glanced round. As in the room they had first entered, the oak beams were so low that both men had to walk warily to avoid knocking their heads against the great centre beam. Unlike that other, first room, however, the walls were panelled. Apart from an easy chair which stood in front of the small fireplace, a high, leather-padded stool, a rich carpet on the floor, and some coloured sporting prints hung upon the walls, there was no furniture in the room. It was strictly utilitarian. Three of the walls were occupied by benches, on which were the wireless sets, component parts and tools which Terhune had noted upon the occasion of the house-warming party. The fourth wall was the outside wall. Part of this wall was occupied by two small windows, which were just below the eaves. The left-hand corner was occupied by a projection, somewhat more than a foot in depth, and four feet wide. The radio work bench had been built so as to fit exactly against the width of the projection.

"There is our missing space," Sampson said in a disappointed voice. "It is no use our looking for a secret hiding place behind that part of the wall."

"Why not?" Terhune asked.

Sampson approached the corner, and banged the bench with his fist. "Because of this solid piece of woodwork." He tapped the width of the projection with his knuckles. "To get inside here one would have to move the bench out of the way. If Andrés Salvaterra were trapped behind here he couldn't have moved the bench back again."

"I agree. That is no priest's hole, señores," Salvaterra confirmed sadly. "Many of the rooms, on this side of the main building, both upstairs and down, have projections similar to that one." He walked across to one of the windows and pointed down below. "If you look out of this window, señores, you will see that the buttresses of the house have been carried through the main wall and into the house. This projection is the top of the nearest buttress."

Sampson and Terhune joined Salvaterra at the window, and looking out, saw that he spoke the truth.

"We may as well return to the surveyor's plans," Sampson suggested.

Terhune did not move; he stood still staring at the part of the buttress which was within the room.

"What are you looking at, Terhune?" the Inspector asked sharply.

"The side of the buttress inside the room is about sixteen inches, isn't it, inspector?"

"We can soon make sure." Sampson stepped back to the projection, and applied the measure to the wall. He nodded. "A fraction over sixteen inches," he confirmed.

"Then it is wide enough for Andrés to have stepped through."

"You mean sideways?"

"Yes."

"Any reasonably slim man could squeeze through sideways, even allowing for one thickness of brickwork," Sampson agreed. "If there is any sort of an entrance, of course!"

"Naturally."

"But, señores, surely a buttress must be composed of solid brickwork," Salvaterra interrupted despairingly.

"It should be," Terhune pointed out. "But that is not to say that it is. That part of the buttress which is outside could be solid while still allowing the portion inside the house to have a space of about twelve inches by more than three feet."

"It could," the inspector confirmed crisply. "So we will leave nothing to chance." Without further ado, he began running his hands over the panelling while Terhune and Salvaterra stood by watching.

Several minutes passed, during which time nobody spoke, and the only sound to be heard was that of Sampson's knuckles tapping upon the woodwork, or the rubbing of his finger-tips as he tried to push one panel after another first to the right, then to the left.

Presently he stepped back two paces. "You had better have a shot, Terhune. To me the panelling feels as solid as the Rock of Gibraltar. By the way, Dr. Salvaterra, haven't you had the central heating installed on the upstairs floor?"

"But yes, señor, of course I have?"

"It isn't in this room, is it?"

"But certainly it is, señor. It is behind the panelling, under the bench, and close to the door. Why do you ask?"

"There seems to be a cold draught in the room, doctor, but maybe I am imagining it. I hope I haven't caught a cold."

Meanwhile, Terhune was examining the panels which concealed the side of the buttress. He noted, immediately, that the design of the panels made it possible for the entire depth to open inwards, assuming, of course, that there was a space behind, and not solid brickwork. In the right-hand corner, where the outer wall joined the side of the buttress, there was an upright length of beading which stretched from ceiling to skirting board. Another upright occurred in the angle where the side and the back met. Either of these up-rights, he thought, was capable of bearing the hinges upon which the intervening panel-work could hang.

Placing an ear against one of the panels he rapped his knuckles against the woodwork. The sound given back was by no means hollow. Nor, on the other hand, was it quite as solid as he would have expected from any real depth of brickwork behind. As an experiment, he applied his ear to one of the panels of the outer wall, and rapped with his knuckles. This time the sound was undeniably "dead."

He crossed the room, and repeated the experiments with each of the remaining three walls in turn. All were similarly dead. Here returned to the buttress, and again rapped upon the woodwork. The noise was undeniably different.

With a mounting conviction that the buttress was not above suspicion, he began to hunt for the means of opening the presumed door or entrance. With meticulous care he covered the area of the side of the buttress, panel by panel, inch by inch. Minutes passed, and then more, but he was no more successful than the inspector. Yet more minutes passed. Sampson began to fidget, and Terhune almost despaired.

Then another idea occurred to him. He turned his attention, instead, to the panelling of the outer wall, immediately to the right of the buttress. At first, with no result, but he continued his efforts, with a persistence which surprised him as much as it did his audience.

His patience was eventually rewarded. As he pressed one of the panels which was situated about half way along the wall between the buttress and the window he felt it yield to his pressure. The complete panel moved backwards a matter of an inch.

Behind him he heard both Salvaterra and the inspector exclaim with excitement. He did not turn, but peered closely at the small space thus made visible to him. There was nothing to be seen. To all intents and purposes, the panel was one which had shrunk with the years, and had become loosened from its frame. Notwithstanding appearances, Terhune persisted, firstly because mere shrinkage could not account for the inch-deep space behind the panel, and secondly, because he seemed to feel a counter-pressure to that exerted by his finger-tips.

He took his hand away from the panel. As he did so the panel rebounded against its frame.

"The panel must have a spring behind it," Sampson said in a voice sharpened by excitement. "Try it again."

Terhune repeated the performance. When he pushed against the panel it moved backwards; when he took his hand away the panel moved forward to its customary niche.

"There must be some reason for that panel to have springs behind," said Sampson's voice again just behind Terhune's ear. "What can you see?"

"Nothing, the light is too bad. Will you strike a match, inspector, while I keep the panel open?"

Sampson struck several matches in turn, and held them close to the panel, but neither he nor Terhune were able to distinguish anything beyond the fact that the panel was set in a square frame, which explained the reason for its not falling downwards when it was pushed back.

"That's damn funny," the inspector muttered presently. "It doesn't seem to do anything. In any case, isn't it too far away to have any connection with the buttress?"

The inspector's question spurred Terhune's memory. "You've given me an idea," he muttered. With his right hand he held the panel pushed back; with the other he fumbled with the panel on the left of the one he held open. He felt it move slightly; the next moment it slid smoothly to the right, filling up the space (as he took his right hand away) of the one he had pushed back. Where the second panel had been was now revealed a small square of bare bricks.

"What the devil!" Sampson ejaculated.

Salvaterra cried out: "*Caramba!*"

Convinced now that he was working on the right lines, Terhune next applied his hand to the panel on the left of the last one he had just moved. As in the case of the second panel, the third likewise slid along, to the right, to occupy the place of the second.

"Ah!" the inspector exclaimed sharply.

One by one Terhune shifted the small square panels along to the right, until he reached the last in the line. As he shifted this one, which was immediately next to the buttress, there was repealed, behind, a piece of lock-mechanism in the shape of a small but substantial iron hook, the pin of which was inserted in an iron eye, and kept there by the tension of a strong spring attached below.

There was no doubting the purpose of the mechanism; not, at least, to the three men who, for a brief second, stared at it amid tense, dreadful silence. Then the momentary spell of hesitation was broken by a sharp cry from Salvaterra. The few words he spoke were in Spanish; Terhune did not even guess their purport, but he acted, spurred by an anxiety not to torture the unhappy father longer than was necessary. With an intuitive conviction that the mystery of Andrés's disappearance was about to be solved, he inserted two fingers below the iron hook and released it.

As the pin of the hook left the eye the men heard the sound of a click; of its own accord the hook continued to move upwards, out of sight, until the spring was stretched to its limit.

Slowly, fearfully, Terhune pushed against the side of the buttress. It yielded to his hand; the whole side of the buttress swung inwards, and revealed a dark, shadowed space from which came a cold, fetid draught.

A gasp of anguish burst from Salvaterra's lips. "What is there, señores? For God's sake tell me quickly. I have not the courage to look."

Sampson stepped quickly to Terhune's side; together they peered into its dark space. There was little to be seen save a narrow tunnel like aperture which descended to black depths, and a large iron rung driven into the outer wall of the aperture, and below it another: both men were sure that a line of rungs continued downwards for some distance.

The inspector struck a match and held it inside the aperture. The flame flickered and went out. He struck a second. Once more the draught from below was too much for the tiny flame.

"What can you see, señores? What can you see?" Salvaterra pleaded frantically.

"Nothing, doctor. It is too dark."

"Señores, I do not understand. Surely you can see if—if there is—is anything—on the floor?"

"There is no floor, doctor."

"Mother of God!" Salvaterra gasped. "Mother of God!" He spoke again, but his words were incoherent.

Sampson turned. "Have you a torch, doctor?" he asked gently.

"I will fetch one, señor." The Panamanian hurried from the room; the two men inside heard his tiny feet pattering hurriedly along the passage outside.

"Shut the door, Terhune, for God's sake," Sampson muttered. "The air is pestilential."

Terhune released his hand. As he did so the door swung to: there was a clicking sound; the pin of the iron hook descended and slipped into its eye, the line of panels slid back into their accustomed places; the sprung panel shot forward...

The two men stared at the panelled wall.

"My God!" the inspector exclaimed. "Of all the devilish contrivances—Terhune, you win your bet a dozen times over. I take back all I said. This house is about the foulest place I have stepped into. There is something—I cannot tell you what—I cannot put my feelings into words—but that draught from below seemed to come straight from hell."

Terhune made no comment—the inspector's sensations were his own. Could he have been satisfied that Andrés was nowhere in the house, he would have been content to leave matters as they were, and so fasten the entrance to the priest's hole that nobody would ever again succeed in releasing its polluted atmosphere. But he could not leave the priest's hole unexplored; every canon of decency dictated this course of action, regardless of his own wishes.

In memory of a likeable young man, Sampson and he must descend the iron rungs into foul, evil depths.

It was tragically easy to see how Andrés's body could have got there. No doubt, Andrés had discovered the method of opening the side of the buttress. In a moment of excitement he had stepped inside, probably on to the uppermost iron rung. Recklessly, foolishly, accidentally, he had relaxed his hold upon the door, which had immediately swung to, trapping the unfortunate man. Possibly Andrés had been unable to find any way of opening the door from the other side, whereupon, no doubt, he had hammered upon the door to attract attention. Unhappily, without success, possibly because his knocking had been drowned by the music from the radio set. Or he might have fallen below, and have broken a limb in doing so. Unable to climb up the awkwardly placed rungs—

"Hold on to yourself, Terhune!" Sampson exclaimed sharply. "Don't let your imagination run away with you."

Terhune realised that his face must have betrayed his thoughts. "I am damned afraid, inspector" he began.

"So am I. You had better let me go down there, Terhune. I am used to tragedies. Besides, I didn't know the lad."

"No, inspector. We will both go down. The sight of a corpse won't mean anything to me; I saw too many during the War. It is how he may have died that worries me more than the fact that he has died."

Sampson nodded understandingly. "I know! But try not to think too much."

The conversation was interrupted by the return of Salvaterra, carrying two electric torches. He gave one to each of his visitors. His face was a sickly, chalky white, and it was quite obvious to the others that his thoughts had been travelling along similar paths to their own.

He did not say anything, but just looked, at them in turn, pleadingly, pathetically, and they realised that he was begging them to continue their exploration of the priest's hole without him.

Terhune nodded in answer and turned towards the wall. It was a matter of a few moments only to reopen the door of the priest's hole. Once again the foul draught chilled his already cold face. He had to call upon his reserve of courage to face the ordeal in front of him.

He turned to Sampson. "Before we both go down, inspector, I think we had better look for the means of opening the door from the other side. I will get inside, while you remain on this side of the door. If I cannot find any means of opening the door I will knock."

Sampson nodded. "A good idea, Terhune."

Reluctantly, Terhune took as firm a grip as possible of the jamb of the door with his right hand and, keeping the door open with his back, turned sideways, to face the outer wall. Squeezing halfway through the narrow entrance, he advanced his left foot to the rung, then his right.

Pressing his back firmly against the door, which was his only method of keeping upright, for he could find nothing for his left hand to hold on to, he moved down two rungs so that only the upper part of his back now kept the door open. He was then able to grip the topmost rung with his left hand. As soon as he was satisfied that he was reasonably secure, he let go of the jamb of the door with his right, and bent his body to the left, to release the door. Immediately, the door closed with a loud thump, leaving Terhune in a blackness so intense, so cold, so enveloping that he experienced a momentary sensation of hysterical panic, which only the certainty of Sampson's presence a yard away helped to allay.

Terhune pulled the torch from his pocket and directed it upwards. The brilliant white circle of light revealed a solid oblong of oak which fitted snugly into the jamb, and the strong spring which automatically closed the door. Nothing else. No handle, no mechanism, nothing whatever by which to open the door.

He raised his hand to signal to Sampson, then hesitated, as an impulse to know the worst prompted him to direct the light of the torch downwards.

The worst was there, plainly to be seen. Sprawling in an ungainly posture was a still, slim body, unmistakably that of Andrés Salvaterra.

Chapter Twenty-One

I

When the tragic news of Andrés's death reached the ears of the inhabitants of Bray and Wickford and Willingham, it was no surprise. From the moment of hearing the first rumour of the poor lad's disappearance, they had anticipated the tragedy, claimed the majority of the inhabitants. This was not so much an instance of being wise after the event, but rather the previous certainty that the House with Crooked Walls would inexorably live up to its reputation. They had been born and reared in the belief that the house was accursed and evil, and although, a few months ago, no one had been able to give a reason for his horror of the place, there had been an illogical belief that the house would take its revenge upon Salvaterra for disturbing its grisly solitude.

For these people, already prejudiced by an inherited, subconscious fear, Terhune's book had crossed the "t's" and dotted the "i's" of their repugnance. They had learned, for the first time, of the strange disappearances of Robert the Hermit, and, much later, Reuben Douglas, neither of whom had ever been seen again. When, therefore, they had heard of Andrés's disappearance, they had been immediately convinced that Andrés, also, would never be seen or heard of again. They did not try to explain why, or how this could be—they only knew it would be.

In spite of this certainty, quite a number of people were genuinely sorry to hear that Andrés had been found dead. Sympathy worked upon their feelings; they spoke of how much they had grown to like the young man, despite their limited acquaintance with him. For the same reason, they deluded themselves into believing that Salvaterra meant far more to them than, in actual fact, he did. They tried to share the bereaved family's sorrow in every possible way, by sending letters of condolence, and flowers, and by attending the funeral in large numbers.

At the same time, there was considerable speculation about the future of House-on-the-Hill. Many rumours circulated as to what Salvaterra intended doing with the place: these varied from one which announced from the usual authoritative source that the Panamanian was presenting the house to the British nation, as an expression of gratitude for the kindness shown to him by the British people, to another which asserted with confidence that Salvaterra was returning to his native country, but that, before doing so, he proposed to raze House-on-the-Hill, and distribute its bricks and beams to the four corners of the county, so that no other person should ever be allowed to suffer from the consequences of living beneath such an accursed roof.

Eventually Salvaterra put a stop to all further rumours by announcing, through the local Press, that he intended returning to Panama long enough for his wife to recover from the shock of his son's death, but that later, probably in the following spring, he would return to House-on-the-Hill and resume permanent residence. In anticipation of the surprise and possible criticism which this decision might cause, he went on to explain that, despite the death of his son, and the past history of the house, he still did not believe in superstition. On the contrary, the death of Andrés, though tragic, was undoubtedly not abnormal, and went far to disprove the suggestion that the disappearance of

Reuben Douglas could be ascribed to supernatural causes. No doubt, Doulgas had died in similar circumstances. Continuing, Salvaterra explained to the reporter that, before returning to England he proposed to have House-on-the-Hill exhaustively examined, not only for the purpose of thoroughly sealing up the fatal priest's hole, but also in order to search for any other traps of that nature, that they might be dealt with in a proper manner. He terminated the interview by asking what would happen to civilisation if everyone refused to live in a house wherein a death had taken place?

Salvaterra's reasoning was sound, and the national Press accepted it as such. So, therefore, did their readers. But not so the people of Bray and the surrounding villages. House-on-the-Hill always had been accursed, and would always remain so.

Meanwhile, an inquest was held on the death of Andrés Salvaterra. The proceedings did not take long. Medical testimony showed that death had been caused by heart failure, following a fall and mental shock. Terhune and Sampson also gave evidence, during which they explained their reasons for believing that Andrés might be found in a secret hiding place somewhere in House-on-the-Hill. Salvaterra testified to Andrés's intention to search for the priest's hole, of finding him measuring up the house, and lastly, of the half-smoked cigarette, the half-finished glass of sherry, the light in the radio-room, and the music from the radio set.

One fact of minor importance came out during the course of Salvaterra's evidence. Andrés, it seemed, was not his son, but his stepson, being the issue of Señora Dolores Salvaterra by her first husband, Manuel Rojas. Salvaterra explained that, on the occasion of the marriage two years previously, Andrés, out of affection for his stepfather, had chosen to adopt the name of Salvaterra in preference to his own.

Although this item of evidence was in the nature of a minor surprise to the Court, it made no difference to the verdict, which was that of Misadventure.

Two weeks later, Salvaterra, together with his wife and his sister, sailed for Panama.

I I

Some three weeks after Salvaterra had left the country, a small number of men booked rooms at the "Almond Tree." These proved to be members of a firm of surveyors and architects, commissioned by Salvaterra to inspect and search House-on-the-Hill.

They began work on a Monday. Two days later Terhune was called to the telephone.

"Are you Mr. Theodore Terhune?"

"Yes."

"This is Ackworth, of Ackworth and Company, architects, of Grosvenor Square, London. Probably you already know that we have been engaged by Dr. Salvaterra to carry out work of a certain nature at House-on-the-Hill?"

"Yes."

"Well, Mr. Terhune, one of Dr. Salvaterra's instructions was, that if we made a discovery of any importance, we were to get into immediate touch with you; so that it might be shewn to you as soon as possible."

"That was generous of Dr. Salvaterra."

"Quite. The point is, Mr. Terhune, that we have just made a discovery which should be of interest to you. Would you care to come along some time soon?"

Terhune was glad Ackworth had made the discovery on a Wednesday. "I can come along early this afternoon."

"Good. At what tine?"

"About two-thirty."

"Excellent. Then I shall expect you about two-thirty."

Just before two that afternoon Terhune set off for House-on-the-Hill. He arrived there a few minutes before time, but as he propped his bicycle against the wall of the main building a tall, middle-aged man came out of the porch. He had greying hair, and walked with a slight limp.

"Mr. Terhune?"

Terhune nodded.

The man held out his hand. "I am Ackworth. Will you come in?"

The two men passed into the house. As Ackworth closed the door behind them, for there was a chill wind blowing from the south-west, he said: "I take it that you are the Theodore Terhune who wrote that book about this place?"

"Yes."

"I read it last week, and thoroughly enjoyed it. I might have thought you had rather drawn the long bow if I had not already experienced the uncanny effect which this place has on one."

Terhune grinned. "So it's got you, too?"

"If you are referring to my experiencing an uncanny sensation of feeling myself to be in an atmosphere of—of evil, the answer is definitely, Yes. That grotto affair below must be just about the foulest place there is this side of Africa. You found out a tidy bit about House-on-the-Hill, but I think there are some things about the house which even you do not know or suspect. In that book of yours, you talk about House-on-the-Hill as being crazily built. I go farther than that. I say that parts of this house were built, not by a man who was just crazy, but plumb insane. And not merely insane, but fiendishly insane."

"What do you mean?"

"I'll shew you. Come this way."

The two men went up the staircase to the gallery, where Ackworth turned right, and then left. Ackworth stopped at the first door on their right, threw it open, and gestured to his companion to enter. Terhune did so, and found himself in a room somewhat similar to that which Andrés had used as his radio-room. There was this difference though; the room was tastefully furnished as a bedroom. As in the case of the radio-room, one of the corners (but this time the right-hand corner) of the outer wall was occupied by the top part of a buttress.

Ackworth crossed the room towards the right-hand inside wall. Bending almost double, he manipulated first one of the panels, and then its immediate left-hand neighbour. The panel slid along to the right, whereupon Ackworth pushed along the line of panels until he reached the one closest to the buttress. When this, too, was pushed to the right Terhune saw revealed lock-mechanism resembling that which had opened the side of the buttress in the radio-room.

The architect pushed up the pin, and set the mechanism working. The hook sprang upwards, was caught, and held fast by another piece of the mechanism. Ackworth pushed against the side of the buttress, which swung inwards, to reveal a black-looking aperture, from which blew a chill, fetid draught.

"Here is another of your priest's holes for you, Mr. Terhune, but you will note that the mechanism by which it opens and closes is situated in a spot quite different from that which you found and opened."

Terhune looked down into the black depth of the shaft-like aperture. "Is there—is there—anything down there?" he muttered.

"Only a few bucketfuls of dirt." Ackworth let the buttress door slam, whereupon the line of panels slid along to their accustomed places, and the original panel sprang forward. "That job is as neat and simple a secret contrivance as one would find in a month of

Sundays," he continued. "The entire system is based upon springs. By the way, judging by architectural evidence, I should estimate that this side of the house, the south side, was built a good many years after the north side, and later than the east wing."

"How many years?"

"Roughly, a century and a half. About the period, according to your book, when the house was occupied by the Ingletons."

"Then the two priest's holes aren't genuine priest's holes?"

"Well, they were not made for the purpose of hiding priests, if that is what you mean. By the middle of the eighteenth century religious tolerance was more or less recognised."

"Then what was the builder's purpose in contriving these deathtraps?"

"God knows! Except, as I said to you downstairs, that in my opinion they were designed by a maniac. Possibly—as you have described so exactly—as death-traps. But I haven't shown you everything yet."

"There are more?"

"Every buttress in the house is false."

"Good God!"

Ackworth chuckled at Terhune's astonishment, and led the way back to the gallery and, by way of it, to the other side of the house, past the tragic radio-room. Together the two men entered another room in the front of the house, which also was furnished as a bedroom. Once again part of the outer wall was occupied by the top of a buttress. Once again Ackworth manipulated the panels (this time high above his head) and pushed open one side of the buttress, to reveal the usual aperture.

"There is something at the bottom of this shaft which I should like you to see. Do you mind accompanying me down?"

"I am not keen," Terhune admitted frankly. "I was hoping never again to be anywhere near such a place. But if it is necessary—"

"It is not necessary, but I think you will be interested."

"In that case, of course."

"Good. Here is a torch. I will go down first." Ackworth put one foot inside the priest's hole, but unexpectedly turned round again. "By the way, I ought to have asked you this. Are your nerves fairly sound?"

"I think so."

"Right. Would you prop the door open with that chair when I am inside? I have no wish to meet the same fate as that poor devil you found. And just in case of accidents, I have arranged for one of the staff to check everyone off every two hours because there is no guessing what may happen next in this damned house."

Ackworth stepped into the priest's hole, and held the door open while Terhune arranged a chair in such a manner that the door could not slam to. Then he squeezed past the chair, and stepped on to the rungs above Ackworth's head.

As he neared the bottom rung Ackworth said: "Just a minute, Mr. Terhune. Do you mind my guiding your foot? I want you to be careful where you stand."

"Go ahead," Terhune told him.

Ackworth guided first one foot and then the other. "Now look," he suggested in a low voice, directing the light of his torch on the ground.

Terhune glanced downwards. Lying in a crumpled heap was a human skeleton.

III

"Reuben Douglas!" Terhune exclaimed presently.

"Without a doubt." Ackworth pulled something from his pocket which he passed over. "I found that penny underneath the pelvis bone. There are some other coins there, but I didn't want to disturb anything until you arrived. You see the date of the coin?"

Terhune examined the penny in the light from his torch. It was dated 1839. Just three years before the date of Douglas's disappearance. There seemed no reason for doubting the identity of the skeleton. It was fairly obvious from the grotesque, contorted position of the bones that Douglas had fallen to the ground, probably from the topmost rung, and had died instantly.

"If ever you revise your book, you will have something to add," Ackworth said presently. "Shall we go up? There is nothing more down here."

"What do you propose doing with the skeleton?"

"I shall telephone the coroner, and let him make arrangements to inspect and remove it."

They returned to the bedroom above, and closed up the side of the buttress. As they walked along the passage towards the gallery, Terhune thanked Ackworth for his kindness.

"Don't mention it," the architect protested genially. "Quite apart from the fact that Dr. Salvaterra asked me to get in touch with you, I know how interested you are in this house. As a matter of fact, your book has made this business of resurveying the house doubly interesting. If I had known something of its past history, I might have looked for priest's holes before the business of reconstruction was begun."

"Did you plan the reconstruction?"

Ackworth hesitated. "I did," he confessed, embarrassed. "But please do not regard the result as typical of my work. Salvaterra wouldn't allow me a free hand. He had very definite ideas on what he wanted, so I had, more or less, to follow them. He was dead set upon having the interior restored, as far as modern amenities allowed, to what it probably was in the days of Good Queen Bess. Nor would he let me alter the exterior: he maintained that House-on-the-Hill had a character of its own, and didn't want it changed. So it had, by George! but why anyone should want it to keep that particular character is beyond me." He shrugged his shoulders. "But Salvaterra paid the piper, so he was entitled to call the tune."

"How did it happen that the builders' men didn't discover that some of the panels were sprung when they stained and polished the woodwork of the bedrooms?"

The architect halted abruptly—they were half-way down the stairs—so Terhune also came to a stop.

"Didn't you know that each of those sprung panels was controlled by some sort of locking device from the frame above?"

"No."

"Well, they were. In each case, the carved wooden rosebud was partly turnable. When the rosebud was half turned to the right, the panel was locked; when it was half turned to the left, this freed the locking mechanism, so that one was able to push the panel in, and start, the ball rolling, as it were."

Terhune shook his head reflectively. "That explanation conflicts with your theory about the priest's holes, so called, being deliberate death traps. If the constructor had wanted people to find them so that they could be trapped inside why did he take so many precautions against the holes being discovered in the first place?"

"I hadn't thought of that." Ackworth grinned. "Perhaps he wasn't fiendishly insane after all, but just plain insane."

Terhune did not respond to the architect's light-heartedness, for he was pursuing another chain of thought. "Another puzzling question, Mr. Ackworth. Seeing that Douglas was trapped inside the priest's hole, he couldn't have worked the locking device. Therefore, why was the sprung panel in that room never discovered?"

"The answer to that question is, I regret to tell you, very mundane. The panel was warped. I had some trouble in making it work in fact."

Terhune grinned his disappointment at this commonplace explanation, and resumed the journey down the stairs. Ackworth kept pace with him.

"May I ask you a personal question, Mr. Ackworth?" Terhune asked as he reached the ground level.

Ackworth chuckled pleasantly. "There is never any harm in asking."

"When you first surveyed this house did you experience a feeling of—of—evil?"

"Did I? By George! I certainly did. If Salvaterra's complete immunity from comparable feelings had not shamed me, I should have refused the commission, even though it was one which greatly interested me."

By this time the two men had reached the door. Terhune held out his hand. "Once more, many thanks for sparing me your time, Mr. Ackworth."

The architect's reply was interrupted by the appearance of another man from the rear of the hall.

"Mr. Ackworth! Mr. Ackworth!"

"What do you want, Collins?"

"We have found something else suspicious."

"Where?"

"In the grotto."

Ackworth glanced at Terhune. "Would you care to remain, Mr. Terhune?"

"If I may."

"Come along, then."

Excitedly, the three men proceeded towards the grotto. As Collins opened the door leading down to the grotto, the cold, fetid draught blew against their faces with the force of a strong wind. But by now the draught was familiar to them all, and they were not especially conscious of it. Terhune's attention, indeed, was taken up by the fact that the crude stairs were now amply lighted by a temporarily installed electric light.

Two men in workmen's overalls were in the grotto. With meticulous care, they were removing the ragstone from part of the wall.

"There is space behind here," Collins explained breathlessly. "When I pushed a rod through the mortar it went in three and a quarter feet before meeting with an obstruction. At the same time it moved something which jangled."

"Jangled?"

"Yes, sir, like—like—"

"An iron chain," one of the workmen suggested.

"That's right," Collins agreed. "An iron chain."

"Carry on, then," Ackworth ordered.

In a tense silence which was disturbed only by the sound of their scraping tools, the two workmen, aided occasionally by Collins, proceeded with their task of removing more of the ragstone. The hole which they made grew appreciably larger. Meanwhile, the five men present carefully avoided meeting one another's glance, each one in fear lest, with the slightest encouragement, he should be the first to suggest a retreat from the unhallowed spot.

"Cripes!" shouted one of the workmen.

The suddenness and loudness of the exclamation made the other men start.

"Lord lova-duck!" the other workman gasped. "Shut up, Bill! You nearly made me jump out of me skin."

"Look!" Bill pointed his unsteady hand in front of him. "Look at that. It fair makes me flesh creep it do and all."

"What is it?" Ackworth snapped.

"A skelington, that's what! A skelington, as true as me name's Bill Bartlett."

"Another!" the architect exclaimed in a low voice. He stepped towards the black hole in the wall. "Mind out," he rasped.

Collins and the workmen moved aside. Ackworth directed the light of his torch inside the aperture. Then he half turned his head.

"Look, Mr. Terhune."

Terhune stepped close to Ackworth and peered inside the hole. Beyond the wall was a space less than three feet square by six feet high. In it was a skeleton, held in an upright position by a chain which, suspended from the wall, had been passed under each armpit and round the chest. Round the neck of the skeleton was a rosary and crucifix.

"Good God!"

"Robert the Hermit?" Ackworth queried.

"It seems as though it may be," Terhune agreed. "But why the chain, and the upright position?"

For a moment Ackworth did not reply. He flashed the torch upwards, sideways, and lastly, downwards.

"What is that?"

"That" was a small oblong iron box. Ackworth inserted his arm into the hole in the wall and, stretching down, picked it up. He handled it carefully as he pulled it out of the aperture, and it was as well that he did so, for when they examined it the men saw that centuries of dampness had corroded the surface of the iron until it was no more than a series of rusted flakes which crumbled into powder as it was touched.

Ackworth tenderly handed the box over to Terhune.

"This is really your pigeon," he explained generously.

Terhune tried to open the lid, but it would not lift, probably because rust had fused the lid to the box.

"Give it a knock with this, sir," Bill suggested, passing over a small hammer.

One sharp knock did the trick. Terhune lifted the lid. Inside was a length of rolled parchment.

"Be careful how you handle that piece of parchment, in case the weather has affected it," Ackworth warned.

The advice was good and worth following. Using extreme care, Terhune began to unroll the parchment, to find that it was still in reasonably good condition: evidently the iron box had protected it from the worst ravages of time. When the roll was fully unwound, he was amazed to distinguish the faint outline of writing. He peered more closely at the writing, and was delighted to see that many of the words were legible. Unfortunately, the words were in a language unknown to him.

He passed the parchment back to Ackworth. The architect examined the writing, his face became puzzled.

"It is not Latin," he said presently. Scarcely were the words uttered than he followed them up with an excited: "I have it! Norman-French! Do you know any French, Mr. Terhune?"

"School French only."

"Same here, but we might be able to make something of it."

With their heads close together, the two men peered at the parchment. Slowly, and with an effort, they puzzled out the writing, sometimes speaking alternately.

"Be—it—known that"—here the writing was illegible—"that Robert the Hermit—shall—(illegible)—his sins and abominations—(illegible)—have therefore taken—it—upon ourselves to—punish him—(illegible)—walling him—(illegible)—alive to die—by slow—(illegible)—and declare that—this—hide of land—shall remain forever—accursed—if his grave—(illegible)—disturbed—"

That was all.

Chapter Twenty-Two

I

From House-on-the-Hill, Terhune proceeded to Willingham Manor.

He was fortunate in finding Julia on her own, as Alicia had left the house to have tea with the Rector.

Julia greeted him warmly. "Hullo, Theo, my sweet! I am glad you have come along. I have been trying to telephone you for the past two hours, but I could not get any reply."

"I have been out since two o'clock," he explained. "At House-on-the-Hill."

She was immediately interested. "Has something happened?"

"Yes. I have news for you, Julie. Plenty of it."

"I have news for you, too: that is why I wanted to see you this afternoon."

"What is your news?"

She shook her head. "Yours first, my pet."

"Ladies first."

"Several people have assured me that I am no lady."

"You are to me."

"Flattery does not come naturally from your lips, Theo," she informed him coolly. "Tell me your news before I get angry."

As usual, Julia had the best of the argument. Terhune related the events of the past few hours. She listened calmly until he spoke of the translation of the writing; then, even her cool imperturbability was disturbed.

"Theo! You don't mean that the villagers buried the Hermit alive!"

"I can't guarantee our translation; some of the Norman-French words bear very little relation to their modern counterpart. But with the help of our school French, Ackworth's Latin, and about fifty per cent guesswork, that is what we made of the writing on the parchment. No doubt, Salvaterra will arrange for it to be examined by a Norman-French expert."

She shuddered. "Never mind what his crimes were. It is horrible to think of that poor man being bricked up alive and left to die."

"You cannot altogether blame the villagers. Being bricked up alive was quite a popular form of death in Norman times. Besides, he had asked for trouble."

"No wonder House-on-the-Hill has been haunted by evil throughout the centuries," she said in a low voice. "For the first time in my life I am almost ready to believe in spirits. Somehow, I can understand the Hermit's tortured spirit seeking admittance to the other world, and being denied the solace of peace because of the curse, seeking revenge on all who dared to disturb the sepulchre of his human remains." She saw Terhune shake his head doubtfully. "Don't you dare laugh at me, Theo," she added furiously.

"I am not laughing at you, Julie. I wouldn't dare after my own experiences in House-on-the-Hill. What I cannot understand is, why, if the place is accursed, the Mulhollands and the Ingletons were not affected by the curse. After all, between them, the two families and their descendants lived there for the best part of two hundred years. That doesn't sound as if the curse was very effective. Do you know, Julie, the discovery to-day of those two skeletons has helped to clear up several puzzling features about the past history of House-on-the-Hill, but we still do not know why those priest's holes were constructed, nor the nature of the tragic circumstances of Caroline Drummond's death."

"The news I have for you might help to do that."

"I had forgotten you had news for me, too. What have you discovered?" he questioned eagerly.

"I have not discovered anything, but I received this just after lunch." She passed him a square of paper which she produced from her handbag.

Unfolding it, he saw that the paper was a cable from Australia:

MACFARLANE COMPANY HAVE TRACED DESCENDANT DRUMMOND FAMILY FULL STORY CAROLINE PRUMMONDS DEATH TOLD IN KILLED BY THE PAST BY ROGER GASKELL PUBLISHED EIGHTEEN THIRTY-TWO WRITING SOON MUCH LOVE ELSIE

"*Killed by the Past!*" Terhune repeated. "It sounds a cheerful piece of work. But I have never heard of it. Nor of Roger Gaskell, Something tells me a visit to the British Museum must be arranged."

"Then something is lying to you, my pet," she said sweetly. "*I* am going to the British Museum. To-morrow!"

I I

The following night Terhune was disturbed, during the reading of the nine o'clock news, by the sound of his private door bell. On his way downstairs he wondered who could be wanting him at that late hour—Miss Amelia? Mrs. Mann? Or Nurse Tweddie, perhaps, to ask if he would do her the favour of lending her a couple of books to while away boring hours on night duty?

It was Julia who wanted him, a weary Julia with tired eyes.

"Julie! You are the last person I expected to see."

"Why? Don't you want to hear the result of my visit to the Museum?"

"Yes, of course, but—"

"But it is so very late!" she mocked. "Theo, there are times when I could cheerfully take you by the shoulders in the hope of shaking you out of the rut of country life. I suppose you were preparing for bed? Well, you are not going to bed yet. You are going to ask me in, you are going to make me one of your very nicest cups of coffee, and you are going to listen to what I am going to tell you of that book, for I am far too excited to sleep until I have shared the story with someone else—which means you!"

He took her up into his study, poked the fire into a cheerful blaze, made preparations for the rite of making real coffee, then sat down and glanced expectantly at her.

"When I didn't hear from you by 'phone, Julie, I concluded that you hadn't much news of real interest."

"I got back late. By the time I had changed, eaten a meal, and satisfied Mother's curiosity, it was too late to 'phone to say I was coming. So I just came."

"You look very tired."

"I am, my pet. I am not as quick a reader as you. It took me all day to finish reading that terrible book."

"Terrible?"

"I had never realised that an author could write such nonsense. No wonder I haven't any real interest in books. I must say, too, for my pains, the type was smudgy—"

He interrupted, with a quick nod of his head. "I know. You needn't tell me." He stretched out his arm and pulled a book from the shelves, which he opened and showed to her. "Something like that?"

"Worse."

"Poor old Julie! Anyway, tell me about *Killed by the Past*."

"Give me a cigarette first, my sweet."

He offered her a cigarette, then a lighted match. After a preliminary puff or so, she snuggled into the chair.

"*Killed by the Past* is a novel—save the mark!"

"A novel? But I thought—"

"Don't be so impatient! And don't interrupt! In a preface the author—he was an American, by the way—explains that, although the story as a whole is a work of fiction, all the facts and most of the characters are—or were—real. The novel, he goes on to say, is based on a story that was told him, during a recent visit to Australia, by a descendant of the family who once lived in Crooked Chimneys—"

He disobeyed her recent instructions. "House-on-the-Hill?"

"Yes. And the family, which he names Duncan, were obviously the Drummonds. Well, the story starts with the first meeting between Charlotte Duncan—Caroline Drummond, of course—and Lord Kenneth—or Lord Kenelm.

"I need not bore you with the details of the nonsensical romance between Charlotte Duncan and Lord Kenneth. Lord Kenneth is ostracised by his fellow peers for daring to fall in love with a girl who wasn't, even distantly, related to somebody with an hereditary title. As the Duke of Cornshire drawls to his fellow club members: 'It was not as if, gentlemen, Lord Kenneth were content to make the wench his mistress. No, by Gad! gentlemen, no. The irresponsible young whelp speaks of proposing marriage to her. Marriage, gentlemen! Zounds! He needs a horsewhipping to bring him to his senses, and I should be the man to administer that chastisement—were I thirty years younger, adzooks!'"

Terhune chuckled. "'Sdeath and odzookens! You didn't plough through all that tripe?"

"I did. Every 'hoity-toity!' and 'lo and behold!' of it. Anyway, our gallant hero fights a duel to uphold the good name of his beloved, beautiful soul-mate, and pinks the rascally Earl of Seahaven in the forearm with as skilful a parry as was ever witnessed in the history of duelling. So honour is satisfied, and Lord Kenneth departs by chaise to spend Christmas at Crooked Chimneys, the lovely but modestly small home of his charmer.

"So the story carries on, Theo. On Christmas night the exciting game of hide-and-seek is suggested, and enthusiastically welcomed. Presently Charlotte trips away to hide, her lovely face blushing at the thought of her handsome noble lover seeking for her—" Julia stopped abruptly.

"What's wrong, Julie? Why that expression?"

"I am a pig! I am forgetting that what Charlotte did in that terrible book, poor Caroline Drummond also did—in actual fact. You see, Theo, Charlotte creeps into a huge clothes closet which has been built against a wall. While she is fumbling about in the dark behind the dresses, she touches something, and feels the wall beside her move. She decides to investigate—you can guess what happens. She is trapped. After a time, when Charlotte remains undiscovered, the family become worried. Candles are lighted, a search is made throughout the house. But she is not found that night. Nor the next day, or the next. Only after five days' continual search is a clue found, inside the clothes closet. It is a little golden ornament which Lord Kenneth has given her. As a result, the priest's hole is discovered, and Charlotte is found dead."

"And Lord Kenneth, I presume, departs from the house and commits suicide?"

"Yes. Oh, Theo! It is horrible to think of poor Caroline Drummond finding herself trapped in one of those ghastly priest's holes, and dying of fear and privation. No wonder the very air of House-on-the-Hill is tainted with evil and tragedy. I wish a German bomb had blown it to bits during the war. At least one more tragedy would have been averted."

Terhune nodded, and rose from his chair to pour out the coffee.

"So now the death of Caroline Drummond is accounted for, and the strange suicide of Lord Kenelm."

"I haven't finished yet."

"What?"

"I have a lot more to tell you."

"You have! Concerning what?"

"Jeremiah Ingleton—who is called Joshua Irving in the novel."

"What on earth has Jeremiah Ingleton to do with Caroline Drummond?"

"Well, in *Killed by the Past*, Charlotte's father is Valentine Duncan, nephew of Sir Calvin Fitzherbert—"

"Constant Fitzwilliam?"

"Yes. Duncan, or Drummond, had been staying with his uncle. Upon his uncle's death he takes possession of the house, and because his right to remain there is unchallenged, he ultimately establishes squatter's right to the freehold. After the tragic death of his daughter, he is so upset that he proceeds to have the place properly examined, In consequence he finds so many priest's holes, any and every one of which is a death-trap, that he is surprised many more people had not been killed during the previous years of his residence there. Even so, another skeleton—of a young boy of about thirteen years of age—is found, also the skeletons of three cats and two dogs."

"But I don't understand, Julie! How could a cat or a dog work that mechanism?"

"You will understand in a minute. First let me explain that the skeleton was that of a servant, a boots boy, who had worked for Sir Calvin—or Sir Constant, if you prefer—who had disappeared in Sir Constant's time, but who was believed to have run away.

"During the search for the priest's holes, Valentine Duncan finds a document written by one Joshua Irving. It was he who constructed the priest's holes, death-traps, or whatever you wish to call them."

"Jeremiah Ingleton! In Heaven's name, why?"

"Because he was mad, Theo."

"Good Lord! Then Ackworth was right when he maintained that the man who constructed the false buttresses was mad."

"Yes, but I haven't finished yet. Wouldn't you like to hear what drove Ingleton mad?"

"Of course."

"In seventeen sixty-three House-on-the-Hill caught fire. The fire did extensive damage to the south façade of the main building, but not to the rest of the house, so the family resolved to continue living in the house until repairs were executed. But the fire had done something else besides damage the south façade. The morning after the fire Jeremiah's wife visited her preserve cellars. She found that a portion of the wall had collapsed. Her curiosity being aroused she investigated. There she saw the skeleton of Robert the Hermit."

"Good God!"

"The shock killed her. And her death—and perhaps, also, the cursed remains of Robert the Hermit—brought on Jeremiah's madness. He suddenly decided that the world was persecuting him, and resolved to have his revenge. Being himself a master builder, he resolved to do all his own repairs to House-on-the-Hill. First of all, he rebricked up the skeleton of Robert the Hermit. Then he constructed the false buttresses and the death-traps. Lastly, he wrote out what he had done for the benefit of posterity, and hid the document in one of the buttresses, together with a second document in which he solemnly cursed any man, woman or child who should ever attempt to destroy the priest's holes.

"Unfortunately, this curse had its effect upon Valentine Drummond, who was extremely superstitious. He did not dare to do away altogether with the priest's holes, but he was not prepared to leave them as death-traps into which anyone was liable to fall. He therefore compromised with his superstitious fears and his conscience by making the means of opening the priest's holes so concealed, and so complicated, that they would not easily be found."

"But he still left them as death-traps," Terhune pointed out.

"I know. I was thinking of that on the way home. Probably he was too afraid of the curse to remove them altogether. Meanwhile, of course, the news of what had happened to Caroline Drummond, and to Sir Constant's 'boots,' added to rumours about the house being cursed, began to circulate through the district. With what result you know. Evidently the local fear of House-on-the-Hill must have originated towards the end of the eighteenth century.

"Valentine Duncan, or Drummond, died within a year of his daughter's death. His son inherited the place, but, according to *Killed by the Past*, everything went wrong for him from the moment of his doing so. Being of an obstinate nature, and, unlike his father, not superstitious, he remained at House-on-the-Hill for the rest of his life. But when he died, and the property descended to his son, Rupert—Gaskell calls him Roland—decided to sell House-on-the-Hill and emigrate to Australia, where, shortly afterwards, he met Gaskell, to whom he related the facts which Gaskell so cruelly maltreated in transforming them into *Killed by the Past*."

"Well, I'll be damned!" Terhune grinned ruefully. "What a lot of time and trouble we should have been saved if we had previously known about *Killed by the Past*. By the way, Julie, did you take a note of the publisher's name?"

"I did, and therein, I think, lies the reason for no author's having bridged the first gap between Nathaniel Ingleton and Sir

Constant Fitzwilliam, and the second gap between Sir Constant and Winstanley's great-grandfather."

"Why?"

"It was published in Boston, U.S.A.," she replied wearily. "Another cigarette, please, my pet, before I fall completely asleep."

Chapter Twenty-Three

The following morning Terhune telephoned Detective-Inspector Sampson at New Scotland Yard.

"Good morning, Mr. Terhune."

"Good morning, inspector. I thought you might be interested in hearing some fresh facts concerning House-on-the-Hill which have come to light."

"Are they urgent? What I mean is, will they keep until Sunday morning?"

"Yes; they only concern items of past history."

"Then they will interest me more if you pass them on when we are together. Unless anything turns up in the meantime, I shall be free again on Sunday. Will it be convenient if I drop in round about ten-thirty?"

"Yes, if you will agree to have lunch with me at the 'Almond Tree.'"

"Gladly. I'll play you darts again. I have been practising lately. By the way, I may have some news for you, too."

"About House-on-the-Hill?"

"Indirectly, yes."

During the intervening days, Terhune puzzled over what the news could be which Sampson had for him. On one occasion he wondered whether the inspector had chanced upon a copy of *Killed by the Past*, and hoped to surprise him with it, but then he recollected that the novel had been published in the United States of America, and that there were scarcely likely to be any copies in the world outside the national libraries.

He did not waste much thought on the problem, however, for there seemed very little left of the past history of the House with Crooked Walls which wanted elucidation. To make sure of this, he wrote down in chronological order the names of all the people and families who had occupied the place. The only gaps in this list were: one between 1842, the date of Reuben Douglas's disappearance, and 1861, when Oliver Finlayson moved in; one between 1882, when Finlayson died, and 1893 when Noel Middlemass purchased the property "blind"; and lastly, one between 1893 and the date of Salvaterra's purchase. To the best of his knowledge, during all three gaps the house had remained empty.

With his customary punctuality, Sampson rang the private bell of Terhune's flat at 10.28. Within a very few minutes he was toasting his toes at the fire and smoking a cigarette, while Terhune told him briefly of the finding of the skeletons of Reuben Douglas and Robert the Hermit (which had already been sensationalised in the daily Press) and later, of the reason for the construction of the priest's holes, and of Caroline Drummond's death.

To this long account Sampson listened with an interest so marked, that, in contrast to his normal, unemotional expression, it seemed to his companion to be exaggerated. His eyes appeared to glow with an inward fire, the reason for which Terhune, frankly, could not understand. Yet, when the story was finished, he made no comment, but offered Terhune a cigarette, lighted one for himself, and gazed into the heart of the fire in deep reflection. Then, when at last he did speak, he ignored House-on-the-Hill and its history, and spoke, instead, of Salvaterra:

"Do you know, Terhune, although several weeks have gone by since my last meeting with Salvaterra and his sister, I cannot forget them. They were the two most extraordinary people I have ever met, and I have met many, I can assure you: a police detective meets more peculiar people than the rest of the civilised world realises. For all that, the two Salvaterras head the list; firstly, because of their likeness, which I have never before seen between two people of the opposite sex, and secondly, because of the adoration which each bore for the other.

"I realise that a partial explanation lies in the fact of their being twins. Twins are popularly supposed to resemble each other, and to have unusual affection for each other, although I have met twins who neither looked much like the other nor possessed more love for each other than is felt by normal brothers and sisters. But that such likeness should persist for a lifetime must be, I imagine, something of a freak of Nature. Still more so, their mutual love, in the light of Salvaterra's marriage." He paused abruptly and, turning his head, faced Terhune with a questioning glance.

"Why did Salvaterra marry, Terhune?"

The question stumped Terhune. "Heaven alone knows!"

"Do you think he married his wife because he fell in love with her. Personally, it seems incredible to me that a bachelor should—I presume he was a bachelor—"

Terhune recognised the question mark in the inspector's voice. "I don't know."

"Well, if he were, then, as I was saying, it seems incredible that at that age, he should wish to marry, particularly considering that he was deeply in love with his sister, who was apparently capable of fulfilling every wifely function save one. As you know, I never had the opportunity of meeting his wife. Do you think the marriage was a happy one?"

Terhune shrugged. "Is one ever able to assess another person's marriage? All I can say is, that Señora Salvaterra did not have the appearance of being a happy woman. And I am not particularly surprised."

"Why not?" Sampson snapped out.

"He allowed not his wife, but his sister to run his life and his home. The impression I received of the household was that the Señora was practically ignored by everybody, save her son, and she was completely under her husband's... and her sister-in-law's... thumb. I must confess I felt rather sorry for her."

Sampson's vulture-like expression became marked. "What was his attitude towards his stepson?"

"He seemed more fond of Andrés than of his wife."

The answer seemed to disappoint the inspector. He angrily pursed his mouth; his thin lips almost disappeared from sight. Then his attitude relaxed. "Do you think he was clever and deep enough to have simulated that affection?"

"My impression of Salvaterra was that he was intelligent enough, and deep enough, to have simulated any emotion he wished. But why should he have pretended to be fond of Andrés, if, in fact, he was not?"

Sampson did not directly answer the question. "Did I tell you that I am friendly with a member of the staff of the Panama Pacific Line? He is nearly fifty years of age. For more than thirty-five years of that life he has lived in Panama. I doubt whether there is any person of importance living in Panama who is unknown to Gilmore. I had lunch with him last Monday."

Terhune began to feel curious as to what the inspector was leading. "Well?"

"I took advantage of the opportunity to ask him whether he had ever heard of Dr. Salvaterra."

"Had he?"

"No."

"Perhaps Salvaterra was not of sufficient importance."

Sampson chuckled. "You can bet your life he wasn't. Then I asked him if he had ever heard of Manuel Rojas."

"Manuel Rojas?"

"Señora Salvaterra's first husband—Andrés's father."

Terhune grinned in a shame-faced way. "I had forgotten the name."

The inspector wagged an admonitory forefinger. "You cannot afford to forget names if you hope to be a first-class amateur detective—"

"Don't start that again," Terhune pleaded.

Sampson's eyes twinkled. "All right, young fellow-me-lad. Well, when I mentioned the name of Manuel Rojas to Gilmore he nearly split his sides with laughter at the mere idea of his not knowing the name. Rojas, it appeared, was one of the richest men in Panama. 'Worth anything over a million pounds sterling' was Gilmore's estimate."

Terhune stared hard at his companion, and realised suddenly that his heart was not beating quite as steadily as usual. "Well?"

"I asked Gilmore if he would care to send a cable on my behalf to Panama, asking for information concerning Rojas's will. He did so, and received the reply Friday afternoon. Rojas had left his entire fortune to his wife in trust for his son Andrés upon reaching his majority. If poor Andrés had lived a few more months he would have inherited a cool million pounds or more."

"The poor devil!" Terhune exclaimed feelingly. "Who gets the money instead?"

"Señora Salvaterra—the woman whom you believe to be in complete subjection to her husband and Inez Salvaterra. Taken by and large, the death of Andrés was rather—timely, don't you think?" Sampson asked casually.

"For the love of Mike, inspector, surely you are not suggesting that—that Salvaterra murdered his stepson to prevent the million pounds passing from his wife's control?"

Sampson frowned. "How can I suggest such an outrageous theory?" he replied irritably. "I am not really serious, Terhune. I am afraid it is just a case of my suspicious mind trying to make two and two add up to five. If Salvaterra could have known that those damned priest's holes existed, then one might have had good reason for wondering—especially in view of the claustrophobia from which, according to Gilmore, the boy suffered—but damn it all! after all the research work you put into tracing the past history of House-on-the-Hill, it was only when Andrés fell down that priest's hole that you learned of, or suspected its existence."

"The present Drummond knew of its existence."

Sampson shook his head. "We must not try to make facts fit in with theories. It would be stretching the long arm of coincidence too far to suggest that Salvaterra went to Australia, met Drummond, and so learned all there was to be known of House-on-the-Hill."

"It might not have been necessary for him to have left Panama to have learned all the necessary information," Terhune muttered.

"What the hell do you mean?" the inspector demanded roughly.

"I neglected to tell you, inspector, that the book from which Miss MacMunn learned the story of Caroline Drummond's death and of Jeremiah Ingleton's insane constructional work was published in the U.S.A."

"Then Salvaterra might have known of the priest's holes before he left Panama. The swine! The cunning, fiendish swine!"

Terhune glanced somewhat helplessly at the detective. "I cannot believe it possible."

"It is all too damned possible!" Sampson asserted aggressively. "Listen, young fellow-me-lad, and see whether you can pick holes in this theory. Rojas dies, leaving his money to his wife in trust for his son, she to inherit entirely in the event of the son's predecease before reaching his majority. Salvaterra and his sister plan to lay their hands upon this money. Somehow or other, he persuades the widow of Rojas to marry him—fill in the blanks as you please.

"Meanwhile, until the money passes completely to the son, the widow has control of the interest, a tidy sum at that. Salvaterra is not satisfied with living handsomely on his wife's money for a few years, and then, afterwards, on the uncertain charity of his stepson. He makes plans to kill Andrés so that his wife will inherit the estate absolutely—which would give him almost virtual control of it. But he is a cunning devil. He does not mean to suffer the consequences of his crime. Not he! He intends to use that super-intelligent brain of his to perpetrate the perfect crime.

"He comes across the story of House-on-the-Hill. Perhaps he had once read the book in a museum or national library; perhaps a stray copy comes into his possession. But how he comes across the story does not matter. It is enough to guess that the story suggests the germ of an idea to him—for had not Andrés already a highly strung, nervous disposition. Was he not a victim of acute claustrophobia? Salvaterra realises that, if he could inveigle Andrés into one of the priest's holes, one of two things could easily happen. Andrés could die of an attack of claustrophobia. And if not of claustrophobia, then of starvation. Had not Caroline Drummond died in like circumstances? And the boots-boy?"

"Nobody could be quite as cold-blooded as that, inspector," Terhune protested.

Sampson ignored the interruption. "Salvaterra's first move is to sail for England, accompanied by his sister, but leaving his wife and stepson in Panama. On his arrival in this country, he pretends to be looking for a country house. He makes enquiries, circulates estate agents. In due course, House-on-the-Hill is brought to his attention. He visits it, and ascertains that the priest's holes still exist. Fine! Then he hears of the fear and repugnance with which the house is regarded locally. Better and better! His cunning brain shews him how to use this reputation to his advantage. He begins negotiations for its purchase, and, at the same time, pretending to be interested in discovering why local inhabitants loathe the sight of the house, asks your solicitor friend, Howard, how best to obtain any information on this subject. Howard swallows the bait, hook, line and sinker; he speaks of one Theodore Terhune, of Bray-in-the-Marsh, who not only specialises in selling books of local interest, but who dabbles occasionally in local detection—and I am not pulling your leg, this time. I am being perfectly serious, Terhune. Whether you like it or not, local people are convinced that you are a first class detective—"

"That is absurd! Just because I read and write detective stories—"

"I know! I know!" Sampson broke in impatiently. "But rural communities make the most of their local celebrities. Anyway, Salvaterra is convinced that you are the very man for his purpose. He visits you, and persuades you to undertake a particularly interesting commission. He has a secondary reason for doing this; he guesses that all the old rumours about House-on-the-Hill being evil and accursed will be revived."

"You did mention something to me, didn't you, inspector, about not making facts fit in with theories?" Terhune asked weakly.

Sampson grinned. "Guilty, me lord! I don't usually let myself go to this extent; but I confess I am enjoying myself, in not having the Director of Public Prosecutions pull me up every few seconds, asking for proof. To continue. When Salvaterra hears that, almost within living memory, Reuben Donald vanished mysteriously—"

"Reuben Douglas," Terhune commented.

"Douglas, then! When he hears of Douglas's disappearance from House-on-the-Hill, Salvaterra is overjoyed—he was, wasn't he?"

"Yes," Terhune admitted.

"He realises that everything is proceeding according to plan. He arranges with you to write a history of House-on-the-Hill, believing—with good reason—that the more the public knows of the history of the house the less they will be surprised—and what is more important, the less they will be suspicious—if House-on-the-Hill claims one more victim. He does everything possible to foster and draw attention to local superstition, even to the extent of having a stained-glass window specially designed, and restoring the grotto as much as possible to its original state. Unlike any murderer I have ever heard of, Salvaterra deliberately sought publicity, in order to make that publicity serve his own ends."

Terhune shook his head. "The theory is too fantastic to be true."

"Fantastic, I grant, but true? I cannot say for sure, but so far, can you find fault with it?"

Terhune chuckled. "As a work of fiction—no!"

"You appear to assume that you and I have exchanged respective roles for once, and that I am drawing upon my imagination, while you have become the coldly calculating disbeliever."

"Not—not exactly disbeliever, inspector. Say, critic."

"Then criticise the continuation of my theory! Having purchased House-on-the-Hill, Salvaterra makes arrangements for the house to be made inhabitable, and then returns to Panama, to bring his wife and stepson back to England. And mark this well, my critical friend. Even apart from the fact that House-on-the-Hill is the ideal place for the murder which he plans, he deliberately takes his small family away from Panama. In Panama the son of Manuel Rojas is an important person. His demise might cause the wrong kind of publicity. Friends of the father might think his death, before reaching his majority, a fortunate chance for Salvaterra. They might even ask awkward questions; at the best, they might interfere with his subsequent plans by influencing Señora Salvaterra to watch her money carefully—that is, assuming that a Panamanian woman has the right to own separate property. I don't know Panamanian law. Perhaps it follows Continental law, and gives the husband the management of the estate. But if Andrés dies abroad there is a chance that his death may not even be reported in the Panamanian Press.

"Salvaterra returns to House-on-the-Hill, and settles in. He now conceives the idea of holding a house-warming party, to meet all the more influential people of the district, to give those people the chance of seeing for themselves what an extraordinary place House-on-the-Hill still remains, and to give him an apparently innocent opportunity of circulating your history of the house which, in the meantime, he has had printed and bound."

"You should be a barrister-at-law, inspector, not a detective."

"I should like to be for once, to get my own back during cross-examination. However, the house-warming party serves its purpose; Salvaterra makes himself more or less popular, because he is wise enough to know that the more open his life is, the more the neighbours like him and his family, the less likelihood there will be of suspicions being aroused when Andrés dies.

"Everything develops as planned. The time approaches for Andrés to die. And on the first convenient night he disappears. What happens? Salvaterra deliberately encourages the Press to make the most of the sensation; he even agrees to allow your book to be serialised. Why? Because he realises two things; the first, that nobody is likely to suspect a man so willing to publicise the disappearance of his son, of being that son's murderer; the second, that everybody will immediately ascribe the disappearance of Andrés to House-on-the-Hill. Until the body was found, were not many people already suggesting that the evil atmosphere of the place had affected the mental balance of the highly-strung young man, so causing him to flee as far from it as possible, or even to commit suicide?"

"Then you believe that our finding the priest's holes upset Salvaterra's plans?"

Sampson shook his head. "Definitely, no, Terhune. Salvaterra wanted the body found, because, even had there previously been the slightest breath of suspicion against him, the discovery would have freed him from that suspicion. The circumstances made it apparently so obvious that Andrés's imagination had been fired by your history of the House with Crooked Walls, that it seemed quite natural for him to have searched for a possible priest's hole. Salvaterra must have realised that, sooner or later, somebody would suggest the possibility of Andrés's having been trapped in a priest's hole, and that a search would be suggested, a suggestion which would be immediately welcomed."

Following these words there was a long silence in the small, book-lined study. At last Sampson said impatiently: "Well, are you still not satisfied that Salvaterra may have murdered Andrés?"

"No," Terhune admitted bluntly.

"Why not?"

"Your theory has one very serious weakness."

"What is that?"

"You make Salvaterra out to be an inhumanly clever and cunning man, who has conceived and executed what popular novels call 'the perfect crime'?"

"I do."

"Well, in spite of his cunning and cleverness in contriving an alleged murder of which he was never likely to be suspected, nevertheless, he is suspected by you, and for no apparent reason. That must mean that Salvaterra has not, after all, committed the perfect crime. What made you suspect him in the first case, inspector?"

"The merest, millionth chance—Gilmore's mention of the claustrophobia. I could not understand how a highly strung young man, suffering from acute claustrophobia, had dared to squeeze sideways into a narrow, dark aperture. But when I learned from you that Salvaterra might have had knowledge of those priest's holes before buying House-on-the-Hill, well, nebulous suspicions began to take definite form."

Again there was a pause in the conversation. With a growing sense of horror, Terhune began to realise that the inspector's theory was not so far-fetched as he had, at first, believed. When he recollected the nervous mannerisms and characteristics of poor Andrés Salvaterra, he could not reconcile them with the supposed acts of a young man eager to explore the narrow, dark and unwholesome priest's hole. It was extremely unlikely that Andrés would have had the courage to enter the priest's hole even in the company of others; still less, on his own.

"What are you going to do about your suspicions?" he asked huskily.

"Nothing."

"Nothing! But, inspector—"

"Listen, Terhune," Sampson began harshly. "I know that you have some knowledge of English law—I once heard you spout quite a mouthful to a station sergeant on the subject of *animus furandi*. I may believe that Salvaterra read *Killed by the Past* before he sailed for England—but can I prove it? Salvaterra has said that Andrés spent two days looking for a priest's hole. Can I prove that Salvaterra lied? I believe that Salvaterra went to Andrés's room the night of the lad's disappearance, opened the entrance of the priest's hole, persuaded Andrés to peer inside, and gave the lad a push which caused him to fall down the shaft. But can I prove that he did that? For all I really know, Andrés *might* genuinely have searched for the priest's hole. He *might* really have fallen down it by accident. His death *might* be nothing more than a lucky break for Salvaterra. After all, Salvaterra is not a young man. Would he take the chance of eternal damnation just to spend the last few years in luxury and plenty? Without proof I can do nothing. And there is no proof, not a shred, not an atom of proof."

"Is Salvaterra, then, to go unpunished for his crime?"

"Only God can answer that question," Sampson replied sombrely.

Chapter Twenty-Four

I

The weeks passed. The coroner held a necessary but useless inquest on the two skeletons found at House-on-the-Hill. Ackworth continued his examination of the house, and discovered a genuine priest's hole, also a small, secret cupboard containing a packet of love letters from a certain Mr. Nathaniel to Adelaide Ingleton, dated 1723 and 1724. Nothing else of consequence came to light, however, so, in due course, he and his workmen left the house after filling up the Hermit's tomb, the false buttresses, and the genuine priest's hole with rubble.

It did not take long for the excitement caused by the events at House-on-the-Hill to die away. Presently it ceased to be a subject of conversation—except when a stranger visited the district. The house itself was still regarded with misgiving, even though the remains of Robert the Hermit and Reuben Douglas had been removed to a more fitting resting place. Nobody would go near the place—except Randall, the butler, and his wife, who were from East Ham, and didn't hold with such silly country nonsense. They weren't frightened of no ghosts, nor of no curse neither, so they took rooms at Keppel's Farm, where they slept at nights, and visited the house each day for the purpose of keeping it clean and aired pending the return of the family.

Terhune soon relapsed into his own way of life. He saw Julia often, and Helena often, and Lady Kylstone often, and Winstanley often: indeed, he saw most of the local people often, for sometimes they visited his shop to buy or exchange books, and sometimes he visited them as a welcome guest. But to none of these people, not even to Julia or Helena, did he mention one word of Sampson's suspicions of Salvaterra. That was a secret sacred to Sampson and himself.

Towards the end of January the Salvaterras returned to House-on-the-Hill. So did Mr. and Mrs. Randall. Later, three women servants arrived from Scotland to work there; a week later, two men from Wales. Meanwhile, all the guests who had attended the house-warming party called, somewhat reluctantly, and always in full day-light, for the purpose of expressing politely their happiness at the family's return, and the hope that they would pay a return visit at the first opportunity. This Salvaterra promised to do when the Señora had properly recovered her health.

Life in Bray-in-the-Marsh, in Willingham, in Wickford remained its usual placid, serene existence, little different from that of the past centuries, little different from that of the future centuries. Weeks lengthened into months, and nothing untoward happened. Not even at House-on-the-Hill. Randall swore to all his cronies at the "Three Tuns"—which he visited on his "nights off"—that the house was altogether a different house now that all the skeletons had been removed from it. He laughed at the idea of its being still cursed. So did the rest of the staff. Why, they asserted, singly and collectively, House-on-the-Hill wasn't no different from any other blinking house. Leastways, it needed just as much keeping clean!

Bray (and Willingham and Wickford) almost began to believe that the curse had been lifted from the House with Crooked Walls.

Almost! But not quite. Rural communities are slow to change their ideas and opinions, especially when they are centuries old.

I I

One night, about the middle of February, Terhune was awakened by the noise of shouting from the direction of Market Square. He jumped out of bed, hurried across to the window, and looked out. Quite a number of dark shadows were to be seen, all hurrying in one direction. People in Market Square at two o'clock in the morning!

Something must have happened. Something extraordinary.

He opened the window, and leaned out.

"Hey! What's up?" he yelled.

Somebody heard him—Mrs. Mann, as a matter of fact.

"A fire, Mr. Terhune."

A fire! "Where?" he called back anxiously, hoping that the fire was not at Timberlands (the Kylstone home). Or Willingham Manor. Or, for that matter, at any of the homes which he was in the habit of visiting.

"House-on-the-Hill," a man's voice squeaked back—Mrs. Mann's small husband. "You can see it from the bottom of Windmill Lane."

Terhune dressed hastily. He didn't know why. Staring at a fire from some miles distant was a useless occupation. Then he slipped into a heavy overcoat and hurried downstairs. He hurried across Market Square and down Windmill Lane as far as Clover Farm. There he joined the large group of people who were clustered together in the middle of the road, staring at the distant red glow.

There was little talking. Nobody had to be told that the House-on-the-Hill was doomed. No small fire could glow so redly at that distance. The place must have been a raging inferno. Nevertheless, a few returned home for their bicycles, Terhune among them—the local fire brigade might be glad of extra help...

For a full hour the fire blazed fiercely. Then it began suddenly to die down, and people remembered that there was not much time left for sleep. In twos and threes, they drifted back to their homes and beds, anxious for the dawn to bring them news of what had happened to the occupants. The house didn't matter—the danged place were better in ruins, that it were, what with curses and skeletons and corpses, and what not! But the occupants now, poor devils! It would come as welcome news to hear that they all escaped safe and sound.

And with the dawn came news, but not such as the sympathetic people of Bray had hoped. Of the entire household—Salvaterra, his wife, his sister, and the seven servants—Mrs. Randall alone was saved. The rest were dead.

The House with Crooked Walls had lived up to its evil reputation.

THE END